Always
and
Forever

ALSO BY SORAYA LANE

Always and Forever

soraya lane

LAKE UNION
PUBLISHING

Text copyright © 2016 Soraya Lane

Published by Lake Union Publishing, Seattle
www.apub.com

Amazon, the Amazon logo, and Lake Union Publishing are trademarks of Amazon.com, Inc., or its affiliates.

ISBN-13: 9781503948464
ISBN-10: 1503948463

Cover design by Lisa Horton

Printed in the United States of America

I am so fortunate to work with some amazingly talented women.

For Emilie Marneur, Sammia Hamer,
Sophie Wilson & Laura Bradford—thank you!

1.

I'm not going to waste time making small talk, because I can tell
you're desperate to find out."

Lisa squeezed her husband's hand. Hard. She was staring at
their OB/GYN without blinking. Was that a hint of a smile or was
he just being polite? Her heart was racing, palms sweaty as she tried
to keep her skin connected to her husband's. She could feel that
Matt was burning up, too, his hand hot in hers.

"You're pregnant."

What? Lisa's other hand started to shake, the one her husband
wasn't pumping in the air, still linked to his. "Are you sure?" she gasped.

Matt let go of her hand and slung his arm over her shoulders
instead, pulling her in tight and smacking a kiss to her cheek. "I
don't think he's joking." He laughed, jumping out of his seat and
trying to yank her up with him. "You're not joking are you, doc?"

"Mr. and Mrs. Collins, I can assure you that I'm not joking."
The doctor was smiling back at her, the bearer of news she'd been
waiting so long to hear. "You're only just pregnant, so it's still early
days, but as of right now you are most definitely having a baby.
Congratulations."

She was numb. Her body had frozen, her mind stuck on that
one word that was playing over and over like she was incapable of
thinking of anything else. *Pregnant.* It had been so long, two years

of trying naturally before two grueling rounds of IVF, and now she was actually pregnant? She was *actually* going to be a mom? *They* were going to be parents?

"Lisa, say something." Matt had a grin on his face so wide she was sure she could see all of his teeth. "Are you okay?"

"*We're pregnant*," she whispered.

He was laughing again, eyes bright as he sat back down. "I guess we'll have to wait a while before we can pick the nursery colors, huh?"

Lisa let out a big breath. She really needed to get a grip. But she was pregnant! "So what are our chances of this working out? I mean, I don't want to be negative, but I don't want to shout it from the rooftops if there's a chance we could lose this baby either." She placed her hand protectively over her stomach, which was still flat like there wasn't anything changing within her body, already stressing out that something bad was going to happen.

"There is a chance of miscarriage—there *always* is this early on—but we see no reason for you to be at any higher risk than any other patient."

Lisa nodded, watching Matt's face. He was always so easy to read. His face was bursting with happiness right now, one corner of his mouth permanently kicked up into a grin. Sometimes he was still such a boy. His puppyish enthusiasm hadn't changed since she'd met him as a teenager.

"We're havin' a baby!" he muttered. "We're having a *baby!*" Matt spoke louder the second time, not giving her any warning before jumping up and dragging her up with him, pulling her into his arms and twirling her around.

"Matt!" she protested, struggling to regain her balance. "Matt, put me down!"

He swung her around again before finally setting her on her feet. She should be used to his exuberance after almost ten years together, but he still managed to catch her by surprise.

"I'll see you both again in another few weeks, but if you have any concerns at all, please don't hesitate to contact me." The doctor's smile was kind. "Go about all your usual activities and don't worry too much."

Matt took her hand again, tucking her against him as they walked out.

"You know you're my rock, right?" Lisa tilted her chin to look up at him, nestled under his arm, the top of her head reaching only to his shoulder. "I mean, you're crazy, but I wouldn't want to be doing this with anyone else."

"You know it's okay to get excited, *right*?" He asked her in return, giving her a wink.

Lisa sighed and held on tighter to his waist. "I just don't want to believe it's real and then be disappointed."

"Me neither, but we won't be," he said, stopping so he could look at her, his body curved as he dipped down for a kiss, eyes trained on hers. "We're having a baby, and if this doesn't work, then we'll just try again. Okay?"

Lisa shut her eyes for a beat, pushing the doubts away, forcing them from her mind. Worrying wasn't going to do her any good. She loved Matt's positive spin on life, but she didn't want just any baby, she wanted *this* baby. "No baby clothes yet, and no telling *anyone*, okay?"

"It'll be our secret until you're ready. I promise." Matt was grinning again. "But I *am* going to take you out for lunch to celebrate."

"Okay. But no champagne," she told him, finding it impossible not to share his excitement even if she was more cautious than he was. Butterflies were beating their wings in her belly, her skin flushing as she buzzed with happiness. "I'm pregnant, remember?"

He laughed and caught her up in his arms, swinging her around. "Baby, that's not something I'll ever forget."

"Matt, you know I hate when you pick me up!" she protested, trying not to laugh because she knew it would only spur him on. "This is the second time in less than fifteen minutes!"

"You love it," he said, still swinging her around.

"Matt!"

"What?" he asked, voice husky as he set her on her feet and locked his hips against hers. "You gonna tell me off?"

"Yeah, as a matter of fact, I am," she whispered, chin tilted as she looked up at him. "I'm the boss, and I say no more picking me up."

"No, sweetheart, you just *think* you're the boss."

Lisa laughed when he grabbed her again, hating that she was light enough for him to manhandle.

"Matt . . ."

"If you weren't pregnant, I wouldn't be giving in this easily," he growled, tucking her under his arm.

"Very funny," she said. "Almost as funny as you thinking you're the boss in this relationship."

They both laughed and bumped together, grinning away like a pair of idiots. They were pregnant and her husband was crazy-silly sometimes, but she wouldn't want it any other way.

❦

Lisa walked through her shop, running her hands along the brightly colored fabrics, loving the soft textures against her fingertips. It had been her lifelong dream to design clothes and have a little store somewhere filled with her own creations, and she'd lived that dream for five years now, since just before they were married. Every day she jumped out of bed, excited to get dressed up in clothes she'd designed and made herself, happy to open the doors and walk into her store. She'd sit out back and design, or sometimes lean against the counter and sketch, always thinking about the next season, the next collection of pieces that would put smiles on the faces of her customers. It was her happy place, and she couldn't imagine it not being a part of her life.

"What are you thinking about?"

Lisa turned and looked at Matt. It always cracked her up how out of place he looked in her pretty shop, dressed in his faded jeans, work boots and t-shirt. He was all man, and the shop was insanely feminine.

"I always thought I'd sell this place when we had kids. But now, I'm not so sure," she told him.

Matt leaned against a rack of clothes and she cringed, expecting him to accidentally push it over. "So keep it. You can do both."

Lisa laughed. "Easy for you to say." But he was right, there was no reason she couldn't be a great mom and still run her own business. If she wanted it that badly, she could make it work.

"The thought of not designing or seeing my customers anymore just kills me," she said, looking around slowly, taking in every inch of the store. The soft pink-painted walls and the chandelier in the center of the space, the wall-to-wall racks full of dresses and skirts and cute tops, the dressing rooms hidden by thick, luxurious drapes. "I love this place, but I want to put everything into being a mom, too. I guess it's the choice that all modern mothers face. I just haven't had to confront it until now."

"Lis, it'll work itself out. Just see what happens," Matt said, shrugging and acting like it wasn't that big a deal.

Lisa sighed and walked to the counter. Standing behind it, she looked down the shop at Matt where he still stood. He was the kind of guy who just took life one day at a time, so relaxed it was a wonder he didn't fall over half the time. They always joked that he'd be late to his own funeral. But she was a planner, liked to know what was happening and when, was used to running her own business and keeping her always-late husband in line. She'd grown so much since she opened for the first time, her collections becoming more mature as she moved closer to thirty, but featuring the same pretty, whimsical fabrics that had always appealed to her. She knew it would be impossible to walk away completely.

"Come on, let's go," Matt said, coming around the counter and scooping his arms around her, body hard to hers.

"Do you take anything seriously?" she muttered, laughing when he nibbled her ear.

Matt kissed her neck. "Sure do. Like how much I'd like to strip you naked on the counter, how much I'm looking forward to dinner at Kelly's tonight because I'm so damn hungry . . ."

Lisa swatted at him, punched his arm and escaped. "You're terrible."

He winked. "I know."

She loved that Matt wanted her, that he was so much fun, but she also would have liked to have a serious discussion about her work with him. Lisa sighed. "It's such a first-world issue, I know, but all I've ever wanted is a family. And on the other hand, I have my dream career going on here, and that's important to me, too. I just don't know what to do. I don't want to be caught between the two and end up doing nothing well."

Matt planted his hands on her hips, smiling down at her. "If anyone can have it all, it's you," he whispered. "Trust me. And besides, you've got me. You kind of do have it all."

Lisa stood on tiptoe, torso pressed to his as she kissed the smirk off his face, used to his teasing. "Oh yeah, I forgot."

"You forgot the most important person in your life?"

Lisa pushed him back, hands flat to his chest, and looked down at her stomach. "Most important or second most important?" she teased. "Actually, I can't forget the dog, so maybe you're third most important."

He grunted. "Hey, I'm most important until the day this baby is born."

Lisa hugged him tight. "I can't wait for the baby to come. It's going to be the longest eight and a half months of my life."

"By the time we paint the nursery, renovate some furniture, buy all the little clothes and fix up the house, the months will fly by in no time."

"I'm scared that I want this too bad," she whispered, listening to the steady beat of his heart against her ear.

His lips touched the top of her head. "Nothing's going to happen. I promise."

She knew it wasn't a promise he could keep, but she was happy to take his word. Everything felt right, everything had happened in the right order. She could keep running her business to stop her going stir-crazy when she was up to her eyeballs in diapers, just as long as she could figure out how to balance the two, and she was married to an awesome guy who was going to be an amazing dad. Matt was right: everything was going to be okay. She needed to take a leaf out of his book and chill out, stop worrying so much.

"I love you," she said, kissing him again before letting go. She walked out back and collected her things together: her design book, plus her favorite pen and pencil zipped into a little baby blue case.

She looked around, smiled at every pop of color, every garment hanging, every piece of jewelry on display. She was going to keep the shop. There was no way she could walk away.

"Let's go," Lisa said.

Matt held out his hand and she clasped it after flicking out the lights. It was time to go home.

❧

"Surprise!"

Lisa burst out laughing as they walked into her big sister's house. It was always chaotic at Kelly's place, but today there were streamers and paper lanterns hanging from the ceiling, a huge sign covered in glitter that she'd bet anything her little nieces had made. And it was obviously all for her. She'd only found out she was pregnant a week ago, but obviously Matt hadn't been so good at keeping their secret.

"*Ohmygod*," she muttered, glancing at Matt.

His face was as surprised as hers, and she knew he'd never throw her a party without her knowing.

"Don't look at me," he muttered straight back.

"Surprise, Aunt Lisa!"

Lisa let go of Matt's hand and dropped to her knees, wrapped her arms around her youngest niece, Eve, loving the feel of her skinny little arms hugging her back.

"Thanks, sweetheart," she said, dropping a kiss into her hair before pulling away.

"Daddy says you're gonna be real angry, but Mama wanted you to have a party."

Lisa laughed. "First, I'm gonna blame Uncle Matt for telling her in the first place, and *then* I'm gonna kill your mom," she replied, imitating her niece.

Eve burst out laughing and ran off giggling.

"Matt! What happened to keeping this quiet?" Lisa demanded.

He looked guilty as sin. "Okay, guilty as charged, but I didn't think she'd throw you a party!"

"Guess this is what I deserve for marrying my sister's best friend, huh?" Lisa teased, letting it go and grinning up at him as she looped her arms around his neck. He bent and kissed her on the mouth, making her sigh and forget all about telling him off. So what if her family knew? Maybe she needed to let go and not worry so much. What did she have to hide? She'd always counted on their support, so maybe it wasn't so bad that they knew the news a little early. She bet Kelly had told their little sister, too, which meant she'd have Penny on the phone before the night was over.

"I know you hate surprise parties," Matt whispered as he touched his lips to hers one last time, his touch so light he always left her craving more. "I would have told you if I'd known—I promise. No way I'd have kept this to myself."

Lisa pulled back when a hand landed on her shoulder. She spun around, giving her sister a big hug, then her brother-in-law, Richard. It was only a family affair, and even though she wanted to kill Kelly for the surprise, it was kind of nice.

"We all wanted to celebrate," Kelly said, holding her hand. "You've tried for so long, and when Matt told me, it was like finding out that I was pregnant. It means so much to us that you're going to have a family."

Lisa dropped her head to her sister's shoulder for a minute, just wanting to savor the moment. "I'm scared of losing my little bump," she confessed. "I don't want anything to happen to him. Or her. That's why I didn't tell you straight away."

"You're not going to lose it," Kelly replied, using her bossy big sister voice. "I promise."

"You can't make that promise," Lisa whispered back, tears in her eyes. "Not you or Matt, even though he thinks that he can somehow pretend like he can."

Big hands wrapped around her from behind them, followed by a warm, solid body pressed to her back. "I can," Matt murmured. "I can promise you, because I'm not going to let anything happen to you *or* Bump. Okay?"

Lisa met her sister's gaze, swapped smiles with her. She knew there was nothing Matt could do to protect her from a miscarriage, even if he actually wrapped her in cotton wool, but she loved that he cared so much, that he was so sure he could look after her and the baby.

"Come on, let's go say hi to everyone," he said, keeping an arm around her.

Lisa pushed away her worries, clung on to Matt. *They were having a baby.* Five words that hadn't stopped running through her mind since the day they'd found out. And finally, finally she felt like she had everything that she'd ever wanted, that the pieces of her own personal jigsaw puzzle were in place.

She had Matt. They had their house. Their dog, Blue.

And soon they were going to have their baby.

Life didn't get any better. Which was why Lisa had woken in a sweat every night since they'd had the news, waiting for something terrible to happen, waiting for something to crash. She knew it was stupid but she couldn't help it. Maybe it was because she was so used to being in control and this was so frustratingly out of her control.

"Come on, sweetheart, follow me." Matt's voice snapped her out of her thoughts.

Lisa smiled up at her husband and let herself get swept away in smiles and laughter, the hands reaching out for her belly; became lost in the bubble of good wishes. Her husband's humor was contagious; the smiles he kept flashing her reminded her why she loved him so much, how much fun they had. He balanced out her anxious tendencies with his positive attitude and zest for life. She might feel like she'd have two children to look after once the baby was born, but Matt was going to be a fun dad, and as long as they were all happy together, that was all she cared about.

"Hey, come give me a hand," Kelly called out, catching her eye.

Lisa was happy to take a breather and disappear into the kitchen. "You do realize that I hate surprises, right?" She slung an arm around her big sister and gave her a hug. "Just in case you've missed that fact our whole lives."

"The girls wanted to do it when I told them, and Matt was so cute when he spilled the beans. I was going on about the girls already asking for Christmas presents months ahead of the event, and he blurted that he couldn't wait to play Santa next year before he even realized what he'd done."

"Well, I wish you'd warned me, but thanks," Lisa said. "It means a lot that you did this for us."

"You look worried," Kelly said, moving away from her and taking cling wrap off some large plates. "Have you been sick?"

Lisa moved closer, leaned forward and stole a sandwich, narrowly avoiding Kelly's hand slapping at her. She popped it in her mouth and sighed. Kelly's tiny sandwiches were perfect as always.

"No. Actually, I'm just nervous, I guess. So many things keep playing through my head—worries, things that could go wrong . . ." She shrugged and went to take a blini, the cream cheese and salmon topped with capers making her mouth water.

"No!" Kelly said, grabbing it from her before she could eat it. "No salmon! You need to read up on what you're allowed to eat with that baby on board."

Lisa shut her mouth, trying to stop herself from actually drooling. "Oops. I forgot."

"It doesn't get any easier. With your first, you worry about everything, then with your second you start to think about what would happen to your first if you didn't make it through childbirth. It's awful."

"Oh, thanks for being so positive," Lisa said sarcastically.

Kelly stopped what she was doing and gave her the "big sister" look that she always did so well. "I'm just trying to say that what you're feeling is normal. Everything will be okay, but the worry never stops, even if nothing goes wrong."

"I know. Hell, I should know—I've seen you go through it twice!"

"Yeah, but it's not until you're a mom that you get that feeling, that . . ." Kelly threw her hands up in the air. "It's terrible. Suddenly you can't watch a news story that involves something happening to a child without crying. Everything just affects you differently. It's impossible to describe how it changes you."

Lisa nodded. "So the emotions are normal, even now?"

Kelly stopped what she was doing and came closer, held both Lisa's hands tight in hers as she stared into her eyes. "Sweetheart, it's normal. The ups and downs of what you're feeling right now are all normal, and it's worth every second."

"You didn't sound that grateful for your little rug rats when you called the other morning to say they'd woken for the third time in a row at five a.m.," Lisa said wryly.

Kelly shrugged. "Some days I'd give them to any orphanage with a spare bed, and I'm not kidding! But others?" her sister smiled. "Seeing the smiles on their little faces as we made decorations for you and talked about the baby, or the way they ran into my arms after school today? Worth every crappy moment. A hundred times over."

"Thanks." Lisa pulled her sister closer, needing a hug. "Matt's insanely excited about being a dad. You should see him stripping the walls in the nursery."

Kelly hugged her back tightly, not letting go. "I have no idea how you found a husband who's so thrilled about being with his wife after so long. It's not just the baby that he's excited about."

Lisa let her sister go, but this time she moved around into the kitchen to help her, happy to take cling wrap off and make sure the plates were arranged all pretty, just how her sister liked.

"Everything's okay with you and Richard, isn't it?"

"Of course! I love Richard. He's . . ." Kelly shrugged. "Richard is Richard. We're like any other married couple with kids, I guess. We have fun together; we parent as best we can and get through each day."

"I'm not following," Lisa said, laughing at the just-as-puzzled look on her sister's face.

"You must be blind. Have you not noticed how Matt looks at you? Like he wants to eat you up? After years together, you guys still have that 'first love' spark. We all laugh about it."

Lisa planted her hands on her hips, trying not to laugh and struggling. "Who's 'we'? Kelly!"

"Everyone! My friends see you two at a party or something and talk for days about how lucky my little sister is with the big burly husband who can't take his eyes off her."

Lisa knew she was blushing; her face was on fire. What could she even say in response to that? "He doesn't look at me like he wants to *eat me*," she muttered. Although she did have to admit that Matt always had his hands on her, still acted like they were teenagers sneaking around sometimes. And she did kind of like it.

"Sorry, did I need to spell it out? By *eat* I mean . . ."

"I know what you mean!" Lisa hissed. She was trying to be angry with her sister but she couldn't stop giggling.

"What's so funny?"

Lisa tried to stop when she heard Matt's deep voice but it only made things worse. She hadn't laughed so hard in forever.

"Your wife has crazy pregnancy hormones, that's all," Kelly said, cracking up again and making it even harder for Lisa to stop.

When she managed to look up at Matt, his eyebrows were raised.

"What's going on, you two? Spill."

Lisa smiled at her husband, forgetting the sandwiches she'd been busy arranging.

"Nothing," she said. "Just two sisters forgetting their age and being silly."

"Hey, there's nothing wrong with silly," Matt said, grinning. "I've been telling you that all along." He held out a hand and tucked her tight into his body when she went to him, under his arm and warm to his chest, her favorite spot in the world.

"And there he goes," Kelly murmured.

"Kelly!" Lisa scolded.

"I'm missing something here, or else you guys are actually going crazy," Matt said.

"Kelly has this silly idea that you give me a look all the time that most husbands don't give their wives after five years of marriage. Like you want to *eat me up*," Lisa confessed.

Matt wrapped his arms around her in a big bear hug and growled deep in his throat. "But I *do* want to eat you up all the time, Lis. Your sister knows me too well."

She went to protest and he grabbed her tighter, lifted her up into the air in his arms. She squirmed, fighting against his hold. They'd always been like this—always goofing around, and she loved that Matt didn't treat her any differently now.

"Matt! Put me down. I thought I'd told you enough already with picking me up!"

"Did you? I don't recall. There's something about you being preggers that makes me want to hold you."

He play-growled again and kissed her, melted away all her struggles until she was like marshmallow in his arms. Nothing felt better than Matt's touch, his kiss, the way he held her and gave her all his attention like nothing else in the world mattered.

"Make the most of it before the baby comes," Kelly called out. "And please, *please* keep your clothes on in my kitchen!"

Lisa indulged in one last kiss before reluctantly pulling away. "It's time to take the food out," she said.

Matt blew her a kiss back. "I'll do the drinks. I'm ready for another beer."

She watched him walk out of the room, couldn't take her eyes off him. She didn't realize her sister had been staring at her.

"And that's why the rest of the female population is jealous of you."

Lisa shrugged. "I'm not going to lie: I hit the jackpot with Matt."

He was infuriatingly laid-back sometimes, drove her crazy when he arrived home late after beers with the guys when he'd promised a date night, but she couldn't imagine being with anyone else.

"You know I'm only teasing, right? There are no two nicer people in the world than you guys. You deserve each other."

Lisa nudged her sister with her shoulder and picked up the plate of sandwiches. "Thanks for all this."

"Sweetheart, you've been the best aunty to my girls. This is a big deal and we're so happy for you." Kelly smirked. "Besides, you keep me in clothes. As long as I can fit your sample sizes, you'll always be my favorite sister!"

Lisa walked out through the same door her husband had disappeared through, a smile on her face that she doubted anything could crack.

2.

THREE MONTHS LATER

Lisa held on tight to Matt's hand, but he didn't seem to mind. Something about squeezing his palm hard was making her less anxious.

"We're going to do a scan now to check the baby," the sonographer told them, her smile kind as she faced them. "I'm going to squirt a little of this on your tummy and then we'll get started."

Lisa adjusted her pants so they were low, jumping when the cold jelly-like liquid touched her stomach.

"Cold?" Matt asked with a laugh.

"Freezing," she muttered.

"Your doctor tells me you've had some bleeding?" the sonographer asked. "That can be perfectly normal during pregnancy, but we'll check everything out just to make sure. We'll also be able to check all the baby's measurements and make sure everything is okay in there."

Lisa let her breath go as something appeared on the screen, a blur that turned to something more recognizable.

"That's our baby," she whispered.

"Sure is. And that bit there that's gone red on the screen—that's the heart, so you don't have to worry that your bleeding has been related to a miscarriage. Give me a sec and I'll play the heartbeat for you."

Lisa looked up at Matt. He was grinning like crazy. She closed her eyes and smiled as the strong little heartbeat played out.

"Unreal, huh?" he said.

They'd had one scan already, but this one was different. This one looked like a baby and not just a little bean. This time felt so much more real.

"Can you tell what gender the baby is?" Matt asked. "It's killing me not knowing."

"Let me just do all the vitals first, and then I'll tell you whether you'll be picking out dresses or toys for the sandbox. You should be just far enough along for me to see."

Lisa laughed, her worries falling away. She'd known that bleeding was normal sometimes, but it hadn't stopped her worrying like crazy. Her doctor had done a Pap smear just in case, but now that she could see their baby, see the little heart beating, she knew everything was going to be okay. It was the baby she'd been worrying about, not herself—she could deal with anything as long as her baby was okay.

They both stayed silent as all the measurements were tracked, parts of their baby enlarged and marked, and then the sonographer stopped and turned to them.

"So you definitely want to know the gender?"

Lisa grabbed Matt's hand again. "Yes."

"*Hell, yes*," Matt added.

They all laughed and then Lisa took a deep breath. She didn't care either way; she just desperately wanted to know.

"It's a boy."

"Yes!" Matt fist-pumped the air and made Lisa laugh, shaking her head.

"How am I going to deal with you and another boy?" she moaned, secretly thrilled.

Matt shrugged. "You'll do it. Maybe I'll grow up."

"No way. I'm counting on you to be like a human playground for this little man."

A boy. A gorgeous little boy to snuggle and kiss and adore. If he turned out anything like his dad, she'd be lucky.

The sonographer handed her a cloth. "I'll leave you with this to wipe your stomach down, and you can come out once you're ready."

"So everything's okay? Nothing out of the ordinary at all?" Lisa asked, starting to wipe.

"As far as I can tell everything looks fine with the baby. But I'll be forwarding these scans on to the specialist to check, as well as your OB/GYN."

Lisa nodded and passed Matt the cloth she'd used, pulling her jeans back up and sitting upright. He came back to stand beside her when he'd thrown the cloth in the bin, holding his hands out. She took them and stood, leaning in to him, breathing deep.

"We're having a boy," she murmured. "It feels so real now."

"You're not upset that it's not a little girl?" Matt asked, kissing her as he stared down at her.

"Not for a second. I just want a beautiful little baby," Lisa told him honestly. She hugged him tight.

"We can try for a girl next time. We're still planning on having a football team of kids, right?" he asked. "I don't want you backing out of the plan now!"

Lisa laughed. "Whoa, slow down. Maybe a quarter of a football team. You're not the one throwing up every morning."

"Oh yeah, sorry." Matt kissed her again, his touch soft, lips melting against hers. "As long as we have kids, I'll be happy. I'm ready to goof around with little people, spend more time at home. It'll give me an excuse to go to kids' movies, make little huts, eat ice cream and . . ."

"What are you talking about? You already goof around all the time!" Lisa burst out laughing.

Matt just shrugged. "You love it. I know you do."

Lisa turned around and headed for the door, ducking under Matt's arm when he pushed it open ahead of her. He'd make a great dad, and she could tell how excited he was. Besides, they'd always talked about having kids. It had always been part of their plan; it had just taken them a bit longer to get pregnant than they'd expected.

"So do I have permission to buy blue paint and get the room finished now?" Matt asked, holding her hand as they walked toward reception.

"Sure thing. Just make sure you get the same soft blue that's on the sample," Lisa said, no longer worrying, excitement taking over. "I'll order the fabric today for the blinds, and there was this super cute blue gingham giraffe that I'd love to put beside his crib."

Matt jumped in front of her, taking her face in both of his hands. "*You're* so cute sometimes," he muttered, dropping his mouth to hers.

There were people all around them, but today Lisa didn't care. She liked that Matt's enthusiasm was rubbing off on her. She kissed him back, laughing when he tried to dip her backward. They'd just found out they were having a little boy; if her husband wanted to kiss her in public, then she was damn well going to let him.

"If you get to buy blue giraffes, I get to go buy diggers. And mini tool belts," Matt told her.

"Deal," she said.

She knew next to nothing about boys, but as far as she was concerned, it was just going to make the process even more fun. Even if she had to take a crash course in trucks and diggers from her crazy-happy husband first.

3.

Lisa's hands were trembling. When Matt reached for her, staring straight ahead but his hand locking over hers, fingers linking tight, she held on like he was her only lifeline. She couldn't breathe. Why couldn't she breathe?

How were they here? Why were they here? What had they done to deserve this? Would anyone notice if she just got up right now and walked out?

"Thank you for your patience."

Lisa gulped, swallowing what felt like a rock in her throat as the oncologist walked into the room and shut the door behind them. She didn't answer, just sat. A few months ago, she'd sat in a room just like this and heard the best news of her life. Now she was waiting to find out if she was dying. If she had cancer. If she . . . Lisa swallowed again, pushed the thoughts away, looked up at Matt. But he was impossible to read, and he was staring at the man who was now staring back at them. Surely the news couldn't be that bad? She'd seen the baby; everything had looked fine. He'd looked perfect.

"I'm not going to lie. The prognosis is worse than we expected," the oncologist said, sitting on the edge of his desk, not even taking a proper seat. "News like this is never easy to deliver, but I want you to know that I will do everything I can to help you beat this." He paused. "The short of it is that you have cervical cancer, and because it's at a more advanced stage than I'd hoped, we have some tough decisions to make."

Lisa stared at him, fingers digging hard into her palm. *What kind of tough decisions?*

"Lisa, I'm confident we can beat this long term, as long as you follow my immediate recommendations for treatment. The bleeding you experienced was related to the cancer, not your pregnancy, and although the baby is healthy, we need to focus on you and the right course of treatment for you."

Lisa glanced at Matt, tried to speak, opened her mouth, but no noise came out.

"Is treatment going to affect the baby?" Matt asked, asking the question she needed the answer to, the only question she cared about right now. The question she'd begged Matt to ask for her in case she froze and couldn't get it out. "Will he be okay?"

Her heart beat too fast, her palm sweaty against Matt's as she stared at the doctor. Waiting. It was all they'd done the past week. Waited for news, waited for treatment options. Waited. Her mind was racing. *She couldn't hurt the baby. She couldn't have any treatment that would hurt him.*

"Unfortunately, I can't sugar-coat this. There's no way to effectively treat you for advanced cervical cancer while you're pregnant, not from what I've seen of all your results, and not if we want to save you." The doctor folded his arms, looked uncomfortable. "It depends what is most important here, what you decide as a family. As your oncologist, my focus is you, Lisa. I want to do everything I can for you and that's what my treatment plan is based upon. I want to start treatment immediately, and we can't do that while you're pregnant. I'm so sorry, but there's just no easy way to say that."

She felt like she was going to be sick. She ducked her head down, sucked back air. But Matt never let go of her hand and she clutched him tight. Tighter and tighter.

"What are you trying to say?" Matt asked. "That I have to choose between my wife and my baby?"

But Lisa didn't need to ask . . . She could see from the doctor's gaze, from the way he couldn't maintain eye contact with her. She knew what he was going to say, what he meant.

"Essentially, yes. My recommendation is to terminate and begin her treatment immediately with surgery. We can discuss the actual treatment plan, but until . . ."

Lisa ran. She caught her shoe, heard her chair tumble as she stumbled and yanked open the door and ran. The waiting room was full, the smell of flowers overpowering, the receptionist's eyes wide as she planted her hand over her mouth and kept running, slamming into the restroom door.

She only just made it to the toilet, doubled over as she vomited. She was sick over and over again until there was nothing left, hands on her belly as she sank to the floor. Her body was still heaving, the pain like knives stabbing every inch of her skin.

"Lisa?" Heavy footsteps echoed out. "Lisa!"

She couldn't say anything, couldn't push out a single word. Tears started to rain a steady beat down her cheeks, slipping into her mouth on their way down her face.

"Sweetheart," Matt whispered, pushing the door open, hitting the ground as he wrapped her in his arms, held her tight, one hand stroking her hair, comforting her, loving her. "Hey, it's all right. Everything's going to be okay."

"He wants to kill our baby," she sobbed, her words barely audible as she choked them out.

Matt was silent, held her, pulled her onto his lap on the floor of the restroom as he cradled her to his chest.

"He wants to save you," Matt whispered. "*I* want to save you."

Lisa sobbed, the noises so loud they sounded more animal than human. She clutched his t-shirt, cried so hard that she soaked right through it. She didn't want to save herself: she wanted to save her baby!

"Lis, it's going to be okay. I promise."

"Our baby," she sobbed. "I want *our* baby." Lisa pulled back, grabbed his hand and put it over her stomach, looked up at him through tear-blurred eyes. "Feel it. Feel our baby. I can't just not be pregnant anymore, just get rid of our *child*." She was hysterical, wished she could calm down but couldn't. "We're talking about our *baby* Matty. Our baby. *Our boy*."

He stayed silent, kept hold of her and rocked her.

"Uh, is everything okay in here?" a voice echoed out.

"Leave us," Matt yelled, holding her tighter, protecting her from the world.

Lisa caught her breath, got ahold of her tears, leaned into her husband and listened to the steady beat of his heart.

"Do you want me to do it?" she whispered. "Do you want to terminate?" She needed to hear him say no. She needed him to tell her that he'd never let that happen.

Matt's big breath pushed his chest out against her cheek, but she stayed tucked against him, needing him more than anything else in the world.

"You know what I want?" he murmured into her hair.

She pulled back, met his gaze as she looked into his impossibly blue eyes. She knew this was hard for him too, but he was different. He was a man. Their baby wasn't inside of him; it was inside of her, a part of her body right now. "What?"

"I want my wife *and* our baby. I want to flip the clock and figure out how the hell to change everything."

Her eyes welled with tears again. "Me too," she whispered.

"But you know what I want more than anything in the world?"

She blinked up at him.

"You. I want my wife. You're what I want. You're what I need."

A shudder trawled her spine, sent goose pimples rippling across every inch of her skin. "You want me to do it? To abort our baby?" she asked, hardly able to believe what she was saying.

"Lisa, if we have this baby . . ." He didn't finish his sentence.

She knew what he was going to say. She'd been up all night reading about options, praying that she wasn't at an advanced stage so they could treat her after she'd given birth. "I might die," she rasped. "If we have this baby, I could die, or he could end up delivered too early if I have treatment while I'm pregnant."

She watched as he steeled his jaw, then looked away as his eyes filled with tears and he cleared his throat. Lisa knew what he was saying, knew that he was right even though she was so desperate for a different answer, for a different solution. How could she have cervical cancer? How could this be happening to her? She was so healthy. She'd always been so careful to stay fit and eat well.

"Lisa, you can't die. Not on my watch, not if there's a cure."

"Because you want me more than you want the baby," she finished for him, wanting to hate him, wanting him to say that he wouldn't let anyone take their unborn child, that he didn't care what the stakes were, that it was the baby he wanted to fight for. But she couldn't.

Matt's grunt told her she was right. Her skin had that stabbing feeling again, the pain in her heart so severe she wondered if she was having a heart attack.

"I can't breathe," she gasped, struggling for air, pushing back from him.

"Come here," Matt commanded, scooping her up as he stood and kicking the door back open. He marched through the restroom, impossibly strong, impossibly heroic as he stormed out into the corridor to get her outside. She might not agree with him, might want to save their child instead of herself, but right now she wanted him to take charge, to get her the hell out of Dodge. She needed to get away from this building and she never, ever wanted to come back.

"I'm taking you home," he muttered, not letting go, not putting her down for a second.

If only he could keep her safe forever, protect her and their baby from the big bad wolf banging on the door.

Her lungs finally felt like they were filling with air, her gasps no longer blindingly desperate. But she knew that the pain in her heart would never disappear, not until the day she died, not if she had to make the decision to say goodbye to a baby she hadn't even had the chance to meet yet.

4.

Matt didn't know what to do, but he could only stare out the window for so long. He wanted to get in his pick-up and drive to work, spend a few hours hammering nails and helping his guys get the framing up on the new house they had under construction, but he couldn't. Lisa needed him and he somehow needed to figure out what to do for her. Their lives had changed so quickly. It had only been two weeks since the diagnosis and the awful decision they'd been forced to make.

He pulled out some fruit from the refrigerator and grabbed a knife, roughly chopped up some pineapple and watermelon. He knew Lisa usually made up super smoothies—hell, she made them for him all the time—but he hadn't exactly been paying attention when she was doing it. He turned, reached for a banana and added that to his pile of fruit, before scooping it all up and putting it in the blender. He let it buzz away for a while before taking a tall glass down and pouring the smoothie in for her, then crossed his fingers and hoped he'd gotten it at least half right.

He forced a smile and walked down to their bedroom. She wasn't there.

"Lisa?" he called out, wondering if she was in the bathroom. He looked in but still didn't find her.

"Lisa?" he called again, walking back down the hall.

Then he saw that the door to the nursery was open, instead of slightly ajar like he'd left it. He looked in and saw her curled up on the big armchair she'd planned on using for feeding.

"Hey," he said softly.

She looked up. The skin under her eyes was dark, her face pale, hair pulled back into a tight ponytail. Lisa had never been the sweatpants kind of girl, always in a skirt or dress or pretty top that she'd designed, but today she was wearing sweatpants and one of his t-shirts, which swamped her body.

"You, uh . . . you okay?" He cringed, knowing from the look of her that she was definitely *not* okay.

She didn't reply, just turned and looked away. Maybe she was staring out the window, maybe at the crib.

"I made you this," Matt said, closing the distance between them and holding out the glass. "Made with love, but it might not taste as good as the ones you make."

She didn't turn so he put it on the dresser beside her.

"Ha ha. You've had a lot of practice, though. I've still got my training wheels on." His voice sounded hollow.

When she still didn't turn, Matt looked skyward, wished someone up there could help him. He stood and waited, turned to scan the room. He'd spent so much time in here, had been so excited about getting it ready for their little boy, and it hurt to know that wasn't going to happen. But it wasn't a patch on the pain he felt at seeing his wife suffer.

He mustered some courage and put a hand on Lisa's shoulder. "Hey, turn around."

At first she didn't move, then she slowly angled her body back toward him. He could see tears in her eyes.

"Drink this," he suggested, reaching for the glass and passing it to her. She took it, but she didn't drink it. "Are you in pain? The doctor said there would be bleeding, so if there's anything I can do . . ."

"I had milk," she suddenly gasped. "I know they told me it could happen, but my boobs are so sore and then milk came out and I had to use the breast pads I had for after the baby."

Matt dropped to his knees. He had no idea what to do, what he was supposed to say.

"Sweetheart, I . . ." He was lost for words. The day of the termination would haunt him forever, knowing his baby was being born, only to die immediately. That it was too early for him to even have a one percent chance of survival. The pain on Lisa's face that day, seeing the light go out in her eyes as she was wheeled away from him.

"But there's no baby. My body doesn't even know that."

"I, um . . . We need to keep up your fluids, right? I mean, we were supposed to make sure that you had lots of water, and . . ."

"I don't want fucking water, Matt! I want our baby! Did you even hear what I just said?"

Matt stared at her, wasn't used to hearing her swear like that. "I'm just trying to help. Look, I know this is hard on you—hell, it's hard on me, too, but we'll have another baby. This nursery isn't going to sit here unused, because we're going to get you better and then we can try again, as soon as the doctor gives us the all-clear."

Lisa just stared at him and he didn't know what she was thinking. He took her hand and pressed a kiss to it.

"I love you, Lisa."

She gave him a sad smile, tears falling down her cheeks. He gently brushed them away with his thumb.

"We're so lucky that we caught this early enough to treat it. I'm so lucky I still have you."

She stayed silent, looked so lifeless staring back at him.

"What can I do? Just tell me what I can do for you."

Lisa looked away again. "Just leave me. We terminated our baby less than two days ago, so just let me sit here alone and grieve for our little boy."

Matt stood. He couldn't see the point of staying if she didn't want him. "So should I leave the smoothie?" he asked.

Lisa didn't answer him so he just left it, closing the door behind him. He walked back into the kitchen and leaned on the counter. Maybe he would have been better off just going to work. This wasn't the Lisa he knew, and he sure as hell wasn't used to their roles being flipped. Lisa had always been the one looking after him, only until now he hadn't realized just how much he relied on her.

5.

Matt held Lisa's hand as she was wheeled past him from oncology on her way through to surgery. He felt helpless. Completely, infuriatingly helpless, and he hated it. It brought back too many memories, made him want to just run away to avoid what he knew might be coming. What could happen. They'd been in a hallway just like this only weeks earlier when she'd so bravely gone through with the termination, and now they just had to hope they'd caught her cancer early enough that the surgeons could work their magic.

"Matt," she whispered when he bent to kiss her.

He held tight, smiled down at her. "You're gonna be fine. Absolutely fine."

"Tell him I need to be able to have kids. Please tell him how important that is to me."

Matt took a deep breath. "Baby, he knows that. We've told him already."

"But . . ."

"Lisa, the most important thing is beating this. Kicking cancer's butt, yeah? He's already told us that there is a small chance they'll have to be more invasive, but they're not going to do that unless they have to. To save you. Nothing is more important than saving you."

She looked away, but not before he saw tears fill her eyes. He stroked her face, wished she got the fact that he didn't give a damn about anything other than saving her. Sure, he wanted kids, but he wanted kids with Lisa around; he wanted to raise them together, or not at all. He wasn't going to lose her.

"Okay, I'll tell him," Matt said, not wanting to say the wrong thing before her surgery. She was scared and he needed to step up and show her that he was there for her. He just wasn't used to feeling like they were on different teams.

"Promise?" she whispered.

"Promise," he said, giving her a little wave as he stepped back. "You'll be great; it'll all be okay."

Her smile was small but it was there. Matt watched her go before turning around and heading for the waiting room. Then he changed his mind and decided to go grab a coffee. He made his way to the hospital café and ordered, then sat down and pulled out his phone. He had jobs to organize, calls to make; he'd rather keep busy instead of thinking about what Lisa was going through. He'd been there in another lifetime, seen his mom suffer and then silently, strongly end her battle with the disease. But Lisa was going to be fine. Because she'd had the termination, the oncologist and surgeons were confident they could eliminate the cancer.

He went on the Internet instead, stared at his Google homepage and forced himself to smile when the waitress bought his coffee over. Lisa was so damn upset about not being able to have kids, but all he cared about right now was not losing her. Cancer wasn't going to take his wife, not on his watch.

Adoption. Matt grinned when he saw how many links came up. If she couldn't carry their kids, then they could adopt. There was another link to fostering. *Hmmm.* He frowned. It wasn't something he'd have chosen to do, taking in an older child, but . . . He kept scrolling. *Surrogacy.* Why the hell not? So what if they had to take a different route to have kids? He'd have to read more about it, but he was pretty open-minded.

Matt sipped his coffee. Everything was going to be fine, he told himself, over and over. If she couldn't carry a baby, if it was worse than they thought during surgery and it ended up being more radical, he'd find a way to give them a family. To keep Lisa happy. This was his time to look after her, and everything was going to be okay. *Smiles and fun*, he reminded himself, swallowing a lump in his throat that he didn't want to acknowledge. Just because she had cancer didn't mean he couldn't make her laugh while he was looking after her. Once this surgery was over, everything was going to go back to normal and they'd be fine.

Because everything was going to be fine. She was going to be fine. He couldn't cope with losing her, not after what he'd been through in the past. Lisa was the bright light that had kept shining when he'd needed it most, and once this was over he hoped like hell he'd get his wife back. Because she'd been nothing like the woman he was used to since her diagnosis, and he wanted her back so bad.

∾

"Matt?" Lisa was groggy, her lips so dry that it felt like she'd had to crack them apart just to speak.

She opened her eyes, slowly lifted her head to look around. But the room was empty. Where was he? She was sore. Her whole body felt weird, and she wasn't sure if it was the surgery, the anesthetic or a combination of both.

The door suddenly flung open just as she turned to look at the full water jug beside her bed, desperate for a drink.

"Hey!"

Matt burst in, a blur as he rushed toward her bed, a big balloon in his hand that he let go of as soon as he met her gaze.

"Hey," she managed, voice hoarse.

Matt kissed her forehead and smiled down at her. "Water?"

Lisa nodded, pushing herself up on her elbows. She vaguely recalled the nurses talking to her, but she must have fallen asleep again soon after.

"Did everything go okay?"

Even though she was hazy, she saw Matt's face change, knew that something was wrong. He passed her the water, a smile still plastered on his face. But she wasn't buying it. It was the same face he used when she caught him out coming home late after a beer with the guys, or when he'd made crazy decisions to buy expensive things for the house when they were fixing it up.

"Matt?"

"Baby, you're here. You're good." He held the water for her to sip, a straw facing up at her. "They're confident that they got it all, that it was picked up early enough."

Lisa swallowed, her throat dry despite the water she'd just drunk. "Matt, tell me."

He looked guilty. Or . . . ? She gripped his hand, stared at him. "Did they do the surgery as planned?"

"No," he admitted, raking his hands through his hair, jaw like steel as he stared down at her. "Lisa, they saved you. Isn't that all that matters right now? You're alive and talking to me."

Her hands were shaking, her body stone cold as she pulled up to a proper sitting position. She felt sore down below, tender as she moved.

"Will we be able to have children?"

Matt wouldn't meet her gaze, looked away.

"Matt!"

"No," he said, finally staring into her eyes. "No, Lisa, we can't have children. They intended on doing the cone biopsy, but they found out it wasn't enough during surgery, so they had to do a more radical procedure. But they got it. They got it, Lis."

Her eyes were burning, tears hot and piercing as they flooded her eyes.

"Baby, we can adopt, foster, have a surrogate. We can still have a family one day. It doesn't mean we can't be parents."

Lisa wanted to be sick. How could he say that? How could he just dismiss what had happened to her? Did it even hurt him that they'd lost their baby? That she'd never have the chance to feel a flutter in her belly from her own child ever again? All these weeks she'd told herself that once she was pregnant again, the pain in her heart wouldn't be so bad. That as soon as she got pregnant for a second time, everything would be okay.

"I don't want to adopt, Matt," she said quietly as tears started to drop silently down her cheeks.

"Hey, if we don't have kids, we can go on motorcycle convoys and jump out of planes. We could make a whole list of awesome stuff that . . ."

"No," she whispered. "No, Matt. Just go."

He reached for her hand, slipped his fingers between hers, but she pulled away. His face was forlorn, mouth downcast, but she didn't care right now, didn't have the energy or will to comfort him. This wasn't a time for his stupid jokes or pretending like everything was okay when it damn well wasn't.

"Lisa, please. You're alive, you're . . ."

She turned away, her tears soaking the pillow beneath her head. "Just leave me alone." Right now, the mere fact she was alive didn't seem like a decent consolation prize.

Matt had always made her smile, had always been so much fun. There had never been a time when he hadn't been able to make her see the bright side of life. But not now. She didn't want to know what they could do or what great ideas he'd come up with; she just wanted to cry. For the babies she'd never birth. For the children she'd never see grow, their eyes the same color as hers or Matt's or their hair the same blonde shade as hers.

Matt was so damn worried about saving her, and yet all she could think about was the baby she'd already given up just to go through the surgery today. The surgery that had stolen something from her that she wanted almost more than life itself.

6.

"Can I get you anything?"

Lisa shook her head, stared at Matt. She wished he'd stop trying to look after her when all she really wanted was to be alone.

"No, I'm fine."

"You're sure? I could make a sandwich or do one of your smoothies. I've got a whole ton of fruit I can use."

"I'm fine, thanks," she managed, looking out the window, not wanting to connect with him.

"You look great," he said, coming closer and slinging an arm around her shoulder.

"I don't feel great." She actually didn't care how she looked. It was the last thing she was worried about.

"Want to watch a movie? I've got all your old favorites ready to go." Matt laughed. "I'm even prepared to watch *Sex and the City* with you."

She didn't want to laugh back but she managed a small smile. "Thanks."

"Or that movie *Dear John* if you want to go all sappy. Otherwise I'm thinking back-to-back viewings of *The Hangover* movies if you feel like laughing."

She wanted to strangle him and yell that she doubted she'd ever want to laugh again. But she didn't. Something inside stopped her.

But she couldn't stop wondering if he just didn't care as much as she did about what had happened.

"Can we take a rain check? I think I'll just go lie outside in the sun for a bit. Don't you have work?"

"Uh, yeah, but I want to look after you. Come on, we can have fun, can't we?"

She shook her head. "Just go to work. I'll be fine, and I'm tired. That way I can sleep."

Matt watched her like he wasn't sure what to do, so she managed another smile, wanted to convince him to leave her without having to scream at him that he was suffocating her. She wasn't used to being fussed over or looked after, and she hated it.

"Okay. Well, I'll head out for a bit. I won't be long."

Lisa hoped he would be. She could do with an entire day of not having to answer to anyone. Not having Matt watching her every move, waiting like she was miraculously going to morph back into her old self. No amount of homemade juices and pats on the head were going to magically make her happy again, even if she craved the exact thing that Matt wanted—for everything to go back to normal again, for her to be herself, for them to be happy without having to try. Maybe she should have just gone to Kelly's place and let her sister look after her.

෴

Matt was starting to feel like it was *Groundhog Day*. Over and over and over. It had been two weeks since Lisa's cancer surgery now, but every day had been the same. There hadn't been a flicker of the old Lisa yet, not even a hint of her improving. He was terrified it was always going to be like this, that he wasn't ever going to get her back. And he was just as scared that he had no idea how to make things better.

Then he'd remind himself what Lisa had been through, the shit she'd survived. He deserved a punch in the face for even thinking that what he was going through was hard. He had her; his wife had survived. It cut deep to think they couldn't have kids, but nothing would change the way he felt about her. He knew what it was like to lose the most important person in his life, and he didn't ever want to face that again.

❦

"Matt, we need to talk."

Matt looked up, dragged his eyes from the television screen. His mom sat down on the sofa beside him, had a look on her face he couldn't read. He sat back and waited, saw his dad walk into the room and wondered what the hell was going on.

"Matt, there's no easy way to tell you this, but I've been diagnosed with a type of cancer."

Matt froze. He looked from his mom to his dad.

"You're kidding, right? Is this a bad joke to see how I react?"

"Matt, this isn't something I'd joke about. I just want you to know so you understand what I'm going through."

He sat up, ran a hand through his hair. Looked back up at his dad again.

"What . . . I mean, how . . . ?" He didn't even know what he was trying to say.

"Darling, I'm going to be fine. I promise I won't let cancer beat me, but I might have to have chemo and maybe radiation, and I didn't want to start losing my hair or being tired and you not knowing what was going on."

"Of course I want to know," he choked out, staring at his dad again. He still couldn't believe it, but he could tell from the sad look on both his parents' faces that it was true. "Could you die?"

His mom reached for him and he threw his arms around her, didn't care that he was way too old to be hugging his mom so hard.

"I could," she whispered, her lips brushing his cheek, "but I won't. I'm not leaving you."

He hugged her tight, squeezed his eyes shut when he felt her body shudder and realized she was crying.

"I love you, Mom," he muttered, needing her to know.

"I know, darling. I love you, too."

Matt held her for as long as he could, until she finally pulled back and stared into his eyes, stroking his face.

"We're going to be fine, okay? We just need to get through this as a family."

 ❧

Matt swallowed hard, the emotion lodged in his throat like a rock that was impossible to shift. He didn't want to go back, didn't want to remember. Lisa had been the only reason he'd been able to move forward, get past his mom's death, because she'd given him something to live for, had drawn him in and made him feel alive.

Which was why he was finding caring for his wife so damn tough right now. Because she wasn't the Lisa he knew, and it was sending him back to a time he didn't want to relive.

Something nudged against him and he bent when he realized that Blue was pressing against his leg, nudging him.

"Hey, boy." He bent and scratched the dog's brown head, then patted his body, before straightening and forcing himself down the hall, worried that Lisa was pulling away from him, withdrawing further into herself instead of making slow steps forward.

"Hey, sweetheart," he said, keeping his voice light, not wanting Lisa to know how much he was struggling.

She didn't answer. Matt stepped in anyway, clearing his throat, not sure if she was asleep or just ignoring him.

"Lisa?"

He heard a groan, saw her move.

"There's someone here to see you," Matt said, glancing down at Blue, then pointing to the bed. "Go say good morning!"

Blue didn't need to be told twice. He took off toward the bed and bounded up instantly, jumping on Lisa and saying good morning the only way he knew how—thumping his tail and licking her face.

"Get off!" she groaned. "Blue, get off me!"

The dog hesitated and Matt laughed. "Come on, he misses you. Give the poor guy some love."

"Get him off me!" Lisa demanded.

Matt quickly walked to the bed and hauled Blue down. "Sorry, bud, not this morning." The dog looked dejected and Matt shared the feeling. It was so unlike Lisa not to want Blue; she was usually first to call him up on the bed in the morning for cuddles.

"Sorry, he's been nosing around looking for you," Matt said. He'd opened the blinds earlier and hoped it would rouse her, but it hadn't worked, which was why he was back in the room to coax her out.

"Come on, what do you want? Breakfast, coffee, anything?"

"I'm fine."

"I've told the guys I won't be in to work today. I thought we could have breakfast, take Blue for a nice long walk in the sun, grab a coffee . . ." Matt stared at her, wanting his wife back, the woman who was usually raring to go in the morning and would be out the door faster than him to take the dog out.

She drew the blanket tighter around her shoulders. "You don't need to do that. Just go to work and do whatever you had planned."

"Lisa, come on," he said, sitting on the edge of the bed. "This isn't like you. Let me take you out for lunch or something. Anything."

He was lost. He had no idea what he was supposed to do anymore.

∽

Lisa lifted her head. It felt like it was stuffed with stones, so heavy she could barely lift it. Matt was trying. She got that, and it wasn't that she didn't appreciate it; she just wanted to be left alone instead of him constantly trying to fix her.

He just didn't seem to get that she was grieving. That she needed time to herself, to process what had happened, to just stare into nothingness and not focus on the pain. Each day felt worse than the one before, not better.

Matt was sitting on the bed now. He stroked her hand and she stared at his fingers on her skin.

"Lisa, come on. Let me spend the day with you."

"I'm fine. Don't worry about me," she forced out.

He sighed and stood, arms folded across his chest as he looked down at her. "But I am worried about you. I don't know what to do," he said.

"Could you close the blinds?" she asked.

He obliged, crossing the room and pulling both blinds shut so the room was bathed in near darkness.

"Fine. I'll be home soon, well before dinner," Matt said, stopping beside the bed and dropping a kiss into her hair.

She forced a smile. "Okay."

When he left, she slumped down, head on the pillow. She wanted to get up and take a shower, but just the thought of it made her feel exhausted. But . . . She listened to Matt's footsteps, waited until she heard the jangle of his keys, knew he'd head straight out. Once he was gone, she forced her feet out of bed and stared at the bathroom like it was her target. She just needed to get up and get going, and if she didn't have Matt hovering then she might just be able to get through a day. It was like he was just waiting for her to come back, thinking that he could be all bright and normal and that some of that would rub off on her. Only it didn't, and as much as she loved him, it was starting to wear her down.

Lisa showered, brushed her teeth and put some make-up on. She could wear her glasses so no one could see how bloodshot her eyes were, and she didn't have to talk to anyone, but she did need to get out of the house. She walked down the hall, stared straight ahead and didn't look at the nursery door. Tears threatened, but she didn't let them fall. She grabbed an apple from the kitchen along with her keys and went into the garage. Her work was only a short drive away, and within fifteen minutes she was parked and walking through the front door. It was late morning, so it was already open, and she was grateful to see it was her part-timer, Jules, on, not Savannah, her manager.

"Lisa?"

She didn't take her glasses off, just smiled and kept walking.

"Morning," Lisa said. "I'm heading into my office to work on my next collection. I'd rather none of the customers knew I was in."

"Um, is there anything I can get you? A coffee?"

Lisa stopped walking, found her smile came easier here for Jules than it did at home when she was trying to be upbeat for Matt. "Yeah, sure. Put a 'Back in five' sign on the door and nip down to get me a latte. Grab yourself one, too." She pulled a note out of her wallet and passed it to Jules. "Thanks."

Lisa straightened her shoulders and opened the door to her office, then shut it behind her and went around to her big leather chair. She collapsed into it, loving the way it seemed to mold to her shape almost instantly.

"Hello, old friend," she whispered, running her hands across her glass desk top. She pressed the button on her computer screen and looked around at the piles of fabric samples. She opened her big design book, the one she always kept on her desk, and looked at her most recent sketches.

Lisa took a deep, shuddering breath. A wave of sadness crashed toward her but she fought hard, didn't let it take hold. This was her sanctuary. This was her happy place, where she could be alone and do her work, lose herself in her creations. Somewhere she didn't have to think about children or cancer or the fact she was supposed to be feeling grateful that she'd been cured and didn't have to endure chemo or anything else on top of what she'd already been through.

She opened iTunes and clicked on her design playlist, let the music wash over her, feeling the beat, her lips moving almost instantly to the Macklemore & Ryan Lewis track she sometimes listened to on repeat when she was designing.

She could do this. She could actually do this.

Lisa picked up her pencil and put it between her teeth as she flipped to a fresh page.

She could do this.

7.

Matt gritted his teeth and knocked back the shot of whiskey. If his friends had stayed and he'd been having a few more beers, he'd have been okay. But nothing about seeing his wife suffering with her grief, and wondering why the hell he still felt he was losing her even though she'd survived, was any part of okay. He slid the glass across the bar, swallowing the burn, wishing it hurt harder so it blocked out his thoughts. All he knew was that being here was a hell of a lot easier than being at home.

"Another," he ground out, clearing his throat. He'd told Lisa he'd be home after work, before dinner, but he'd never made it.

His mom had passed away eleven years ago, but the pain was still there, the loss of a parent something that would forever haunt him. But now with Lisa suffering, still recovering from her cancer surgery, the pain was raw, more real. He shut his eyes, thinking back, no longer fighting the memories that had been drifting into his vision every time he tried to fall asleep, every time he stopped thinking about his wife and what he could do for her. His mom was haunting him, the memory of her dying, the feeling of helplessness that he'd long since buried.

Matt walked silently over to the bed. He'd been told not to, that he should remember his mom the way she looked in his mind, but he needed to see her. If he didn't say goodbye and see for himself that she was gone, he knew he'd never believe it.

"Mom?" he said hoarsely as he approached, glancing behind him to make sure the door was still shut, that no one had followed him in. He didn't want anyone to hear him, and he sure as hell didn't want anyone to see him.

"Mom." It was a whisper this time as he stood over her, reaching for her hand and holding it so carefully, afraid he might break her.

She was gone. He could see there was no one there anymore, that it was just her lifeless body forlorn on the bed. Tears started to fall down his cheeks but he angrily brushed them away, sniffed hard and wiped his nose with the arm of his shirt. It wasn't right, her lying there like that, so bare, so exposed. She would never have shown that much skin.

Matt carefully put her hand down, back on the bed; her skin was almost translucent. Before she'd become sick, she'd always had a tan, was outside more than she was in, but now her skin was ghostly white. He was finding it harder and harder to remember his beautiful mom the way she'd always been, her dark hair falling to her shoulder blades, a big smile always firmly in place, making her mouth tilt up every time she looked at him. That was the mom he wanted to remember for the rest of his life, but right now he wanted to give his mom some dignity.

"Excuse me, but . . ."

Matt spun around, glaring at the nurse who'd interrupted him.

"What?" he snapped.

"It's just that we need to clear the room and . . ."

"Get the fuck away from my mother!" he screamed.

His father appeared then, eyes dark, days' worth of stubble on his cheeks. "Son, she's just trying to do her job."

"*Leave me,*" *Matt said, his voice like venom, staring at his dad.* "*Leave me alone.*"

He turned his back, didn't give a damn now whether anyone else was in the room or not, because he wasn't leaving his mom like that. He sure as hell wasn't going to let her be wheeled out like a nameless corpse, dressed in the ugly hospital gown. She had always looked beautiful, never left the house without make-up on and nice clothes, and he wasn't going to let anyone else see her like this. It was the last thing he could do for her and he was going to damn well do it.

Matt glanced behind him, saw they were alone again, and he touched her hand, then placed a palm to her cheek. He might be only seventeen, but he knew right from wrong, and this was wrong.

"*I'm so sorry, Mom,*" *he muttered. Her head was bare, her bald head almost grotesque it was so pale. And she was so, so thin. He hadn't noticed it so much until now, just how bone thin she really was beneath her clothes.*

Matt dragged his eyes from her scalp and looked around for her bag. She never left home without it, and he doubted she would have gotten in the ambulance unless someone had brought it for her. He was right. It was sitting on the floor, kicked halfway under the hospital bed. He pulled it out and found her scarf; the softest silk and in a light pink color. Maybe that's why he hadn't noticed how sick she'd looked, because she'd always had her scarf tied around her head and make-up on her face, her trademark pink lipstick brightening her skin. He lifted the scarf and stared at it, tried to figure out what to do and had no damn clue. So he just folded it in half and placed it over her head, covering part of her forehead, then carefully lifting her head to tuck it under.

He sucked back a sob as his fingertips connected with her skin. It felt too cold, not right. But Matt kept it together, did his best tying the scarf to the side slightly. At least she looked a little more like herself.

Then he found her blanket, one made of soft wool that she'd always had folded in her large bag, slung across the top because she was always getting cold and needing it near. When she'd been to watch his football games, he'd always looked up and seen her with it tucked around her shoulders, but her big smile and even bigger wave had meant no one else probably had a clue how sick she was. Maybe not even him. It wasn't until he'd received the call today, walked into the room and seen her lying on the bed, that it had really hit him. His mom's cancer had been bad; he'd known that, but knowing hadn't prepared him, not even close.

Matt pulled her gown down her legs as far as he could, feeling weird touching her like that when it wasn't something he'd ever usually do. Then he opened out the blanket and placed it over her, wanting to keep her warm even though he knew it was impossible. He even tucked her hands under it, knowing how cold they'd been the last couple of months. She was always calling him over to hold her hands, always telling him how warm he was and how she needed to steal a little bit of it before he left for the day.

He wished he'd skipped school and just stayed home. If he'd known she wasn't going to be around when he got home, he would have. Screw school. Screw football. Screw the whole fucking world.

Matt bent down low over her, wished he knew what to do with make-up so he could have put some on her face, but that was way beyond him. Instead, he held her, let all his tears fall onto the blanket he'd just covered her in.

"I love you, Mom," he choked out. "I love you so much."

He wanted to believe she was watching him from somewhere, that maybe she hadn't even left the room yet and was standing behind him, or drifting up above, before she passed over to wherever it was that dead people went.

And then he stood up, pulled himself together and walked out the door.

"Matt!"

His dad called out behind him as he stormed down the corridor, furiously wiping tears from his face. He didn't stop, didn't want to see him.

"Matt!"

A hand closed over his arm and he turned, angrily shoving his dad's fingers from his jacket.

"Don't touch me," he growled.

"I know you're upset, we all are, but . . ."

"Upset? You're upset? I don't see any tears!" Matt shouted. "Why the hell aren't you crying?"

His father's face was tired, worn, but it sure as hell didn't look upset.

"Matt, you need to calm down."

He raked a hand through his hair. "Did you see her in there? Did you see the way they left her? Or was that you? Didn't you care enough to give her some fucking dignity?"

Matt knew he was making a scene, would never have spoken like that around his mom, but he couldn't help it. Anger thrummed through him, made him want to slam his fist into something, anything.

"I was with her when she passed, Matt. It was very fast. She had an infection that her body just couldn't fight any longer."

"Did you fight hard enough for her? Did you even cry when she died in front of you?"

Matt wiped more tears away, unable to stop the flood of them as they rained down his cheeks. He hated him. He hated his father for not fighting, for not doing something to save his mom. He hated him for never crying, for always standing there silent and stoic instead of acting like he gave a damn. And he hated the look in his mom's eyes when she saw the strain between them. Because he'd loved his mom so bad, had no idea how he was even going to live without her. He was seventeen. He needed a mom. He needed his mom.

"I have some paperwork to fill in," his dad said, taking a step back. *"I'll meet you at home and then we can talk."*

Matt turned on his heel and stalked back down the corridor. He didn't want to go home, didn't want to talk to the man he'd slowly started to hate.

I wish it was you and not her. *That's what he wanted to say to him, only he'd been too chicken-shit to spit the words out.*

∾

Matt clenched the glass hard, stared into the amber liquid before raising the glass and swallowing the entire contents. He'd drunk too much; the straight whiskey no longer stung his throat. It should have numbed his pain, but it hadn't.

His phone rang and he pulled it out of his jeans pocket, stared at the screen through blurry eyes. It was Lisa. Lisa, his bubbly, fun wife. Lisa who had always kept him on the straight and narrow. *Lisa who had cancer. Lisa who stayed in their room all day and didn't want to leave their bed.* He waited until the ringing stopped and pushed it back into his pocket. He was in no state to talk to her, and he wasn't in the mood for a lecture about where he was. He'd tried so hard, but he wasn't used to being the adult, wasn't used to being the strong one and having to care for her. Because since he was nineteen, Lisa had had his back, but their roles had been reversed and he was being a pretty shitty husband right now.

"One more," he told the bartender, pointing to his glass.

He watched as it was filled, stared at it awhile. The bar was quiet now, the noise from earlier long gone, replaced with the silence of a few serious drinkers propping up the bar.

Matt felt hollow, and it was a feeling he recognized well, even after all these years. When his mom had died, there'd been nothing left inside him except pain, no other feeling other than an agony that made it almost impossible to lift his head. And anger. He had been so damn angry he could have exploded.

He lifted his drink and gulped down the shot, slammed the glass down on the bar and heaved himself up. He was wobbly on his feet, the room spinning.

"Hand over your keys," the bartender said. "You can come collect them in the morning but you ain't driving."

Matt shook his head, tried to laugh. "Nah. Then I'd have nowhere to sleep."

The bartender shrugged. "Not my problem, pal. I'll push the button and unlock it if you want to crash in there, but I'm keeping the keys."

Matt threw them on the counter and staggered out. Tonight there would be no Lisa giving him a hard time about staying out too late, no explosive argument followed by him begging to be let in the house. She liked making him sleep on the sofa when she was angry, but not tonight. Because tonight his wife was alone in bed, recovering still, depressed still. And instead of being with her, he'd given up and gone out.

If he hadn't felt like shit before, he sure as hell did now. All because he didn't know how the hell to deal with a wife who had had the same goddamn disease his mom had. And thinking about losing Lisa was impossible. All he wanted was his wife, and yet all she seemed to care about was what they'd lost.

She has no idea what it's like to lose the battle with cancer. Matt staggered, wished he'd had one more drink, another to block out the thoughts, to force him into oblivion. If his wife had seen what he'd gone through as a kid, maybe then she'd understand. *Maybe.* Right now he had no idea what was going through her head, and it felt like he never would.

"Where were you last night?" Lisa tucked her hair behind her ear, wishing she'd washed it. She was used to her hair feeling soft and bouncy, not lank like it was right now.

"Uh, it was a rough night," Matt answered, eyes downcast, voice husky. "Sorry."

She didn't say anything. What was she going to say? That he should have been home with his recovering wife who was about as fun as a bucket of sick right now? There were so many things she could have said with a barbed tongue, but she didn't. A few months ago, she would have headed out with a few girls if he was planning a boys' night, but now she didn't want to do anything.

"Who were you out with?" she asked, hating how needy she sounded.

"Uh, a few of the guys."

She couldn't decide if he looked guilty or just remorseful. "I needed you," she said, her voice cracking.

Matt stared at her and she looked away.

"You've been designing?" he asked as he walked past.

Lisa held her breath. He stank of alcohol. She looked down at the notebook open on the blanket, pencil lost beneath the covers somewhere.

"Yeah. Was better than lying awake worrying about you." And designing was the only thing making her feel alive right now, so of course she'd been designing.

He looked guilty. "Look, I crashed in the Chevy for the night. I'd had a few too many."

At least he hadn't driven home drunk. Truth was, she didn't care, not like she normally would, even though she was interrogating him. If he'd stayed out all night a few months ago, she'd have been beside herself thinking he'd had a car accident or something, but last night she'd almost wondered if he was gone for good, sick of looking after her and dealing with a depressed wife who couldn't even crack a smile without a huge effort anymore.

"Is there, uh, anything I can get you?" Matt asked, standing in the doorway with his thumbs looped through his jeans.

"I'm fine." She was going to snap that him having a shower would be nice but she bit her tongue. He could say the same to her.

"Come on, you need to eat. How about bacon and eggs?" He waggled his eyebrows before giving her a wink.

"Maybe just some toast," she said, trying hard to smile back.

When he left, she forced her legs out of bed, pushed her toes down onto the soft, plush carpet. What she hadn't told Matt was that his being out all night hadn't been okay. She'd sat awake, wondering what he was doing, where he was. She'd called him and he hadn't bothered to answer. So she'd told the dog to get up on the bed and snuggled into him, waiting, hoping she hadn't been so depressed and dark that she'd pushed her husband away for good. There had been something therapeutic about stroking Blue's thick fur, fingers lost in the repetitive motion of kneading him back and forth. But it hadn't been the same as having Matt at home. She sighed; she craved him when he wasn't there, and craved space when he was.

Lisa padded into the bathroom and turned on the shower, staring at herself in the mirror. It was like looking at a stranger. Her eyes were hollow, dark shadows beneath them, hair hanging limp, unloved. Her skin was pale, not the usual golden tan she sported over summer. But today was different. Today she was going to haul herself into the shop and work out front instead of staying hidden in her office designing. Today she was going to make herself look good. Today she was going to force herself to be part of the world again and reconnect with her customers.

Lisa showered, washed her hair and pinned it up as she rubbed a tanning moisturizer into her skin after drying. While she waited for that to dry in, she smothered her face in cream and then went out to get dressed. She reluctantly pulled a blind and saw that the sun was shining, so picked a little striped dress out of her wardrobe. She might feel like dying inside, but to the rest of the world she didn't want to be a pity case. She just wanted to dive back into work head first and try to find herself again. She got out her hairdryer and quickly blasted her hair, head upside down as she dried it.

There was no other way she could see to move forward, unless hiding in bed and in her office for the rest of her life was an option.

Her mobile rang and she crossed the room to look for it, found it on the floor beside the bed. She answered, not recognizing the number.

"Lisa, hi. It's Dr. Lindsay."

She hated hearing his name. Every time she'd ever spoken with him, it had been bad news in some form.

"Hi," she managed, shivering as she wondered what he was going to say. She knew she should be grateful to this amazing man for saving her life, but right now he was just the man who'd made her terminate her baby and robbed her of the chance of ever conceiving another.

"Lisa, I have great news. Your latest results are back in and the surgery was most definitely a success. I can confirm that as of right now we definitely won't need to pursue any further treatments. Everything went as planned."

Yeah, as planned because they'd cured her—he didn't bother to mention what they'd taken away from her. She was silent for a beat before forcing herself to answer. "So the surgery worked? The cancer has gone?"

"Yes, it worked. We never like to use the word *cured* when it comes to cancer, and it's still early days so we'll continue to do tests to monitor you. We'll be vigilant with checking you from now on, but going from these initial post-surgery tests, it's looking good."

What he was trying to say was that what she'd been through had been worth it. Lisa took a deep breath. She hated feeling like such a bitch, but it was like she was slipping into darkness all the time, unable to see the glass as half full after a lifetime of being so defiant in the face of anything bad that came her way.

"Thanks for the call," she said. "It's great news."

So why was she so numb? Lisa ended the call but clutched tight to her mobile as she walked out into the hall and found Matt in the kitchen.

"What?" Matt's face lit up as he put down his mug and stared at her.

"The surgery worked," she mumbled. "Dr. Lindsay's confirmed that I definitely won't need chemo or anything else, just like they expected."

Matt closed the distance between them in seconds, wrapping his arms around her and lifting her clean off her feet. "Woo hoo! Best news ever."

She smiled, fought the urge to snap at him and tell him to put her down. He was happy and she should have been, too.

"So everything's fine? I mean, it's over?" he asked.

Lisa bit hard on her lower lip, so hard she wondered if she might taste blood. "He just said the initial tests were clear but that they'd need to keep checking. I don't think I'm completely in the clear yet, but he sounded pretty positive."

"Baby, it was worth everything. I was so close to losing you." Matt kissed her, his mouth hungrily searching out hers.

Usually she would have laughed and kissed him back, been as eager as he was, but not now. She moved her mouth but the tingly feeling she usually felt from locking lips with him wasn't there.

"Was it worth everything?" she managed, the words whispered, pushing him away with her palm flat to his chest.

Matt frowned down at her. "Yeah, it was. We're together. You didn't die."

A part of me died. She wanted to say it but the words faded in her throat.

Instead of answering she walked past him and had a look at what he'd made. The smell of bacon almost made her gag, but he'd made an effort—she had to give him that.

"I'll just have some eggs if that's okay," Lisa said, hearing him move behind her as she reached for the coffee.

"Lis, I don't get why you're so unhappy. We should be celebrating!" Matt wrapped his arms around her, mouth dropping to her neck.

Lisa froze, tried not to explode. "So I'm alive," she muttered. "But I lost a baby, Matt. A baby I still think about every day, but you've obviously forgotten about him."

His hands fell away and she fought tears. She didn't want to push him away, didn't want to be cruel, but he just didn't get it!

"I haven't forgotten," he said quietly. "But you will always be more important to me than a child I've never met. You're more important to me than anyone else."

The tears were burning, fiery, but she refused to let them fall. "He was my child, *our* child, and I will never stop questioning the decision we made. Never."

Matt moved away, and she turned when she knew he was no longer standing behind her. She loved him—she always would—but right now a little part of her hated him for loving her more

55

than he'd loved their child. It was unfair and it was cruel, but she couldn't help the emotions throbbing through every inch of her body.

"I can't do this right now," she said, squaring her shoulders and deciding to leave rather than argue. It was unfair to both of them. "I'm going into the shop."

Matt nodded, face solemn. "Okay."

It was strange seeing him standing there with a spatula in one hand, skillet in the other. He'd never cooked for her before, never taken on the role of caring for her until now.

Lisa collected her keys and walked out, wanting to be busy, wanting to stop thinking and blaming and wondering. She couldn't stand staying in the house for a moment longer. Her hands were shaking when she got behind the steering wheel, but she forced herself to keep going. It didn't take long to get to her shop, and she immediately saw Savannah, her manager, putting out the sign as she parked.

"Hey!" she called out when she walked in, the smell of her favorite scented candle hitting her the second she was inside.

The colors surrounded her, the fabrics calling to her and wanting to be touched, and she wished in that moment that she could just stay here forever. This was her place. This was where she belonged. This was where she could be herself, away from what had happened and the decisions that had been made.

"Lisa! You look amazing!" Savannah came running to her, arms open as she pulled her in for a big hug. "Are you okay? You don't look like you're just heading to the office today."

"I'm okay," Lisa said, returning the hug, holding her friend and long-time employee close to her body. "But here I don't want to talk about it. The C-word is banned, and so is anything else unless it's work related or gossip that you want to tell me."

Savannah gave her a tight smile. "Understood."

"Now show me all the new stock that's arrived this morning and let me see the pre-orders. I want to know who I'm going to see walking through that door today."

Savvy had known her long enough not to question her, and she took her by the hand and dragged her out back.

"I'll show you everything, but first sit down. You need to show me every single new design."

Lisa laughed and dropped into the chair, ready to kiss Savvy for being so normal with her instead of wrapping her in cotton wool. Work was what she needed. Work was going to be her savior. If only she could hide here and imagine the rest of the world away forever.

❦

"Kelly, it's me."

Matt sat in his pick-up, staring back at the house. He was still parked in the driveway.

"Hey, how's it going?"

"Like shit," he said truthfully.

"I take it you're not having a good day," Kelly said, and he could almost feel her smile down the line.

"Understatement of the century," he muttered. "I have a wife who goddamn hates me, I stayed out all night so I feel like crap, and I have no goddamn idea what to do."

"For the head, I'd recommend Tylenol," Kelly said, voice softer now. "For my sister, I'd say just give her time."

"Kelly, it's been a while now. All she keeps bringing up is the baby, or the babies we're never going to have. I mean, why can't she just get how lucky we are that she's alive?"

Kelly sighed and he did the same, slumping over the steering wheel. He'd always thought he understood her. Yes, they were opposites in many ways, but that had always worked before—he'd understood where she was coming from.

"All her life, she's had this dream of being a mom, having children, so right now she can't stop thinking about what she's lost," said Kelly.

"I know. We always talked about having kids, but . . ."

"Matt, when you're pregnant, you feel so protective of the little life inside of you. Every step, everything you do, you're more aware. Add to that the fact you'd tried for so long. She lost a lot terminating that pregnancy—it must have been a hundred times worse than a natural miscarriage. At least then there's nothing you can do to stop it happening, but this was a choice you both made."

He heard what she was saying, and it wasn't like it hadn't hurt like hell losing the baby, but from the day he'd been told that his wife could be saved, that was all he'd wanted to focus on.

"Maybe I've been a jerk, but I just wanted to save her. I love her."

"I know you do, but just give her time. She's hurting."

"So do nothing?" he asked.

"Think of some things you can do together. Make time for her. There's nothing else I can suggest but just giving yourself to her when she needs you."

"Do you know she's back working?" Matt asked, leaning back in the seat now. "I didn't even realize she'd been back there so often when I was at work."

"The shop is good for her. We both know that. It's like her therapy."

Matt ground his teeth. Therapy for her, but it didn't help him figure out what to do.

"Maybe you should call into the shop. It might be easier for her hanging out with you there instead of at home with all the baby reminders," Kelly said.

"Thanks for all the advice," Matt said.

"You want my real advice?" Kelly said with a laugh. "Don't be an asshole again and stay out all night drinking. You want my sister to recover? Then be there when she needs you. And that means stepping up and pulling your own shit together."

Matt grinned. "Thank god for a sister-in-law to pull me up by my boot straps, huh? Maybe I should call Penny too. Then she can give me a telling off as well."

Kelly laughed. "You better believe it. We expect a lot from our unofficial brother—you know that."

He said goodbye and started up his vehicle. Kelly was right: he needed to sort his shit out and try to understand what Lisa was going through. He'd been so hung up on saving her, on not losing her to cancer, but in reality he felt like he was starting to lose her anyway.

∽

Matt had been in to check on his construction sites, but he decided to head into town and see Lisa before he got completely covered in dirt for the day. He grinned as he jumped into his truck. This way he could take her out for a nice lunch, surprise her.

"Let's go see our girl, huh?" he said to Blue, opening the door and letting the dog jump in first to ride shotgun.

Blue stuck his head out the window as Matt started the engine. It only took a short time to get there, and when Matt pulled up on the other side of the road, he saw Lisa in the window, head tipped back, laughing at something as she dressed a mannequin. Matt sat watching her, slung his arm around Blue to give him a pat. It was nice to see Lisa happy, to see her smiling, joking around and in her happy place. He'd been racking his brain trying to figure out what he could buy her as a nice gift, and it hit him then. A really nice new book to sketch in, something that wasn't too big to carry around. Something she could get started on a new collection with, focusing on the future. Maybe he could ask Savannah to look for something for him. She'd definitely know what Lisa would like.

"Come on bud, let's go."

Blue jumped out with him and followed alongside him as they crossed the road. Lisa had her back turned now as she pulled a skirt onto the mannequin she was dressing, but he could hear her laughing.

"Hey, gorgeous," he called out as he walked in.

Her laughter died as she turned and stared at him. "Matt?"

"Thought we'd surprise you. What're you guys laughing about?"

"Hey, Matt," Savannah said, stepping out of the window as Blue ran toward her, tail wagging.

"Hey, Savvy," he replied, shoving his hands in his pockets and wondering why his wife was suddenly looking so dull, when he'd seen her so happy and full of life from across the road.

"I thought we could go grab some lunch," he said, "or else I could help you wiggle clothes onto those sexy-ass ladies there."

Lisa gave him a tight smile. Clearly his jokes weren't going to make her laugh.

"I'm pretty busy today. Maybe we could take a rain check?" Lisa asked, coming forward to give Blue a big hug, blonde hair falling all over the dog as she bent to cuddle him.

"Ah, yeah. Sure thing," Matt said. "Maybe a coffee instead? I didn't pick up a hammer even for a minute so I could stay nice and clean for you." He gestured at his white t-shirt. He couldn't read her expression.

"It's a nice thought, but I really want to keep going here. I'm behind on everything," she said stiffly.

Matt nodded, but a pang of hurt hit him. "Sure. I get it. Come on, Blue."

He bent in to kiss her but she turned her face. It had been like that since the termination, the loss of connection, her always pulling away. He hated the distance between them but didn't know what the hell to do about it.

The dog reluctantly followed when he turned away and Matt waved to Savannah. "See you at home," he said to Lisa.

"Yeah, I'll see you later."

Maybe it was just him, but he got the feeling that the reason his wife had lost her smile had less to do with how she felt after surgery and a whole lot more to do with him.

❦

Lisa watched Matt go, never took her eyes off him as he crossed the road with Blue and jumped into his pick-up. She raised a hand as he drove off.

She hated the way she felt around him. Why could she come to work and feel like her old self, but not be that same person around Matt? She loved her husband, but when she was with him now . . . She sighed. All she could think about was what they'd lost, what they'd never have. And Matt was a constant reminder, because the overwhelming feelings of failure were amplified whenever she was with him. She hated herself for the way she'd behaved toward him, for being so cold when he was trying so hard.

"You okay?" Savvy asked, putting her hand on Lisa's shoulder.

"Yeah, fine," Lisa said, pushing her thoughts away, looking at the skirt she'd dropped in the window. "Let's get back to making these ladies look fab."

Savvy didn't look convinced, but she didn't ask any more questions and Lisa wasn't about to bring the topic up again. She'd see Matt soon; right now she had work to do, and work was exactly what she needed.

8.
TWELVE WEEKS LATER

Lisa braved a smile and stared into her champagne glass, raising it slowly to her lips to take a sip. The last thing she felt like was celebrating or drinking, but the other option was to give up and sob on her bed. She straightened her shoulders and smiled at her husband, trying hard to make an effort for his sake.

Hell, he deserved a medal for putting up with her. There was nothing she could do to pull herself out of the way she was with him, but he was trying and she needed to acknowledge that, even if it was easier to say than do. The only place she still felt like herself anymore was at work, but she couldn't exactly hide there twenty-four-seven.

"Happy birth day, Bump," Matt said.

Lisa blinked away a fresh flood of tears and nodded. "Happy birth day." She ran a hand over her stomach, something she'd never stopped doing even when the roundness had long since disappeared.

She swallowed the emotion and raised her glass again. After going sugar-, dairy- and gluten-free immediately after her cancer diagnosis, she knew she needed to make the most of the delicious bubbles now that she was easing up on her diet restrictions. "We should have been making a mad dash to the hospital today." Lisa forced herself to push the words out. They hadn't talked about him for weeks now, but today, not acknowledging him would have only made it harder.

Matt's smile was slow. "I bet you'd have been waddling around in bare feet, praying he would get a hurry on."

Lisa swilled the champagne again, held the stem so tight she almost hoped the glass would shatter. *Their little boy. Their darling, sweet little baby boy.*

"Do you ever wish we hadn't found out?"

She nodded. "Yeah. All the time."

"It made the whole thing more real," Matt said, surprising her with his tenderness. "Thinking about what . . ."

Lisa met his gaze. "Our son would be like?" she answered for him. "Maybe just thinking of him as an *it* would have made it easier. We wouldn't have built up such an idea of what he would have been like."

They didn't often talk about what they'd lost, because she always shut down whenever she thought about it. But today was the day they were supposed to have become parents. That she was supposed to have been staying strong and refusing an epidural, learning to breastfeed and refusing formula. Although after everything she'd endured now, she'd happily take the drugs and make up a bottle if it meant being a mom; all the preconceptions she'd held about motherhood were long gone. She just wanted the opportunity, wanted the chance to actually hold her own baby and decide what was best for him.

Instead, they had an empty nursery filled with even emptier cans of paint. Soft blue walls perfectly finished, a white sleigh crib pushed to one side, the big comfy armchair she'd found at a market never to be used for sitting with a baby. A delicate mobile forlorn on the floor where she'd been trying to assemble it. And still she couldn't bear to go in there and take it all away.

"What are we going to do?" Lisa asked, not wanting to pretend any longer that everything was going to be okay when it wasn't. Nothing about their life was going to plan; nothing felt right.

Matt leaned over and gave her that big, gorgeous smile that had made her fall for him over a decade earlier as a crazy-in-love sixteen-year-old. His fingers over her palm had always soothed her, made her so thankful to have her big, burly builder husband at her side. He'd always been so tough and strong, but what scared her the most now was that none of that physical strength had been able to save her when she'd most needed saving.

"We're going to think up a whole lot of fun things to do together, things we wouldn't have done with a baby in tow," he said, as if it was the most logical suggestion in the world. "And then we're going to do them all."

She loved his optimism, even if most of hers had completely run out and left her as a "glass half empty" kind of gal. "You're kidding, right?"

He laughed. "Nope. I've been trying all this time to think of something we could do together, and this is it. We can do a whole bunch of fun things."

She sat back, tried to forget everything else so she could just stare at her man. She wanted to go back to the way she used to feel, only nothing felt the same anymore. "Okay," she agreed, knowing she needed to make an effort. "Or maybe we could just come up with one thing, something we could do now."

"While we're at it, maybe we should think of what we're grateful for."

"You go first," Lisa said, not sure what to say. She was trying so hard not to be negative, to give him a chance.

"Hey, I'm just thankful you've still got your long hair after everything we've been through. It'd be a bummer to be married to the pretty beach-blonde and have you looking all bald and ugly."

Lisa burst out laughing. She hadn't laughed for the hell of it in a long time with him, but something about the way he was looking at her made her crack up. Only Matt could ever get away with saying something like that, and it took her back in time.

"You always did love my hair," she mused, running her fingers through her long locks. They were well past her shoulders, and she was so fortunate to have survived cancer without losing them. "I don't want to say something for the hell of it, but I am grateful to be alive, even if I don't act like it sometimes."

"I know you are," he said, reaching for the champagne bottle and filling up both their glasses with a cheeky wink. "So fire away with your ideas. What fun thing are we going to do?"

"I'm blanking," she confessed, not able to think of anything other than curling up to watch something on television before bed. Which was basically what she'd done every night lately.

"Come on, there must be something?" Matt asked.

"Um, I don't know . . ." She hesitated.

Matt took her hand, squeezed it. "Come on, please. Just have fun with me. For old time's sake."

She felt guilty, knew how hard she'd been to live with lately. She took another sip of champagne and braved a smile. When he touched her hand, she didn't pull away. Instead, she sucked in a breath and didn't break the connection even though that had been her instant reaction lately. "Go on a road trip."

Matt chuckled. "That's actually a brilliant idea."

Lisa raised an eyebrow. "It is?"

"Well it's something that only a couple without kids can do, so hell yes, let's do it!"

"You don't have to drink this just because we're celebrating," Lisa said with a laugh, feeling so much more like her old self now that they were joking around and she was coming up with ideas. "Go grab a beer."

Matt grinned and did what she'd suggested. When he returned, twisting the top on the bottle, he bent to kiss her, tilting her chin up with his thumb. "We're going on a road trip, we're going on a road trip," he said in a stupid sing-song voice.

"I guess we actually could." Lisa laughed, finding it hard to believe that she could even smile, given the way she'd been feeling, given what day it was. Maybe she just needed to take a leaf out of Matt's book, because right now she was feeling better than she had in a long time. "One day," she added, even as the familiar feelings of despair started to bubble up within her now that she'd acknowledged how good she felt. She forced them away, didn't want to think about cancer or babies or . . . She swallowed and took a slow, deep breath.

"If we're going on a road trip then we need a super-cool car," Matt winked.

Lisa leaned back into their outdoor sofa, smiling as she cradled her champagne, no longer in danger of snapping the glass into shards. She'd been dreading the day for so long, but now it was here . . . she had a lot to be thankful for and she knew it. The cancer, the baby . . . They were all stumbling blocks, barriers in the way of what was supposed to be an amazing life. But she had Matt and her family, and she needed to start being grateful instead of resentful, before she ended up losing her husband and becoming all bitter and twisted. Her cancer hadn't just ended her dreams—it had ended Matt's too, and it was hard to deal with the fact that she was the obstacle standing between Matt and his ability to become a dad.

"Can we end the trip in Mexico?" she asked, dreaming of white sand and blue water.

"Mexico?" Matt asked, eyebrow arched. "You're serious?"

"Yeah," she said. "I am."

Matt laughed. "Hell yes. Mexico here we come!"

Lisa smiled. Driving around, heading for Mexico—it all sounded perfect. Maybe a vacation a long way from home was exactly what they both needed. A change of scenery to remind her of all the good things that were still in the world.

They sat for a while, sipping, silent. The light had almost completely disappeared, and as darkness engulfed them, the pretty little lights that Lisa had strung up across the pergola at Thanksgiving the year before, all through the wisteria, twinkled back at her.

"Matt, I don't ever want to sell the house," she said, not taking her eyes off their beautifully renovated bungalow. They'd bought it just after they'd been married. It had been a work in progress for years, but when they'd found out she was pregnant, Matt had spent every spare hour finishing the place. It had been transformed from a house into a home, the whitewashed walls and pretty country-style kitchen everything she'd ever dreamed of, with doors opening out to a big sun-filled patio. Their floors were stained the perfect shade of dark chocolate, gnarled old wood beneath, but made beautiful by sanding, staining and sealing. And she'd chosen every piece of furniture with their renovated home in mind, the home that was supposed to be for a family. "Even after everything, I never want to sell this place."

"I don't want to sell it either, Lisa. It's our home, no matter what. Why have you been worrying about that? There's no need."

She was blinking away tears again when Matt's smile stopped her from choking up, told her that she needed to stay strong. Today was not the day for tears.

"It's just that we bought this home and fixed it up so we could have a family, and now we're not having kids . . ."

"Sweetheart, if we want to have kids, we can have kids. You know I'm up for adoption or whatever it takes!"

She shook her head. "Don't, Matt. Not now."

He shrugged. "I'm not selling this place after all the work I put into it. So don't even worry about it—it's still our home."

She nodded, wished she could be as optimistic as he was.

"I love you, Lisa," he said, taking her by surprise with his words.

Lisa looked into his eyes. "I love you, too." She smiled, trying not to be sad, wishing she felt differently. "*Promise I do.*"

Matt put down his beer and pulled her into his arms, onto his lap. "Baby, I know it. I always have."

It was Matt with tears in his eyes now. Matt who never cried no matter what, who'd stayed so strong. The only other time she'd seen his eyes fill with tears was the day they'd found out they were expecting a son; but on the day he'd been taken from them her husband had remained unflinchingly stoic, strong for her every step of the way, even when she'd sobbed. She'd thought all this time that it was because he didn't care as much as she did, but maybe she'd been wrong; maybe she'd just needed someone to blame.

"I'll be sitting here admiring a tree house one day, for the kids we're gonna fill this house with when you're ready to talk about it," he whispered, holding her hand.

"Matt, don't," she cautioned, not wanting to venture into that territory, not now. "Please just stop with the adoption talk, or anything else that involves kids."

He went to say something, mouth open, then stopped. "You would have made one helluva mom," Matt said, meeting her gaze, not backing down. "I don't care what you want me to say or not: you would have and you still could."

Lisa knew that Matt thought they had other options, but it wasn't what she wanted, wasn't what she'd seen in her future. But it broke her heart to think of Matt never getting that chance to be a dad, of them never getting the chance to be the parents they'd always laughed about being, so casually, like it was their right to have kids one day. Never realizing how damn hard it would be, or that the life they'd started to map out as teenagers might not go to plan.

"You still want it that bad, don't you?" she asked sadly.

"No, what I want is for you to be happy, whatever it takes." He leaned in to kiss her, to comfort her, but she just pushed him away. She didn't want his touch, not now.

∾

Matt stared into the eyes of his wife. He was trying. *He was trying so damn hard it was almost killing him.* He was trying to be in touch with his feelings, trying to say the right thing, trying to save his goddamn marriage.

"I don't care about not being a dad if it means I have you, Lisa. I need you to know that. You've got nothing to feel guilty about."

"But I do and I always will," she said, shaking her head, her fingers clenched tightly together so that he could see the white of her knuckles. "We wanted a family—*you* wanted a family, and now . . ."

"For Christ's sake, Lisa, I just want you!" How did she not get that he was just happy to have her alive?

He'd wanted their son more than anything, still wanted the little boy they'd talked about so much before he was gone, but not if the cost was Lisa. *Never* if he couldn't do it with her. There was nothing he wouldn't sacrifice for his wife, to make sure he didn't lose someone else he loved to cancer. Deep inside of him was an anger so strong it bubbled up like a volcano ready to erupt, a pain that made him want to scream and attack something, anything, lash out and pummel everything in his way. But Matt never unleashed it, refused to let it surface. He wasn't going to smash his fist into anything, because he was way too close to losing her already, and he wasn't about to give her an excuse to kick him to the curb.

"So when are we heading off on our road trip?" he asked, quickly changing the subject, not wanting to argue.

Lisa's gaze was sad. "We can't just head off. Weren't we really just talking hypothetically?"

He put his elbows on the table and leaned forward. "Yes, we can. And no, we weren't."

"But you've got a house to finish and more projects coming through. Don't you have a bathroom renovation to start down the road? And I've got the shop to run, another collection to design . . ."

He reached for her hand, held it. "That's why I have good guys working for me: so I can take time off when I need it."

"Just because you can walk away so easily doesn't mean I can." Lisa shook her head. "This is just crazy. We can't just up and leave. I can't."

"We can and we are," he said. "You can get inspiration for your designs while we're away. Baby, this is one thing you don't get a say in. I'm taking charge."

She blew out a big sigh and slumped forward, hands in his. "No."

Matt wasn't going to back down. "*Yes*."

The tears shining from her eyes did exactly what they always did to him; pulled strength from a reservoir within him he hadn't even known he had until recently. Every tear she shed made him tougher, more determined to support her and be the one to shoulder the load. It didn't stop his pain or make him any less pissed off with the world, but it made him a stronger man for his wife.

"What are we going to do with Blue?" Lisa murmured, her cheek resting against his hand as she lay slumped over the table. "We can't just leave our baby."

Matt chuckled, pleased that she was actually touching him, that she wasn't pulling away like she had been over the last few months. "We're hardly leaving him. Regular people go on vacation all the time and leave their pets somewhere nice."

"My sister might take him."

"Kelly?" Matt said, cringing at the thought of Lisa's big sister having their over-active Labrador along with her two kids. "I guess." He'd been thinking more along the lines of booking him into a kennel so the dog had no choice but to behave and wasn't in danger of getting up to mischief or escaping.

"I can't just abandon him."

As if on cue, Blue came running out, wagging his chocolate brown tail, tongue lolling to the side. Matt groaned when he saw something caught in the corner of his mouth.

"Blue . . ." he growled.

The dog just sat and wagged his tail, the picture of innocence.

Lisa's head snapped up and she stared at Matt first, then slowly at Blue. "Oh no, what's he . . ."

Blue licked his mouth and a piece of bright red fabric dropped to the ground beside the table. The way he was staring at them, so pleased with himself, made Matt groan again.

"Blue!" Lisa screamed at the same time as she leaped up and ran.

Matt glared at the dog. "Very bad," he muttered. "Very, *very* bad dog."

Blue didn't even have the decency to look guilty, but Matt knew it was a disaster, whatever he'd eaten. He followed his wife, stopped in the doorway of their bedroom, leaned against the jamb and watched Lisa bent over something on the ground. When she turned she was holding half of a pretty red stiletto.

"I must have forgotten to shut the closet door," she said.

Matt could have killed the dog. "I'm sorry. They looked cute on you." He remembered her wearing them with a red dress when she'd launched her summer collection in the store.

She sighed. "My sister might actually kill him while we're gone."

"Maybe." Matt knew she would have almost killed the dog herself for eating a pair of shoes a year ago, but things like that didn't seem to affect her quite the same way anymore. "On the plus side, you won't need those kinds of shoes on the road."

Lisa started laughing then and threw the shoe over her shoulder. It hit the wall. Matt crossed the room and dropped to the carpet beside her, laughing, slinging an arm around his wife. Blue poked his nose into the room at the same time, tail starting to thump against the wall in the hall when he got their attention.

"Come here," Lisa said. "You bad dog."

Blue came bounding in, his big body wiggling and making them both laugh all over again as he bowled straight into them, his tongue frantically trying to connect with their faces before he sat down on Lisa and did his best to squash her.

Matt patted his head while Lisa stroked him. Their crazy mutt, who was thick as a brick half the time and hadn't seemed to notice that he wasn't the tiny brown puppy he once was, the way he launched at them and tried to snuggle on their knees still. But he'd just warmed Lisa's heart, got through to her in a way Matt hadn't been able to in awhile, and that meant he owed the dog big time.

"We're terrible parents," Lisa said, still smiling as she lavished attention on Blue. But he saw the smile start to fade, knew he was going to lose her to her thoughts if he didn't act fast.

"Yeah, but look how much he loves us. He thinks we're the best."

Matt didn't need to be told what kind of parents they'd be, or would have been, because there was no doubt in his mind.

He loved their nieces, loved the idea of a little person trailing around after him, of chilling with his kid. And Lisa . . . He steeled his jaw, watching the way she lovingly stroked Blue's fur. Lisa would have been the world's best mom. His wife knew how to love, and she had enough room in her heart for a whole football team of kids.

"So when do we leave?" Lisa asked, surprising him. He'd expected to have to do a hard sell to convince her.

"Tomorrow? The day after?" Matt shrugged. "Whenever you want."

Lisa nodded and gave Blue another big hug. "The day after tomorrow it is. I'll just have to work like crazy to get everything sorted in the shop."

Matt leaned over and tried to kiss her, wanted that easygoing thing back between them that he'd been missing, but the dog took his chance and fell over backward trying to lean back for the affection.

"I'm not going to miss this big doofus," he muttered, grabbing Lisa and pulling her over Blue to get her to himself.

"Take that back! He can hear you!" she protested, shoving at him as he tried to kiss her. Matt ignored her completely, pushing her down to the floor and covering her body with his as he started to kiss her, wanting to show her how much he still wanted her. It had been months since they'd been intimate, since their pregnancy ultrasound when everything had still been happy, and the distance had been weird. He kept his arms locked on each side of her, not letting their pesky dog interrupt.

He was all talk—Blue had ridden shotgun in his Chevy from the day they'd brought him home as a pup, accompanied him to building sites every day. He'd miss him like hell, but this was about him and Lisa, and he was fast realizing how close to losing her he was getting, with or without cancer. Blue would still be here waiting for them when they returned.

Matt pulled back, kissed her slowly this time, her lips soft and pillowy beneath his. "I love you, baby."

She looped her arms around his neck, the look in her eyes giving him hope that he hadn't lost her yet. "I love you, too."

He hugged her tight to him, inhaled the coconut smell of her hair and tried to commit everything about her to memory.

"I know I've been a bit of an asshole, but I'm not used to being . . ."

"The adult?" She laughed.

"We've been together a long time, and it's been easy," he admitted. "Great, but easy. This last year was pretty rough."

"Yeah, it was. Still is," she told him, voice tinged with a sadness that was impossible to miss. "But I never wanted you to wrap me in cotton wool, Matt. I'll get through this. I just need time I guess."

"Yeah, but the local bar could have done with less of our money, and you could have done with a more doting husband." Although doting hadn't exactly worked: he'd felt like he was suffocating her, always saying and doing the wrong thing. Sometimes being apart after her surgery had been easier than being together. Part of him had wanted to treat her like a needy baby bird with a broken wing, but she'd always been the strong one, and another part of him had needed her to stay that way, had had no idea how to turn the tables, reverse their roles.

"I thought I was going to lose you, Lis, and it scared me. It still does. Please let's go away and just *be* us again."

Her smile was sweet, genuine. "Okay, fine. I'm convinced. I'll let Savannah run the shop, and we'll go away and just hit the road. You're right, we need it."

"Damn right we do. Let's hit the road, baby!"

Matt wasn't sure that she was as excited as he was, but it felt like his chance, like he might actually be able to make Lisa happy again if he just got her away from home and all the reminders of what they'd been through. He'd seen the old Lisa tonight, a spark of *his* Lisa, and he wanted her back. He wanted things to go back to the way they'd been, and he had no idea what to do if the road trip didn't work.

9.

Lisa smiled when Matt slapped her on the bottom as he passed her in the kitchen. She looked up, eyes meeting his, and caught him stealing a bagel.

"Matt! Those were for on the road."

"Lucky there're shops all the way from here to wherever we drive," he quipped with a grin.

She groaned, but it felt nice to joke around with him. "You're terrible," she grumbled.

"Don't act like you don't love it."

Lisa cracked another smile and it felt nice. The moments of lightness had been few and far between over the last few months, but something about today was making her feel good. Maybe it was just the fact that they were heading away, that things were going to be different for a while with new places to explore.

"I'm heading to the garage to sort a few things out," Matt said, walking backward and kissing her cheek.

Lisa inhaled his cologne, wished she hadn't found it so hard to feel close to him when she missed him so much. It was stupid, because they were still together all the time, but their usual spark had been missing and she hadn't realized how badly she'd been craving it. She was pleased he hadn't given up on her after all the times she'd turned away. In fact, she was pleased *everyone* hadn't given up on her. She hadn't exactly been seeing much of Kelly or her nieces either.

She watched him go, turning when she heard a car horn, followed by Blue scrambling madly on the timber floor and barking as he ran for the front door. Kelly had obviously arrived.

Lisa followed the dog, opening the door and watching him run toward the car. Her sister jumped straight out, and Blue was all over her.

"Hey," Lisa called out.

"Hey back," Kelly said. "You excited?"

More nervous than excited, but it was making her smile so she guessed she was kind of buzzed. "Yeah. I think so."

Kelly walked closer, still fending off the dog.

"Promise me you'll look after him," Lisa said, dropping down and throwing her arms around Blue one last time. "I'm going to miss him so much."

Her big sister dropped down beside her, hand on Blue's head as she stared into her eyes. "I promise. As long as he doesn't eat my handbag or the kids' toys, we'll be fine."

Lisa grimaced. "And if he does?"

Kelly laughed. "Then he'll be put in a box and sent to wherever you two are!"

Lisa hugged her sister, squeezing her long and hard against her body. They'd always been so close, and she hated that she'd been so distant from her and everybody else. "You know I'm going to miss you and the girls. I love you all so much, even if I haven't seen much of you lately."

She'd tried to tell herself to live in the moment, not to start tearing up, but something about hugging Kelly and realizing what a shitty sister she'd been lately was getting to her. She realized how withdrawn she'd been. If she said anything now, Kelly would fob her off and tell her she'd had a good excuse, but still. She just wanted to break free of the dark cloud that was following her around, shrug it off for good instead of just for a few hours or stolen moments here and there. And she was hoping that the road trip would do that for her.

"Stay strong," Kelly said, holding on to her arm and staring straight into her eyes, looking at her like only a big sister could. "And try to have fun. You both deserve it."

Lisa was pleased Kelly hadn't brought the girls. The last thing she needed was to pack the car and sob at the same time—it was hard enough saying goodbye to Blue without adding Zoe and Eve to the mix. She loved them so bad, but being around them lately had only reminded her of what she'd never have. She hated being that person when she loved them more than anything, but she couldn't help the way she'd been.

"See you, Bluey," she said, trying to sound bright as tears swamped her eyes. She quickly brushed them from her cheeks. "Be good."

Matt emerged from the garage then, but Lisa didn't wait for him, wanting a minute to herself. Instead, she waved to her sister and turned her back, went into the house and straight to her bedroom. She had two big bags almost packed on the bed, but everything was still a mess. She didn't know what to take, what she'd need. And she suddenly wasn't even sure she wanted to leave her house, because it had been her safe place while she was sick. Her beautiful bedroom with the voluminous drapes swept back from the windows, the walls a duck-egg blue that had taken her so long to choose when they'd been renovating the house. Her white waffle duvet cover and over-size pillows that she never failed to love every time she went to bed; the bedroom that had become her sanctuary and her prison when she'd been recovering. All she could say was thank god for work, but even that wasn't going to save her marriage if she didn't start making an effort. *Which was why she had to go on this road trip no matter what.* Because work wasn't enough.

"You okay?"

Matt's deep voice made her turn. She took one look at him and ran into his arms, cheek to his chest, listening to the steady thump-thump-thump of his heart. Why had she kept pushing him away when she wanted him so bad?

"I'm sorry," she whispered, feeling like she couldn't breathe, like every bit of air had been sucked from her lungs and there was no oxygen left to inhale. "I'm so sorry. But I can't do this. I don't want to go away."

"You can. You know why?"

She looked up at him, loving the gruff way he spoke to her.

"Why?"

"Because I'm your person, and it's only a trip. We're not leaving forever," he said, one side of his mouth kicking up into a grin. "And we're doing this together: we need the break. Now come with me."

"Where to?" she asked, blinking away the last of her tears and following him, taking the hand he held out. It was the nursery she didn't want to leave, terrified of forgetting her excitement, the anticipation of waiting for their first baby, of all those memories, even if they were painful. She wished it hadn't affected her so badly, but it had and she didn't know what to do about it. Which was why she was swinging back and forth about wanting to go away on the one hand and hibernating at home on the other.

"Two things," he said. "The first one is gonna be tough. The second is gonna make you smile."

Lisa took his hand and followed him out into the hall, but she dug her toes in when she saw the nursery door open, knew instantly where he was taking her.

"No, Matt," she said, refusing to go any further.

"We need to go in there. Together," he said firmly.

"Why? Come on, just let me go finish packing."

Matt stared at her. "We need to look around that room and then shut the door, leave it behind. Together."

It was so unlike him to be so insistent. "Fine."

She followed him, hesitated, and then stepped into the nursery and looked around. Even though she knew every inch of the room, knew how many giraffes were on the cute little mosaic going around the room and all the colors of the mobile still sitting on the carpet waiting to be hung, she still looked at every little detail, took it all in.

She looked out the window, out into the garden. The sun was shining brightly, but everything was still lush and green from the rain they'd had. If she'd been home with a newborn, she'd have been spending as many hours out there as she could log. Sitting on a picnic blanket on the grass, beneath the shade of the single tree in the corner of the yard. Admiring cherubic little hands and cheeks, laughing with her baby boy, singing even though she was tone deaf, making puppets and telling stories. It was supposed to be her time, the one time in her life that she stepped back from the business she'd built and took time out just for her and her new baby. Lisa turned around.

"This room is just sitting here, waiting to be used," she said sadly. "It's like *we're* still waiting."

Matt put an arm around her shoulders. "You want to stay in here any longer?" he asked.

Lisa was surprised at how thoughtful he was being. "No," she said honestly.

They both walked out and she pulled the door shut behind them, the noise of the latch making her feel sick. All that time she'd avoided going in there with Matt, except that one day he'd found her in there.

"Come on, let's go out and see your present now!" Matt said, tugging on her hand excitedly.

She sighed, not wanting to do anything anymore. Just being in the baby's room had drained all of her energy, and now Matt had gone from sweet and thoughtful to something that felt entirely the opposite, even if he was just trying to be nice. He was like a child sometimes, and although she'd always found that part of his personality fun, lately it had been draining.

"What is it?" she asked.

"An anniversary present," he said, his palm covering hers again.

"What? But we don't do presents. Seriously, I . . ."

"Come on," he said, tucking her under his arm, holding her close. "If you don't like it, we can take it back. This is the fun part."

Lisa followed him to the garage, mystified. Matt never gave her presents, *never*. She'd always hoped he might get more romantic one day, but there were only so many times she could hear him say that he didn't buy into Valentine's Day, birthdays or anniversaries without giving up. "You didn't have to get me anything." She hoped it wasn't a pity present. That would make it even worse.

Matt squeezed her. "It's kind of a gift for both of us."

She groaned. "Like the time you bought me a chainsaw?" It was the only other time she could remember him surprising her, all because he'd been desperate to buy a big, expensive power tool. But at least thinking about that dismal present took her mind off everything else, and even made her smile despite herself.

"Close your eyes," Matt said, leaving her side as she planted her hands over her face. "And no peeking."

Lisa heard a noise that sounded like the garage door going up, then silence. Until Matt's hands were closing over hers and slowly putting them back down to her sides.

"Surprise!"

Lisa's eyes almost popped out of her head. "A car?!" she spluttered, feet immobile as she looked from the car to Matt to the car again. "What the hell?"

"Not just any car. She's a Cadillac." His grin told her that he was insanely proud of the gift. "Bet you didn't see that one coming."

"*Ohmygod*." Lisa finally managed to get her legs moving and walked closer, fisting her hands to stop them from trembling as she approached the shiny red Cadillac her husband had just been crazy enough to give her. She touched the gleaming paintwork and grinned as she looked at the cream leather interior. Someone had either loved the car incredibly well or done a great job of recently restoring her.

"She's beautiful," Lisa said, turning to look at Matt, deciding not to lose the plot over how much money he must have spent. He'd done it for her and she could see how excited he was. She suddenly looked around, seeing his Chevy truck out front but . . . "Where's my car?"

Matt looked guilty. "I figured there was no point in having your boring old Toyota sitting around when I could get us a Cadillac."

"Matt! You sold my car without asking me?!" She planted her hands on her hips, ready to tear into him. Only the look on his face, the smile that had always melted her heart and the nervousness that flashed in his eyes, stopped her. He'd done this for her, for them. The last thing he needed was her getting all sentimental over a car that didn't deserve it. It had been an average vehicle that she'd gotten used to driving, not something she'd loved. "How can we even afford this one?"

"You let me worry about what we can and can't afford. Besides, they gave me a pretty good trade-in price for your car. Now jump in and try her out!"

His enthusiasm was contagious and she wasn't about to be the party pooper at her own party. "I hope it has a roof that works," she grumbled.

"Course it does, baby," Matt assured her, opening the passenger door for her. "Your carriage awaits."

Lisa sat down and burst out laughing, the clouds above her lifting, happiness taking over. "We actually own a Cadillac!"

Matt joined her, sitting behind the wheel. "We sure as hell do."

"This is crazy," she muttered.

"You already said that," he said with a grin. "The day I suggested the road trip in the first place."

Lisa sighed and leaned back in the seat. It was incredible. She'd never been super into cars, but there was something about the Cadillac that made her feel like someone else. "We'll be like Thelma and Louise."

"Thelma and freakin' Louise?" Matt spluttered. "I ain't no Louise."

"Bonnie and Clyde then," she said with a smirk.

"I can roll with that."

"*Ohmygod,* please don't tell me you stole this car? I don't want to *actually* be Bonnie and Clyde."

Matt gave her a long hard stare, one eyebrow raised. "No, sweetheart, I didn't steal the car. Don't be crazy—even I'm not that stupid."

Lisa shut her eyes and rested her head back again. It did feel good. The car was beautiful, her husband was bending over backward to make her happy, and they were about to go on the adventure of a lifetime. It might not be what she'd seen in her future, but she wasn't about to look a gift horse in the mouth, not after all the blows she'd received over the last year. It was time to try, and she was going to make a damn good effort at doing exactly that. For both their sakes. Because she'd been with Matt since she was barely a woman, married her childhood sweetheart. Their problem was that everything had always been easy between them; they'd never had to face any obstacles. Until now. And now life was testing both of them in ways she'd never imagined possible.

❧

"You ready to roll?" Matt called out, shutting the trunk and stretching as he glanced over at his Chevy. He couldn't believe that his pick-up was going to be parked up without him. The only thing about it he did like was that it meant he wasn't going to be working for a bit, and after a busy few years building houses with his teams of guys, it was nice to take a decent break.

"Almost."

He jogged up the two steps of their house and headed down the hall. He stopped when he reached their bedroom. Lisa was bending to pick up a bag and the look she gave him was pure guilt.

"Another bag?" he asked, groaning at the thought of re-packing the trunk to make anything else fit.

"I don't know how long we're going to be gone," she said, flashing him a smile that made him groan again. "You want me to look good though, right?"

"Stop with the guilt," Matt growled, trying not to laugh. "Of course I want you to look good!" It felt good laughing, just joking around. Made him remember how things had always been between them.

"Okay then." The two words sounded like a breath of air, a gentle whoosh as she blinked and fixed her beautiful hazel eyes on him, a peacefulness there that made him smile.

"Come on, let's go," he said, crossing the room and taking the bag from her before she could change her mind.

"You have the camera?" she asked.

"We have the camera. And the iPads and our phones and the list and just about everything from your closet." Lisa punched him on the arm and he jumped out of the way, laughing. "And *I* have a change of underwear, a clean t-shirt and a pair of jeans. We're good to go."

"The fridge is empty and everything's turned off. I think we're actually ready to leave," Lisa told him.

"Me and you in our pretty red Cadillac," Matt said with a chuckle as he threw his arm around her and dragged her down the hall. There was no point saying anything else; all he wanted was to keep a smile on her face and enjoy every second they had together.

"Just me and you and the road," she murmured, hugging him tight to her side as they walked.

He noticed that she didn't even look at the nursery door they'd shut earlier. Going into the baby's room had been tough before, but it was something he'd been wanting to do and he was glad he'd looked around it. Maybe he could get the color changed while they were gone so it was easier for Lisa to come back to.

Matt stopped to set the alarm and then pulled the front door shut behind them, locking it and turning to face the car. Lisa grinned as she walked toward it, swinging open the door and jumping in. He watched as she scooped her long blonde hair up into a ponytail, thinking how gorgeous she still was. She'd been cute when he'd fallen for her, but she was all woman now, and she'd gotten more gorgeous with every year that had passed.

He carried the bag to the car, leaned in to give her a quick kiss on the mouth and then opened the trunk again.

"What was that for?" Lisa asked, looking surprised.

"Nothing. Nothing at all. Can't a guy kiss his wife just for the hell of it?"

"Sure."

He listened to her laugh and found a place to stuff her bag. "And because you're my wife, it means I can kiss you whenever the hell I want."

Matt was trying so damn hard, but at least today it felt natural. Their fights usually consisted of him screwing up, her yelling at him, him waiting her out and eventually them having crazy-good make-up sex. Whatever was going on between them right now was nothing like that.

Matt strode over to his Chevy and started the engine, drove it into the garage before locking it and shutting the garage door. He pushed the keys into his back pocket out of habit and ran back over to jump behind the wheel of the Caddy.

"You're taking the truck keys with you?" Lisa asked, looking confused.

"I ain't risking no one stealing my ride," Matt said with a grin, turning the engine over and leaning back as the car started up. It sounded like heaven to him: endless days driving and no plans. After being settled for years, he was looking forward to some downtime. If he hadn't met Lisa he'd probably have been a drifter, not giving a damn about putting down roots anywhere, after the upheaval of losing his mom. But with her, he'd been happy to do whatever she wanted, and he'd gotten used to following her lead.

"Goodbye, little house," Lisa called out, holding her hand high above her head and waving in the air as he backed out.

Matt took her hand and placed it on the gear shift, putting his on top of it.

"This is it," he said, giving her a quick grin before pulling out onto the road.

"Yep, this is it. Here's to an amazing road trip," Lisa said.

"Damn right."

Matt put his foot down and reached in the back for his baseball cap, loving the way it shaped to his head like it was made just for him. He put his hand back over Lisa's and settled into his seat. They were going to drive for a few hours, eat somewhere good, and then find somewhere to stay the night.

Sounded perfect to him. Or as perfect as they could get right now.

∽

The sun was so bright and beautiful that Lisa was worried she was going to get burnt before their vacation even began, but it was making her feel good. Maybe she'd been seriously lacking in Vitamin D the past few months. Matt had put the hood up for a bit and was putting some gas in, and she did a quick check of her emails, wanting to post a pic of their car that she'd taken earlier. Her customers loved seeing snaps of her life and what she was wearing or doing.

After a little while offline when things were really rough, she'd jumped straight back in to social media, sharing designs, what she was wearing . . . Lisa gulped. Pretending like she hadn't had her heart ripped out of her chest and her dreams shattered had been tough, but there was also something freeing about being another person online. Work was what kept her going, and she liked the contact with the women who frequented her store or bought online, the fact that her clothes made them feel good.

Lisa put her phone back in her purse once she was done and turned as Matt jumped back in the car. He passed her a Coke and put a bag of chips in between them, and she quickly ripped the bag open. So much for her post-cancer diet.

"To hell with no sugar, huh?" she joked.

Matt held up his Coke and banged it to hers. "Cheers to that."

They both sipped, and Lisa loved the taste. She never drank soda and it took her back to the drinks she used to buy at school when she was earning her own money and her mom couldn't stop her.

"Maybe we should have bought a more practical car. Like one with cup holders," Matt said, taking another swig of his soda before balancing it between his thighs and firing up the engine.

Lisa drank some more, not even bothering to feel guilty. She'd done so well with her special cancer diet of no sugar or dairy, but the sugary bubbles were definitely worth it.

"Where are we stopping tonight?"

"Anywhere we like," Matt replied.

She got the map out, a real one instead of the app on her phone. It was like trying to read Braille, but she squinted at it and turned it a few times and tried to look like she knew what she was doing. They'd talked about where they wanted to go but she'd been so anxious packing and worrying about the dog and her shop that she'd left it to Matt to figure the rest out. He was better at working out distances and stopovers than she would ever be. Lisa put down the map and angled her body so she was facing him.

"Do you ever think about how different your life could have turned out if we hadn't met?" she asked.

"Hmmm, not really," Matt said through a mouthful of chips. "If we hadn't gotten together, maybe I would have moved away from Redding, closer to the beach maybe so I could have surfed whenever I wanted."

She put the map down and stared out the window at the Californian landscape as it whizzed past. "Would you be playing football still?"

Matt chuckled. "Baby, we both know I wasn't cut out to go pro, and I sure as hell wouldn't still be playing now, not at almost thirty."

"How do you know you weren't good enough?" she asked.

"If I was, I'd have done it regardless of whether I was with you or not. Are you asking me all this to avoid having to read the map?" he joked.

She bit down on her lower lip and gently chewed on it, ignoring the map comment. She'd always wondered if Matt felt like he'd sacrificed anything for her, whether he had dreams he wished he'd followed that didn't include staying in their hometown. Suddenly she needed to know the answers to questions that she hadn't bothered asking before, didn't want to take for granted how he felt. Because now it wasn't just all that stuff; it was the fact that she couldn't give him a family, too. That she might have made him sacrifice something else. Would he have married her if he'd known? She tried to push the thoughts away but they were hard to shake.

"I was a damn good high school quarterback, but I was never *pro* kind of good. Not good enough to make a career from it. You know that, Lis."

"You would have been picked up by a college team." She wasn't trying to pick a fight or dredge up the past, but suddenly she couldn't stop, needed to know.

Matt glanced at her before quickly looking straight ahead again. "I was, actually."

She had to stop her jaw from dropping. "You were?"

"Yeah, I was," he said softly, eyes firmly fixed on the road as he spoke. "But that was a long time ago, and it wasn't what I wanted. Life was kinda rough then."

Lisa was silent for longer than she meant to be, but she couldn't believe what he'd just told her. They'd been together so long and the fact he'd never mentioned it seemed weird to her. Why hadn't he wanted her to know back then? Why had he kept it from her all this time?

"Look, I knew what I wanted, and I'm happy. I made that decision for me, and it was the right one. I just wasn't in the right head space to be part of a new team. I couldn't have focused and it would have been a disaster."

Matt was three years her senior, which meant that he'd made the decision before they were officially together. But still. The *what ifs* in life had been bothering her since her surgery.

"You know I'd have told you to go," she said wistfully. "We weren't even dating then."

"Like I said, I knew what I wanted. I didn't have to tell anyone because my mind was made up."

"I often wonder who I would have met, what I would have done differently," Lisa told him, finding it hard to consider another life, a different path. "I can't imagine being with another man, not now, but it's crazy to think how different our lives could have turned out."

Matt took her hand and looped his fingers through hers. "I'm happy, Lis. I always have been and I wouldn't change a goddamn thing."

She stared at him. "Really? Even knowing how much pain there was to come, you'd still have asked me to marry you?"

His smile was slow as he glanced over at her. "Even knowing the future, I'd still have kissed you behind your parents' house when you were sixteen."

Lisa clamped her hand over her mouth, remembering. "I can't believe we did that! And then waited so long for a rematch."

"Hey, you didn't see the look on your dad's face when we snuck back around and he was walking out of the garage! It was enough to scare me off a rematch for a while."

Lisa smiled, the memory like a flash of color in her mind, thinking about her old family home and having all her family together. Even though Kelly was only a few years older than her, she was more the mother figure in her life now as well as being her best friend. She'd kind of picked up where their mom had left off when their folks had moved away for her dad's work, and Lisa had missed them so badly when they'd first moved. Her little sister, Penny, was working in New York near their parents, but she was moving back to California sooner rather than later, and Lisa couldn't wait to spend more time with her.

"So you're happy? I mean, you're happy with the decisions you made in the past?" Lisa asked.

"Hell, yeah. Aren't you?"

Lisa sighed. She seemed to do it all the time now; it seemed to be the only answer she was capable of sometimes.

"I'm happy with you, with everything we have, but sometimes I wish I hadn't dragged you into all this," she said. "That I'd taken a different path so I didn't have to cause you so much pain. I know I've been hard to live with, impossible during this treatment, and I keep forgetting how hard it must be for you. We've never really talked about your mom either."

"They're crazy words," Matt said straight back, shaking his head and frowning over at her. "There's no one I'd rather have by my side than you. We've had ten awesome years together, and a tiny part of that time has been crappy." He was silent for a beat. "My mom died and I survived it. You're not the same as her, and what happened to you was not the same as what happened to her."

Crappy was a nice way to put what they'd been through, and she didn't doubt for a second that he hadn't seen parallels between her and his mom. She'd just been so preoccupied with what she was going through that she hadn't asked him, or maybe she hadn't been emotionally available enough to deal with anyone but herself.

Lisa leaned back in her seat as her husband stroked her leg. She knew how lucky she was to have a partner who had been her best friend for so long—they loved each other's company and nothing had changed that over the years. Cracks had shown in so many of their friends' marriages, but maybe having kids had added stress to their lives. Perhaps it was time to feel fortunate that she'd been able to enjoy every second with Matt, that they'd been able to spend so much time together, just the two of them. What they'd been through had tested them, hurt them both, but she was ready to fight, to start over as best she could.

"It feels good to have nothing to do. Nowhere to be," Lisa admitted.

Matt stayed silent a while before answering. "You're not already missing the shop?"

Lisa shrugged and stared out the window some more. "Yeah, I am. But I can't hide away there forever, can I?"

Her store had been her focus for the last six years, something she'd built up from a tiny shop selling her own designs, to a little fashion powerhouse for her creations and more. And then she'd added her online store, which had seen her workload double, but she loved it.

"I'm so pleased you never sold the shop, once we found out you were pregnant," Matt said, glancing over at her.

"Me too, but the break will be good. It'll let me focus on refilling the creative well and working on some new designs." Her design book was packed in the bag at her feet, and she planned on doing lots of sketching and keeping her designs fresh and fun. Even if it was just a few dresses, a pretty skirt and some fun necklaces, it would be good to add to her next collection.

"You do realize that I expect to trawl through vintage markets and look for beautiful fabrics, right?" she asked Matt. "I want to be inspired, to think about what I could design next. I don't want to be a victim; I just want to be the old me again. To feel everything and love life."

"Lis, I've been your husband for a while now. I fully anticipate being tortured at markets on this trip." Matt's words were soft, gentler than usual. "And I want the old you back again, too."

"Me too," she whispered, reaching for his hand again, holding it tight. "I really, really want that, too."

❧

They rode in silence awhile, the scenery whizzing past. Matt felt relaxed, enjoyed just staring out the window and listening to whatever country music the radio station was playing.

"You haven't told me where we're going yet," Lisa said.

He glanced over at her, one hand on the wheel as he settled back into the seat. The Caddy wasn't as comfy as the Chevy, but he wasn't about to complain. Driving it with the top down on a picture-perfect day was good enough for him, and the way they were just chatting was making him feel like he could actually get the old Lisa back. Kelly had been right when she'd told him to make more of an effort.

"Sacramento," he told her. She'd been so busy getting ready to leave that he'd figured it all out himself.

"So you need me to find that on here?"

Matt laughed when Lisa turned the map around, squinting as she stared at it.

"You do realize we'd never have won *The Amazing Race*." He grinned when she dropped the map, clearly exasperated. "You'd have let us down. But Sacramento isn't far and I don't think you need to navigate."

"Me? *I'd* have let you down?" She made a *humph* kind of noise. "I could have been the driver."

He chuckled as she picked up the map again, looking like she was about to kick its butt for pissing her off. "Hey, we'd have come out of it smiling. I just don't think we would have had a shot at actually getting to any of the destinations ahead of the other contestants. And I'd never have let you drive."

Lisa let out a big sigh. "Okay, I admit it. I'm a bad sidekick. Maps just don't make sense to me. I mean, *ugh*."

Matt reached for her hand, linked their fingers together so their connected hands were resting on her thigh. "I didn't marry you for your map-reading skills."

She started to stroke his hand, tickling gently across his skin, and it felt good.

"How long will it take?"

"Just a few hours. I thought we'd head to Sacramento, stay the night there before going on to Napa Valley in the morning. Sound okay?"

He took his eyes off the road for a second again, caught her eye. He knew just the mention of Napa would make her smile. Or at least he hoped it would, because deciding to take her back there was about as romantic as he'd ever been.

"It sounds perfect."

They'd always talked about taking a trip back to Napa. It was where he'd proposed, amongst the vines on a balmy summer's evening after way too much wine, and where they'd gotten married since it had been their special place. He'd checked them into the same room again, and he couldn't wait to see the look on her face when they pulled up outside. He was desperate to tell her, but the surprise factor was too good to miss out on. And he had her gift too, the design book he'd thought about that day he'd been parked outside her shop. She might have shot him down on his lunch offer, but he'd still sent Savvy an email to ask her to look for the perfect book and to fill it with pieces of Lisa's favorite fabrics. He couldn't wait to surprise her with it when the time was right.

"You tired?"

She yawned in reply. "Yeah. I'm exhausted. I've been spending way too long in the shop lately, and then designing into the small hours."

"Just shut your eyes and chill. You don't need to stay awake for me."

"Yes, sir," she murmured, but when he looked at her, she was smiling.

It was his job to take care of her, to protect her. He'd already failed big time, hadn't been able to do anything when the doctor had given them the sucker-punch news, and instead of stepping up, he'd just kept on cruising, expecting everything to be okay, not realizing how tough she was going to find the other side of things, coping with what she'd lost. If it had been cancer of another kind, he knew she'd have been so strong, so determined, but losing the baby had knocked the stuffing straight out of her and he needed to find a way of slowly getting it all back.

After a while he saw she was asleep, and he decided to call his dad. He'd told him they were going, but hadn't exactly had a lot of time to chat before they'd jumped in the car and headed out of town. The night before, when Lisa had been asleep and he'd been lying there, all he could think about was his mom. They were memories he hadn't been able to shake since Lisa had been diagnosed, and the way he'd treated his dad always played heavily on his conscience. Would their own son, had he lived, have behaved toward him that way if Lisa had died? Would Matt have ended up taking the blame? Matt clutched the wheel tighter with both hands, thinking back to what a shit he'd been.

∽

He dug his nails into his palms and stood taller, forced himself to walk into the church with his head held high, not about to be a jerk when it was his final chance to say goodbye to his mom.

He saw his dad, sitting in the front row with his aunt on one side. Matt gritted his teeth, forced himself to move closer.

"Matt, come sit here," his dad said.

Matt stopped at the head of the row and sat alone instead, staring long and hard at his dad. He hated him. He hated him so badly that he wanted to hurt him. But instead he sat, kept a lid on his anger, sucked in a breath as his eyes fell on his mom's coffin. He wondered who'd chosen it, who had decided what his dead mom was going to lie in to be put into the ground.

Then the music started to play, just a piano that sounded haunting in the otherwise silent church. It was full, except for the two front rows. Full of people who'd loved his mom, people he knew and people he didn't. Family who had traveled from he couldn't even remember where. And still all he felt was pain.

His dad hadn't fought hard enough. His dad hadn't cared enough. If it had been Matt's wife, he'd have saved her. He would have found someone to help her, he wouldn't have given up, he wouldn't have stopped until he'd managed to make her better. If they'd only been honest with him, told him that she was going to die that soon. Because he didn't believe for a moment that his dad hadn't known, and they shouldn't have kept it from him. They should have given him the chance to say goodbye.

"We are gathered here today to remember Candace Williams." The words washed over Matt, made him reel. He doubled over, thinking he was going to be sick on his shoes. The pain was so bad; the pain was . . . He sucked back a breath, fisted his hands tight and pulled up so he was leaning against the uncomfortable wooden pew again.

"Candace was a wife and most importantly a mother, and I would like us all to acknowledge that she has left behind a son whom she was so proud of. A promising quarterback with the world at his feet. I know that Candace would want Matthew to grieve and then live his life knowing that she will always be looking out for him."

"Screw this," Matt muttered, jumping up, the inside of the church suddenly spinning as he clutched the back of the pew. He thought again that he was going to be sick, but he forced it down, refused to give in to the nausea.

"Matthew, we feel your pain; we know how badly you hurt. Please don't go," the minister said.

"Matt." It was his father now, on his feet, pleading, holding out a hand to him.

"No," Matt choked out the word, blinded by a blasting pain that consumed him, that made it impossible to even breathe. "You have no idea how hard this is or what she wanted, and I'm not going to sit here and listen to someone who didn't know my mom speak a whole lot of bullshit about her."

"Matt!" His father scolded, taking a step closer.

"You should have fought harder, Dad. You shouldn't have let her go," Matt yelled, oblivious to all the people gathered around them. "You should have saved her!"

"Matthew, please." The minister came closer, but Matt started to walk backward, tripping down the aisle.

"You want to know something about my mom? The truth?" he asked as tears streamed down his cheeks, clogging his throat. "She was the best mom in the world, and she didn't deserve to die."

Matt turned and ran out, needing to get away. I'm sorry, Mom. *He whispered the words inside his head, hoping she could hear him. But she was Mom. She would understand. She was the one person in the world who always got him. They could sit in the same room for hours and she'd never push him, never grill him for information or try to tell him what to do. And when he was ready to talk, she was always waiting, happy to listen and give him a hug, to drop her head to his shoulder and tell him he'd always be her baby. She'd ruffle his hair and he'd laugh and push her off, and then she'd fix him something to eat. She'd been at home waiting for him every day after school, or cheering him on at practice. She'd put little notes in his lunch when he'd gotten his first real job over summer vacation, and even though he'd been red-faced from embarrassment, she'd managed to make him laugh.*

But she was gone now. And that meant there was no one left to talk to, no one to laugh with and chill out on the sofa with at home. No more stupid notes.

Matt gasped in fresh air as he ran down the road. His legs wouldn't stop, feet pounding the pavement. When he finally stopped, doubled over and trying to breathe, the nausea came back and he vomited, over and over. His body shook, stomach heaving.

He didn't ever want to feel like this again. He was never going to get close to anyone else, never going to let himself get hurt again. He didn't care what happened, as long as he never had to feel pain like this again.

Matt ran all the way home, burst in the front door and yanked open the refrigerator. He took out two of his dad's beers and went to his bedroom, still panting, his breath short and sharp. Then he dropped to his stomach and pulled out a little container he'd hidden under his bed, one he'd bought from the stoners at school. He opened a beer and guzzled it, then pulled out one of the joints and lit up, using the matches he'd stored under his bed, too. He leaned back, inhaled deep, coughed as the marijuana filled his lungs.

He might not be able to forget, but he'd discovered what would make him feel better, what could blur the memories and take him to a happier place.

✄

Matt glanced down at the phone on the seat between him and Lisa. Every time he thought back to what he'd done, the kid he'd turned into, it cut deep. He dialed his dad's number and hit the speaker button, then placed the phone on his lap so he could keep both hands on the wheel. Another reason why the Cadillac wasn't practical compared to his Chevy with all its clever technology, but it still wasn't enough to make him regret buying the car.

"Hey, son."

Matt smiled when he heard his dad's gruff voice, forgetting all about the car and the shit he'd done as a teenager. It had taken them a while to get to a good place, but they were pretty solid now and Matt didn't want to screw it up. He'd put so much blame on his dad after his mom had died, made him the brunt of all his teenage anger and hatred, but they'd managed to get past it eventually, mainly thanks to Lisa. She'd made him happy and the animosity had slowly faded away, eventually. A decade later and the guilt still ate him up, but all he could do was make up for it now as best he could, even if he wasn't ready to talk about how much it had hurt losing his mom or how bad it still hurt sometimes. *Or to say sorry.*

"How are you, Dad?"

"Oh, you know. Just been out doing some gardening. Now I've come in for a beer and a crossword."

Matt stifled a laugh. His dad was fast becoming an old man now that he was retired. "Sounds busy. Make sure you put your feet up for a bit."

His dad grunted. "Where are you?"

"Heading to Sacramento," Matt told him, glancing at Lisa to make sure she was still asleep. Her lips were parted, her breathing heavier than usual, or maybe he just hadn't noticed before. She looked perfect sitting there with her hair falling over her shoulder, arm still resting against the window. "We'll head to Napa, then San Fran, maybe a few more stops, then San Diego. We're wanting to reach Mexico at the end, stay somewhere nice."

His dad was silent for a beat, and Matt kept his eyes on the road, cleared his throat. There was so much he wanted to talk to his dad about, stuff he'd held close and not talked about with anyone, but getting the words out always seemed impossible. They still did.

"How's she holding up?"

"Okay, I guess." He sighed, not wanting to lie. "Actually, not great, but we'll get there."

"Just give her some time. Don't push her."

"That's what I'm trying to do. I'm trying, Dad."

"Matt, you and Lisa have been together a long time, but . . ." Matt kept listening, knew his dad was trying to find the right words. "Look, you've never faced anything like this before, but you can get past it. She's a great girl and I know how much you love her."

"I'm glad you believe in me," Matt said, trying to make a joke even though he was feeling somber.

"I'll see you when you're back," his dad said. "You go and have a good time, and come back with a truckload of memories to share with me. It's boring being at home all the time!"

"Did I tell you we bought a Cadillac?" Matt asked with a laugh.

"You bought a goddamn Cadillac and didn't come show it to me before you left?"

They both laughed and it felt good. "I'll give you the keys when we get back. You can take her for a spin and have some fun."

They said goodbye and Matt settled in for the rest of the drive. There wasn't too long to go—it was less than three hours in total from Redding to Sacramento—and he just wanted to take it slow and enjoy the road. He had his wife at his side, the sun was shining a steady beat all around them, and he was driving a kick-ass car. There was nothing he wouldn't do for her; his problem was that he wasn't sure *what* it was she wanted from him.

Things seemed good today, almost normal, but he knew there were way too many things lurking beneath the surface for Lisa to just magically come back to him.

10.
TWELVE YEARS EARLIER

H e's an angry young man," Matt overheard his dad say. "I don't know where I went wrong."

Matt listened but said nothing. Because if he went and spoke to his dad then they'd know he was listening, and then they'd end up arguing, and he didn't want Kelly's parents to see.

"Is he doing drugs? Smoking? Drinking?" Matt overheard.

"I honestly don't know. But he's out until all hours and he hardly speaks a word to me. We're not in a good place right now, and we haven't been since the day his mom died. It's been over a year of hell, and I just don't know what to do with him anymore."

Matt's dad was lying. He'd already tried grounding him for smoking and Matt had just gone out the window and not come home for the night.

"He's always polite here. I know that doesn't help, but it's something. And Kelly seems to really like him; they're good friends. We only see a nice young man when he's visiting and he really seems to look out for her, so I wouldn't worry too much."

"Stop listening," Kelly said, grabbing his hand and dragging him away. "You might hear something you'll wish you hadn't."

"Easy for you to say," Matt grumbled, but he did what she said. He didn't need to hear anything else his dad had to say.

"Want to go for a swim?" she asked, waving him over as she skipped ahead. "The others will be here soon."

"Sure." He nodded and smiled at Kelly. They'd gotten along ever since they'd ended up taking the same classes through senior year, in a definitely-friends-only kind of way. She'd ended up dating one of his buddies, and even though she was pretty, he'd never thought about her like that. He liked hanging out with her because he liked listening to her and she never told him bullshit stuff about his mom, like it would get easier or that he should stop drinking. They all smoked a little, but he smoked a lot, almost chain smoking now to get through each day. And nothing had gotten easier; not one day had been anything like easy, and he couldn't see that changing anytime soon.

He lit up a cigarette, quickly puffing before Kelly came over to drag him into the pool. She was up ahead of him, already pulling her t-shirt over her head, flashing the hot pink bikini she had on underneath as she stood by the water.

"Hey."

Matt turned and saw a girl standing there. Someone he didn't recognize. "Hey," he replied, clearing his throat and dropping his cigarette to the ground and stamping on it with his boot.

"I don't think we've met . . ." he said, fighting the urge to look her up and down. She was so pretty, with long blonde hair that fell all the way down her back, beautiful blue eyes that seemed to twinkle at him. She appeared to be younger than him, but she looked confident as hell and it knocked him off balance for a beat.

"I'm Lisa. Kelly's sister."

Damn. It was Kelly's *younger* sister. He'd only been over at Kelly's house a few times now over summer vacation, and he'd never met her siblings, but he did know them by name just from hearing her talk about her family.

"Uh, you going to swim with us?" he asked.

She laughed. "I don't think Kelly invited me." Lisa twirled a strand of beach-blonde hair around her fingers, smile wide. "She'd kill me if I crashed her little party."

"No way! You have to. Come on." He held his hand out, waited for her to clasp it. When she did, he had to kind of drag her along, her eyes wide as she stared ahead to her sister. She was seriously cute.

"You sure? I mean, don't you want to finish your cigarette? Or start a new one?"

"Me?" He laughed, surprised by how sassy she was when she looked innocent as hell. "I don't usually smoke. It's no big deal." Now he was a liar as well as flirting with Kelly's little sister, but the words felt kinda true. He wasn't going to smoke around a girl like Lisa, not for a second. Maybe he *could* quit if he wanted to. He smiled to himself. Maybe he just hadn't had a good reason before now.

"I might be her younger sister, but I'm not her *dumber* sister. You stubbed that out like you're used to doing it, and I saw you sucking back hard."

Matt shrugged. "So maybe I just quit."

"Doubt it. But it's gross, so you should."

"So you don't date smokers?" he asked.

"I definitely don't date smokers. Or old guys."

Matt laughed when her lips kicked up into a cute grin, liking the sparky younger version of his best friend. He'd never had any chemistry with Kelly; they just liked hanging out. But Lisa had the same directness that he liked in her sister, along with a sassy attitude and sparkling blue eyes that were making him feel all kinds of interested. "For starters, I'm not old, if that's what you're saying. And if you don't like smokers, then hell, baby, I *definitely* just quit."

"Now I can see why Kelly's never let me meet you before."

"Me? Nah, I'm a pussycat."

Her smile lit up her face as he looked back at her. "Speak of the devil . . ."

"Lisa? I thought you were studying today?" Kelly was frowning and Matt quickly let go of her sister's hand. "What are you doing here?"

"I said you wouldn't mind if she joined us," Matt said, squeezing Kelly's shoulder and giving her a big grin. "You don't mind do you, Kel?"

"You're not touching my sister," Kelly said, hands on her hips. "Just forget it. Lisa, leave us alone."

Matt grinned. He hadn't felt so good in forever, not without smoking something he shouldn't or getting drunk. And it definitely had something to do with the beautiful blonde staring back at her sister like there was no way in hell she was being told what to do, her lips slightly parted as she turned her gaze back to him. She was innocent but worldly-looking at the same time, looked like she'd be a lot of fun but wouldn't put up with any bullshit. And he liked her. A lot. Already. It usually took a substance to pull him away from the darkness, but just being around Lisa had made him forget everything.

He stripped down to just his shorts, threw his t-shirt past Kelly, and ran to the edge of the pool, doing a backflip at the same time as both girls screamed. When he resurfaced, Kelly looked furious with him and Lisa was laughing, hand clamped over her mouth.

"Showoff," Kelly muttered as she walked past him and used the steps to get in, swimming over to something floating that he guessed she was going to sunbathe on. Kelly glared back at Lisa. "Stay if you want, but don't get in the way."

Lisa walked over, not replying to her sister, her feet bare. She was wearing a sundress and she sat down at the edge and dipped her feet into the water, then her legs, dress hitched up high to show off a lot of golden, smooth skin.

Matt swam closer, rested his arms on the edge of the concrete and looked up at her. He wanted to know more.

"She's only sixteen!" Kelly called out.

Matt laughed, looking at Lisa, not Kelly. "I'm not that much older than you. I just turned nineteen," he said.

Lisa just smiled, moving her legs back and forth in the water. "Old enough to be trouble."

All the anger, the weight on his shoulders that he hadn't been able to shift, the black hole he'd been staring down for the past year—it all started to lift. She might be too young, and she might be Kelly's sister, but there was something about Lisa. Something that he doubted he'd ever be able to forget. She was beautiful, calm, happy . . . the exact opposite of how he'd felt all year. And he wanted to keep making her smile, to see the way her face lit up. To be around her. He liked her barbed tongue too, liked the way she'd already called him out even though she didn't know him.

"Want to come swimming?" he asked, raising an eyebrow as he watched her.

She shrugged, but he saw her smile, knew she was as interested as he was. "Thanks for the invite. It is kind of my pool."

"Oh really?" he replied, trying not to laugh at her.

She kept a straight face, only giving herself away when one side of her mouth kicked up. "Yeah, actually."

"One, two, *three!*"

Matt pulled Lisa down into the water, eyes on hers, drawn like a magnet to this carefree young woman who somehow made him want to get on with life instead of treading water.

"Matt! What part of 'don't touch my sister' didn't you get?" Kelly said as she got out of the pool and stared at Matt.

Matt pulled Kelly on the way past and sent her spiraling back into the water, just as the rest of their friends showed up.

"Hey! Hands off my girl!" Tommy, Kelly's boyfriend, yelled the second he saw what had happened, shoving off his t-shirt and diving in without a second to spare.

Matt let go of Lisa, ready for Tommy when he surfaced, launching at him with his fists flying. It was play fighting, but they were still going to get rough, and he didn't want Lisa getting caught up in it. Sometimes Tommy was less about the play and more about the fight, especially if it involved his girlfriend.

"Leave Matt alone," Kelly moaned, coming up behind Tommy and grabbing his shoulders. "He was just trying to impress my sister, not me."

Tommy was easily distracted and Matt happily turned back to Lisa to find her swimming away from him, her blonde hair wet, dress a blur of color beneath the water. There was something about her that was making him feel a whole lot more alive than he had since . . . He stamped away the thoughts. It had been the worst year of his life, and Lisa was the first *something* other than drugs or drink that made him feel awesome.

"Hey!" he called out, swimming after her.

Her eyes met his and he tried not to laugh. All the beautiful girls he'd met, all the cheerleaders who'd caught his eye before— they weren't a patch on Lisa. She might be young, but dammit, he'd just wait. And by the looks of it, he was going to have to chase her, and it had been a long time since a cute girl had given him a decent chase.

∽

Lisa lay back, stretched out in the sun. He'd joined her, but there was only so long he could lie in the sun beside her without saying or doing something. How the hell had he not known about her, or met her, until now?

"I was going to try a corny line on you, but . . ." Matt started.

Lisa pushed up onto her elbows, wet dress hitched up high, showing off a whole lot of leg. "Just be real. I like you," she said simply.

Matt grinned. "You do?"

"Yeah. I mean, I have no idea why you like hanging out with my sister so much when she's such a pain in the ass, but sure. You're fun."

Matt laughed. "She's not a pain. She's actually the fun one."

"Easy for you to say," Lisa scoffed. "She's not exactly fun to live with when you have to share a bathroom with her."

"Poor you. Anything I can do?"

Lisa raised an eyebrow. "Can you build?"

"Why?"

"Well, if you could build me a new bathroom then yeah, you could do something to help me!"

Matt studied Lisa, eyes moving over her face, liking the way she was just so easy to talk to, so open. "You know, she might be a pain, but I bet she'd be there for you if you needed her."

"What makes you say that?" Lisa asked.

Matt took a long breath, not wanting to bring up his mom, not around Lisa. He liked that she made him forget, and he wanted to keep it that way. "Let's just say she was pretty awesome when I needed someone. Still is. My mom died a while back."

Lisa's face changed, her smile fading. "I did know that. I'm sorry."

Matt forced a smile, wanted Lisa to go back to how she'd been before. He liked the banter, wanted to be lost in her infectious smile again, wanted to divert her attention away from feeling sorry for him.

"So can I come and swim with you tomorrow, since it's your pool?"

Lisa's eyes lit up again as she leaned back on her towel. "Maybe."

"Maybe as in *yes* because you want to hang out again?"

"How about you play your cards right and then I'll decide?" She giggled and Matt laughed, not wanting to move too fast but finding it impossible not to make some kind of move to show her that he seriously liked her, too.

"So can I kiss you?" he asked, leaning in, reaching out to touch her still-damp hair.

"No," she said with a laugh.

"No right now or no forever?" he asked with a cute grin.

"No because we've just met," she said, hand to his chest as she moved him back. "And I'm not easy like your usual type."

"Oh, you think I have a type?" He shook his head. If he'd had a type, he sure as hell didn't now, because the only girl he wanted was Lisa.

Her skin was warm and her eyes never left his as her hand rested against him. His whole body was buzzing with anticipation, wanting her so damn bad, liking the way she made him feel.

"Matt, get off my damn sister!"

Matt dipped down fast, pressed a quick kiss to her lips, desperate for more but not about to push his luck.

"Hey!" Lisa protested, laughing as she shoved him away.

"Sorry. If your sister's gonna kill me I didn't want it to be for nothing."

Lisa laughed, biting down on her bottom lip as she stared at him, making him want her so bad. "So are you going to call me?" she asked.

"Are you going to go out with me?"

They were both staring, both smiling, both waiting.

"Yeah," she replied. "Maybe I am."

"Then *hell yes,* I'm gonna call you," he yelled out, jumping up and running back to the pool, leaping in and sending water splashing everywhere.

When he looked back, Lisa was still giggling and he couldn't stop laughing. He wanted to high-five the world! He'd met a girl. A girl he liked. A girl who was going to rock his world in a good kind of way. And liking a girl had never felt so damn awesome.

11.
PRESENT DAY

Baby, we're here," Matt said, voice low as he placed a hand on Lisa's thigh.

"Huh?" she mumbled.

He knew she was going to be angry with him for letting her sleep so long, but he'd figured that she probably needed it after the hours she'd been pulling at the shop. Besides, it had done him good to have time to think, process his own thoughts and try to get a handle on what they'd been going through. He had so many questions, so many things he wanted to know the answers to, but he was too scared to ask any of them and he certainly wasn't about to bring up Lisa's cancer with her. Or even attempt to talk about kids, or their lack of kids, too soon, after the way she'd shot him down earlier. But he wasn't going to give up about the adoption or fostering options—she might be snappy about it now, but he'd read how long the wait could be for adoption. They needed to get their names down if they were going to do it.

"What?" she mumbled, sitting up straight and stretching out her arms above her head. "No way! You let me sleep?"

Matt shrugged. "You looked so cute all tucked up with your mouth open, snoring."

She slapped his arm playfully.

"I don't snore."

"Yeah, you do."

She went to hit him again but this time he grabbed her hand and dropped a kiss against her skin before she could make contact with him. It had been awhile since he'd just touched her like that, without thinking. "You're so cute when you're angry," he said teasingly.

She laughed and pushed him away, opening her door and getting out. Matt watched as she reached her hands up, shielding her face from the sun. The weather was perfect, and not for the first time since they'd left home, he was so pleased they'd decided to do it.

"Come on!" Matt said. "Let's get this party started." He locked the Caddy, pushed the keys into his pocket and walked around to check that Lisa had done her door. Then he reached for Lisa's hand as she met his gaze and smiled over at him; *like nothing was wrong, like they were still just Matt and Lisa with not a thing in the world to worry about.* But there was something lacking despite the fact they were touching, something he hoped would just magically disappear, a feeling he couldn't shake, like at any moment everything could unravel. He got why she hadn't been interested in sex after what she'd been through, but it was weird for them to not at least touch and kiss easily.

"Want to go investigate where we're staying?" he asked.

"Depends on how long you think we should stay."

He shrugged. "I was thinking just one night here, but we can do whatever you want."

She nodded. "You mind if I go take a walk? Look around for a bit?"

He turned when she pressed a warm kiss to his cheek before letting go of his hand and walking off, glancing over her shoulder and smiling as he raised his hand in a wave. Lisa had always been independent and he loved that about her, but she was different now. Her confidence was so much quieter, whereas before it had been so overt.

Matt headed into the motel. It was one he'd come across doing a quick Google search the night before, and given they were only in town a night, he wasn't fussy as long as the sheets were clean, the room was clean, and they had somewhere safe to park their car.

"Can I help you?"

Matt smiled at the older woman behind the counter. "Sure can. I need a room for two."

She nodded. "One night?"

Matt nodded. "Yep, unless my wife finds enough things to do for longer."

She took his credit card when he held it out, and he filled out a form before taking the keys as they were passed to him. He looked around, thought it looked okay for a night or two.

"Your wife needs help finding places to go, tell her to come see me. I'd be starting with one of our farmers' markets in the morning and I'll bet you'll be coming in and paying me for another night after taking a look around."

Matt groaned. "Now I'll have to tell her about the market." He chuckled to himself. *If she didn't know about it already, that was.* Maybe Sacramento had been the perfect place to bring her—nothing perked her up like fresh produce and pretty secondhand clothes to sort though. And he'd bet that she'd manage to find some of those at any market. It was an obsession she'd turned into a business, and as much as he liked her pretty designs, it wasn't an obsession he even came close to sharing with her.

He headed off to find her, thinking that they really hadn't organized themselves very well. If she didn't have her cell on her, he'd either have to stroll around town looking for her or wait it out and hope she came back before too long. He started walking before pulling his phone from his pocket, crossing the road and heading for the first coffee shop he could see. He needed a shot of caffeine to kick-start his brain. While he was waiting in line, he looked out the window and saw, across the street, a mane of golden blonde hair—it was Lisa, her head tipped back as she laughed at something an elderly woman was saying, hand on her arm.

That was his Lisa. She'd always made friends with everyone and couldn't ever seem to stop talking when she met someone to chat with. He was happy to see her coming back to herself.

When Matt stepped out of the coffee place and waved, catching her eye, she smiled and waved to him just like old times. He watched as she said some final words to the woman she was talking to before hurrying across the road to him.

"You're not going to believe it," she said.

Matt groaned, even though he loved hearing her so excited. "I'm gonna take a guess that it has something to do with tomorrow's market?"

"How do you know about it already?" She reached and took the take-out cup from his hand, sipping as they walked. "Mmm, I need one."

"So, back to the farmers' market," Matt said, taking his coffee back after she'd taken a few long sips. "Do we really need to buy a whole heap of fruit and veggies for the road?"

"We can just handpick a few things, and then there's this woman there who has a whole heap of vintage fabrics, ribbons and clothes. She has a little shop in town too, but she's closed today and might be there tomorrow. Well, according to Hazel anyway."

Matt frowned jokingly at his wife. "Who the hell is Hazel? Since when do we know anyone from Sacramento?"

"Hazel is the lovely old lady I got chatting to before. I told her we might see her tomorrow."

"Ohmygod," Matt muttered. "Tell me again why I married you and *continue* to let you torture me with markets and strangers that you collect like they're animals who need a home?" He was teasing but he loved it, was ready to high-five her for being so happy and normal.

"Matt," she said, taking his coffee again and draining it before passing him back the empty cup, "you know you secretly *love* coming to markets with me. Didn't we already have this conversation?"

Matt laughed; it was the only thing he could do. Lisa was in a happy place, and it was nice to see that old fiery spark that he'd been missing. It was like someone had flicked a switch.

"Market, here we come, then," he said. "*Boss.*"

Lisa laughed. "Matt, thanks for suggesting this trip." She gazed up at him and he stilled as she pressed a kiss to his jaw. "This road trip was the best idea you've ever had. I needed it."

He clasped her hand tightly and they walked side by side through town. At least he'd finally done the right thing.

"So, tell me more about this farmers' market," he said, wanting to hear her talk, to take his mind off the other things floating through his head.

"Well, it's supposed to be incredible," she said. "They have amazing produce here, all grown locally . . ."

Matt hardly heard a word she said. All he cared about was the happiness in the lilt of her voice, and the way her eyes kept darting sideways to catch his.

"Come on, crazy market girl, let's go find something to eat."

"Can you believe they have a drive-in movie theater here? They're showing *Jurassic World* and some kids' movie. What a shame we can't take the girls to it. Eve and Zoe would love it!"

Matt shook his head, trying not to laugh at her. Lisa was back. And if felt so damn good.

༄

Lisa actually felt kind of normal. The sun was shining, and she was in a cool town that she'd never had the chance to explore properly before even though it was only a few hours from home. She hadn't been lying to Matt—it was exactly what she'd needed. Getting away from everything had taken a weight off her shoulders that she wouldn't have thought could be moved.

"So can we go?" she asked, swinging hands with Matt as she looked around the city.

"Where?"

"To the drive-in movie," she told him.

"We sure can."

Lisa tucked in closer to him. "What could be better than going to a drive-in movie in a vintage Cadillac?"

"Says the *Grease* movie fan-girl," Matt teased, grabbing for her.

She laughed. "I always used to dream of being Sandy. I guess I'm still playing dress-up and make-believe with what I do for a job."

She stayed in place beside him, loving the way he tucked her tight, his arm around her so that she could snuggle into the nook beneath his shoulder. When they'd first met, she'd fantasized about being up close and personal with the big quarterback, loved watching him play. Back then he'd been best friends with her sister and she'd lived in fear of Kelly falling for him herself, but she never had. Kelly had been friends with everyone, but for some reason she'd clicked with Matt and they'd spent a lot of time together. Matty had been struggling with his mom battling cancer, and her sister had had a tough time with an old boy-friend—maybe they'd just liked the fact they could hang out and nothing was going to happen, not that either of them had ever talked about it to her. But when Lisa had first met Matt, she'd fallen hard. Every look, every accidental touch . . . He'd made her heart race, her body burn with a fire deep inside her she hadn't even known existed.

As Matt always said, she was lucky he'd been best friends with her older sister. If she'd had an older brother, Matt would have probably been kneecapped before they'd even had the chance to sneak off together, simply because of the way he used to look at her.

"So I'm thinking we might have to stay more than one night," Matt said, pulling her from her thoughts.

"Why's that?"

"Because I did a bit of research before we left home, and I actually made a booking at a really nice restaurant tonight. Which means we'll either have to cancel that or miss the movie."

"Seriously?" she asked. It wasn't like Matt to do anything even remotely romantic, which was why he'd managed to take her by surprise when he'd suggested this trip in the first place.

"What, about staying an extra night or the restaurant?"

"Both."

Matt tucked her tighter against him. "We're going to have din-ner overlooking the river, and yeah, if you want to stay another night to go to the drive-in, then consider it done. I just want to chill and enjoy."

"I thought you'd love the idea of the drive-in."

"I never said I didn't. I'm just not sure about the movie," he said.

"Huh," Lisa murmured.

Matt stopped walking and looked down at her. "What does *huh* mean?"

She smiled and blinked up at him. "Well, drive-ins used to be all about the snuggling and the necking and the . . ."

She stopped talking when Matt placed a finger over her lips. "Stop talking. I need to phone and cancel dinner tonight."

"Wh–"

"We're going to the drive-in *tonight*!"

They both laughed and Lisa breathed out a happy kind of sigh. "This feels nice."

"Yeah," he said, "it does."

They walked in silence, but as she looked around, held on to her husband, the thoughts started to slowly trickle back. Was this enough? Was it okay that they'd never take their children exploring? Never take kids on a road trip and go on adventures? She wished she'd never acknowledged how good she was feeling, because it had made the thoughts come back like a flood into her mind that she couldn't hold back.

Silent tears started to slide down Lisa's cheeks but she gritted her teeth to stop from crying, tried so hard to push them away, to stop her feelings.

"Lis, I think we . . ." Matt said, arm falling away from her as he slowed down. "Hey, what's wrong?"

Matt dipped down, his body instantly engulfing hers, arms embracing her in a big bear hug, chin to the top of her head. She focused on breathing, hugged him back, comforted by the warmth of his chest, the soft rise and fall of it. She waited until she had her emotions back in check, or as back in check as they could be given how she was feeling and what she was going through.

"I'm sorry, I don't know what's happening to me. I just . . ." she took a deep, shuddering kind of breath. "It all comes crashing back sometimes, that's all."

"We're gonna be okay," he said firmly. "You hear me? We're going to be great. We were doing fine just now, just like old times, right?"

Lisa heard him, loud and clear, but it was one thing to be positive and another entirely to simply stick your head in the sand, which was what Matt had been doing. He was trying hard, but . . . she needed to get a grip, refocus.

"Are we still going to get some lunch?" she asked, wishing her emotions weren't so all over the place and wanting to change the subject. It wasn't like her to be that way, but she'd been on a roller coaster of a ride over the past nine months. She was almost ready to admit that she needed professional help. *Almost.* But then it would mean actually admitting what she'd done, that she'd terminated her one and only pregnancy, and she wasn't ready to confront that yet.

"Lunch, then afternoon sex in our dodgy motel room, then dinner," Matt suggested, giving her one of his too-cute winks. Only she wasn't quite ready to play along yet.

"How about we start with lunch?" she said.

"Honey D Café?" Matt asked.

She saw his frown. "It looks good."

"You obviously can't read the sign. They have a tofu lunch special and a roasted milk tea, sea salt latte. I don't even know what that is!"

"Come on Mr. Macho Builder, it's time you tried some tofu."

"No chance," he protested.

Lisa raised an eyebrow, holding on to him tightly as she reached for his hand. She was trying, he was trying . . . she just wished they didn't flip from happy to sad to almost there so often in one day.

"Oh no, not that look," Matt groaned.

"*Please*," Lisa begged. "I want to eat tofu together. And crazy sea salt latte concoctions."

Matt dropped his head. "Okay, fine." He dragged her closer. "Let's get this over with."

12.
TEN YEARS EARLIER

I can't believe we just did that," Lisa whispered against Matt's skin. His chest was slick, damp with sweat, but she didn't seem to care.

"If your dad wasn't going to kill me before, he is now." Matt groaned but slid his arm protectively around her at the same time. Lisa snuggled in tight to him. "Man, is he going to kill me."

"I can't believe you're talking about my dad when we've just . . ." She smiled and he cracked up at the look on her face. "Done it."

Matt laughed. "Yeah, sorry."

Lisa kissed him. "I forgive you. Just don't do it again!"

"I love you," Matt said, brushing his lips across her head.

She pushed up on one elbow, hair falling over her shoulder and down onto Matt's face. Lisa stared at him, and he pushed up slowly to press his mouth to hers again, loving the taste of her. He could kiss her all day and never stop.

"You don't have to say that to me," she whispered when she pulled back.

"I know," Matt said, his eyes lazy, half shut as he stared at her lips. Always at her lips. "I only ever say things I mean."

Lisa kissed him again and giggled when he pulled her arm and made her collapse on top of him. He felt like they were the only two people in the world when they were together.

"Can we . . ." she started, sucking her bottom lip in beneath her top teeth.

"All night long, over and over," he muttered, arms enclosing her as he rolled them so he ended up above her, staring down at her, blowing a strand of hair off her face before closing his lips over hers.

Matt skimmed a hand down her body, caressed even more softly down the inside of her thigh with his fingertips. Lisa had told her parents she was going camping with friends, a group of girls they'd never have expected her to lie about. He felt bad that she was lying for him, *for them*, but having a whole night with Lisa in the middle of nowhere? It was perfect.

Lisa moaned when Matt's mouth left hers and he trailed his lips down her neck, kissing her so slow and sweet, his lips damp as he brushed against her skin, teasing her when he went lower, circling his tongue, chuckling when she moaned again.

"I could do this all night," she whispered, circling her arms more tightly around him and locking her legs around his back, anchoring him against her.

"We're perfect for each other," he muttered against her lips as he started to kiss her again. "Because I was just thinking that *exact* same thought."

Lisa squealed when he rolled them again, putting her back on top, but he wanted to let her take the lead, let her slow things down if she wanted to.

Lisa was his happy place, and he didn't want to do anything to mess that up.

⁓

"Hey, beautiful."

Matt slung his arms around Lisa's waist from behind as he spoke low into her ear. He pressed a kiss to her neck and rocked his body into hers.

"Hey," she whispered back, setting down the knife she was holding and spinning in his arms.

He'd expected her mouth on his, but instead she laid her cheek to his chest and hugged him tight. Matt stroked her back and rested his chin against the top of her head.

"You okay?"

"Uh-huh," she muttered.

He wasn't convinced, but he guessed she'd talk when she was good and ready. Because there'd been a lot of action and not much talking since they'd arrived.

"You didn't have to cook anything," he said. He'd jumped in the shower and by the time he came out he could smell something on the stove. Not exactly what he expected from an eighteen-year-old.

"It's just pasta and a tomato sauce. Nothing amazing."

"So let me help, then," he said.

Lisa looked over her shoulder at him and he stole a quick kiss. "I'm kinda done, but you could be my taste tester."

"Aye-aye, Captain! That's just the type of job I like."

Lisa leaned back into him as she stirred. They'd rented the little cabin for the night, and they'd stopped off on the way to grab a few supplies. Matt grinned as he thought about the car ride up—they'd hardly been able to keep their hands off each other, and after hours lying in bed and doing everything they'd been waiting, *wanting* to do for so long, he could still feel himself stirring with her body so hard up against his. Once they ate, he was definitely going to be dragging her back to bed again.

"Try this," she said, turning in his arms and holding out the wooden spoon. He locked eyes with her as she blew on the hot sauce, lips igniting into a fresh smile as she waited for him to taste it.

"I guess I didn't expect you to know how to cook," he said, laughing to himself. She managed to surprise him constantly; she might be young, but there was something about her that made him feel like the young one.

"Hey, I'm surprised that you haven't run out already, so I guess we're even."

"It's good," he said.

"Yeah?" she asked, looking unsure.

"Hand on my heart," he said, licking his lips. "Damn good!"

Matt waited for her to put the spoon back and turn again. He tilted her face up with his fingers locked beneath her chin. "You're gorgeous."

Her smile was softer now, less sure. "I wasn't sure you'd still want me, you know, after . . ."

"After sex? You thought I only wanted you for that and once I had it I'd let you go?"

"Well, you don't exactly have the best track record," she said, confusing him with the serious look on her face. She dragged her fingers down his chest. "And you can kind of get any girl you want."

"I've been a fricking monk since I met you!" He protested. "And not *any* girl: it's taken me forever to convince you."

Lisa laughed, head tilted back, making it obvious the joke was on him. "Poor baby. I know."

Matt shook his head, a smile playing across his lips even as he tried hard to keep a straight face.

"You have no damn idea, do you? What you've done to me?"

She blinked up at him, her doe-eyed stare making her look so damn innocent. But the way she'd keep resisting him, pushing him, making him wait before whispering in his ear one night that she was ready and wanted him . . . Christ! She drove him crazy. Completely fucking crazy!

"Have you looked in a mirror lately?" he demanded.

Matt grinned when her saw her blush, realized he'd managed to embarrass her. She might be young, but she usually called the shots, and he liked catching her out like that.

"You're so damn beautiful and you don't even know it."

He kissed her back when she rose up onto her toes and pressed a soft, barely there kiss to his lips . . . It made him so damn desperate to shove her back against the kitchen cabinets and kiss her roughly, strip her naked again.

"I can't believe I'm here with you. That I've run away with a man."

"You'd better believe it," he joked.

"There's so much I want to know about you." She snuggled into him again. "You know, you've never told me about your mom. It must have been so hard losing her."

He didn't want to talk about his mom. Lisa had changed the course of his life, taken the anger out of him and made him happy again just by being her, but it didn't mean he wanted to talk to her about losing his mother.

"You're just saying that because you feel guilty lying to your own mom," he said, trying to change the subject.

"Maybe," she said. "But I still wonder sometimes what it was like for you. How you got through it."

"I just did," he said. "It's in the past now. And hey, if you keep going on about it, I'm going to have to run out after all. Let's just have a nice time, just us."

He laughed, pulling a silly face to make her smile when she didn't say anything. "So you really thought I wouldn't want you after this, huh?" he asked, trying harder this time, needing to throw her off topic.

"It's the only reason I cooked for you," she joked, making him crack up. "Thought I'd wow you with my culinary skills to make you stay."

"Very funny," he said, holding her tight against him again. "I ain't letting you go. Ever. Culinary skills or not."

He inhaled the sweet scent of her shampoo, or maybe it was perfume, shutting his eyes as he turned his cheek into her soft hair. He might be crappy at expressing himself, but he wanted Lisa more than anything. When his mom had died, he'd known then he could never go through anything like it again, couldn't deal with losing someone else he loved. He'd made it clear to every girl he'd been with that it was just casual, and then Lisa had come along with her big blue eyes and her soft, long blonde hair. And then he'd started talking to her, had realized that there was a whole lot more to her than how damn cute she was. Lisa was pretty and sweet, strong and capable. He wanted to tuck her close and beat the hell out of anyone who even thought of hurting her. And just like that he'd fallen, done exactly what he'd earned such a bad reputation for not doing in the past.

"We're going to have to tell my parents about us," she said. "I mean, that it's not just us going on some dates."

Matt laughed. "Wait, you want to tell your dad that when he thinks you're tucked up safe in bed at night you're actually sneaking out your window to jump in my car?" Matt shook his head. "Or more importantly now, my bed? With me doing wicked, *wicked* things to you?"

"Well . . ." Lisa looked up at him, eyes bright and full of something so damn intoxicating he couldn't get enough of her. "Maybe not the sneaking out part. But we do need to tell them. I'm old enough for them to have to deal with it."

"Kelly knows," Matt said, watching her face to see how she reacted.

"You told my sister!"

He hadn't had to watch her face after all. Her shriek was enough. "Lisa, until we hooked up, she was one of my best friends. She kind of still is. I can't lie to her; you know that."

"Does she know we're here?" Lisa asked.

"Um, no. I didn't tell her that I was sneaking her little sister away for a dirty night in a cabin with me. But she knows we're together, that I'm not hooking up with anyone else."

Lisa looked relieved. "You still shouldn't have told her about us, not yet."

"Yeah, I should. Because she told me that she's seen the way I look at you, watched me pull my shit together since I met you. She knows you're good for me, and I wanted her to know."

"But?"

He liked how easily she seemed to be able to read him, knew that there was a *but*, that he wasn't telling her everything.

"*But* she's scared I'm going to hurt you. Her beautiful little sister who's never had her heart broken before."

"I'm scared of that too, sometimes," she whispered as he cupped her face, palms to her cheeks as he stared into her eyes.

"I've never loved a girl before, but I love you. Real bad," Matt told her honestly, voice cracking. "You have my word that I'll never hurt you. Promise."

Lisa's lips parted the second before he kissed her, her arms circled around him, warm body pressed to his. He'd fallen for a girl and it felt all kinds of right. Lisa made him forget, Lisa was his new beginning, and he wasn't going to do anything to mess that up.

13.
PRESENT DAY

We are going to be so fat by the end of this trip."

Matt grabbed her hand as they walked into Scott's Seafood. Lisa had half-expected her husband to take her to some grungy little seafood place—he was never one to choose somewhere fancy. But she could see out to the river as soon as they stepped inside, and it was perfect.

"We might be fat, but as long as we're happy, yeah?" he said, winking at her before turning to face the waitress approaching them.

"Are you here for Happy Hour?" she asked.

"We sure are," Matt replied. "Can we sit at the bar for an hour, then grab a table for dinner?"

The waitress smiled and took their names before telling them to head over to the bar.

"Cocktail?" Matt asked as he reached for the menu.

Lisa shook her head. Matt's enthusiasm was always infectious, and today was no different, only lately she'd felt guilty every time she was happy. And no matter how hard she tried to stop herself from thinking like that, she couldn't. "Get me a Bud. I'll have a beer with you." She'd never ordered beer before, usually just had a few sips of Matt's, but she'd been craving it all day. Maybe it was all the sunshine and fresh air she'd been getting, and the fact that she was trying hard to be a fun wife.

She watched as Matt ordered, smiling when he slid a bottle of beer her way.

"I never thought my wife would be swilling beer with me," Matt said with a grin.

"I know. It's a bit of a waste only ordering beer at happy hour, isn't it?"

"It's not a waste if it makes you happy."

His words were sweet, so kind, but Lisa found it hard to meet his gaze. She didn't know what made her happy these days.

"*Are you* happy?" he asked.

Lisa forced a smile, tried to be brave . . . But all she wanted to do was run back to their room and bury her face in a pillow. How did she tell her husband that every day there was a pain in her so deep she didn't even know if she'd be able to walk, talk, *think*? That the bursts of happiness she'd had over the last twenty-four hours were only that—sudden bursts that felt great, but only made the crash back to reality that much harder.

Matt pulled his bar stool closer, legs parted so her knees could tuck inside his thighs. They'd always been like that, always touching, and nothing had ever changed between them, until now. Now there was an invisible divide a lot of the time, an awkwardness that meant she had to think about every movement, every touch, instead of being instinctual. She'd often wondered if things would have been different when kids had come along, that this change between them would have happened sooner, but she was one of those women who'd always adored her husband, couldn't imagine loving her children as much as her man. Until she'd fallen pregnant and had sixteen weeks to think about and fall in love with the little person she was carrying. Then she'd realized that there just had to be enough room in her heart for both.

"I'm happy that I'm alive," she said honestly, because even though she felt guilty, she *was* happy that she was still walking this planet; that she could breathe and be, and not be six feet under or suffering through chemo.

"Good." He sipped his beer and she did the same. "Me too."

"Are you?" she asked. "Happy, I mean?"

"Well, I'm pissed off at the universe for a whole lot of things right now, but yeah, I'm happy enough."

Lisa leaned in to him, made herself connect with him, and Matt pressed a warm, soft kiss to her forehead. When she tipped her head back to look up at him, she watched his lips, parted hers as he moved closer. Matt kissed her once, then twice, and she sighed into his mouth when he finally pulled back.

"I could do that all night," she murmured, a weight lifting, reminding her of how good things had been. Once they touched, it always took her back in time, made her feel amazing. Her problem was initiating it.

"Me too," he whispered back, lips to her ear now, tickling her and making her laugh. "But I'm kinda hanging out for the steak and prawn combo."

Lisa stifled her laughter. "You're turning down sex because you want shrimp?" They hadn't talked about sex, or lack of it, but she was starting to feel like she wanted it again, was craving that connection. She'd bet that no matter what he joked, he was desperate for it, too. But Matt was going easy on her—joking about their sex life made her feel a whole lot *less* bad about the drought they'd been going through.

"I'm a simple man," Matt said, shrugging as he took a pull of beer. "I need some sustenance before I can be expected to satisfy my wife." He grabbed the menu and waggled his eyebrows at her over it. "Talking about food, want to grab some of their calamari?"

"When have I ever said no to sharing calamari?"

Lisa leaned over the bar and ordered, then sat back to slowly sip her beer. It was a weird feeling, being in limbo, feeling like she was having to try when her marriage had always been so easy.

When they'd been on vacation before, it was always for a short time, maybe a week, and she'd always known how busy life would be when they returned home, with so many things to do after taking a break. And then, she'd had no regrets, no all-consuming pangs of guilt.

"So you've definitely chosen what you're having?" Lisa asked, taking a deep breath.

He reached for her hand, tucked his fingers tight over hers and pulled a menu closer. "Yeah. Fillet steak with grilled prawns is my pick. Sounds like my idea of heaven on a plate."

"That's you and me both, then."

Lisa took another sip of beer, liking the weight of his hand over hers, wishing she hadn't pushed him away so much lately. "I know things have been rough, but I love you, Matt."

Matt gave her a slow, sexy wink. "I know. I love you, too."

She leaned in and kissed him, focused only on her lips brushing against his.

"Want to go to our table instead of propping up the bar?" he asked.

Lisa nodded. "Sounds like a good idea."

Matt checked with their waitress as she finished her beer and leaned over the counter to reach for the wine list they'd discarded earlier. More than two drinks and she'd be drunk, but she did like the idea of nursing a glass of chilled wine over dinner.

"Hey, you're drinking more than me. I'd better catch up," Matt murmured, pushing up behind her, his groin to her lower back. "And our table's ready."

Lisa tipped back, let him trail warm kisses down her neck. "Have you been thinking about Blue?"

He chuckled against her skin. "Right now, Blue is the last thing on my mind."

Lisa pushed him away when the bartender came over to take her order. She ordered a chardonnay and then turned back to Matt, twisting in his arms, happy to be there.

"I'm worried about him."

He sighed. "Will you promise not to mention the dog again when I'm kissing you, if I tell you to ring your damn sister and check up on him now?"

She smiled up at him. "Deal."

Lisa pulled out her phone, grinning when she saw the text she'd missed. "Check this out," she said as they walked outside.

Matt leaned in, bumping shoulders with her. "Ha, cute."

The girls were snuggled up to Blue, arms around him, and he had his tongue lolling out, smile on his face like he was the happiest pup in the world.

"I guess I won't bother calling. He looks pretty happy to me."

Matt held Lisa's chair for her, then sat down across from her.

"Sorry to interrupt. Here's your chardonnay."

Lisa gave the waitress who'd brought out her drink a grateful smile. "Thanks."

"I'll take another Bud."

"Tonight feels like a good night," Lisa said, closing her eyes, loving the feel of the coolish wind against her bare skin, the way the beer had taken the edge off whatever she'd been feeling.

"You know, I've been praying," Matt said, chuckling like he'd said something funny.

She laughed even though she knew she shouldn't. But this was Matt: he wasn't exactly the church-going type! "You're kidding, right?" she asked.

"You know, they say that even non-believers pray when they think they're going to die, or basically just whenever things turn to shit."

Lisa gulped. "Have we turned to shit?" She stared into his eyes. "I just feel so lost, like most of the time I can't even catch a breath. But this feels good—*we* feel good right now."

Matt took a long pull of his beer as she watched. "Hey, there's a fifty-fifty chance the big man upstairs was listening, because we're sitting here together now. I might get into this whole praying business."

"You're so cute sometimes," she said, smiling back at him. And he was trying damn hard, she knew that.

"Ditto."

Lisa laughed, and laughed some more. It wasn't even that funny; it had just been a long time since she'd actually felt like laughing for the hell of it.

Matt grinned back at her, liking how relaxed things suddenly felt between them.

"Come here," Lisa whispered, pulling him in close. She kissed him, her lips soft and warm and making him wish they were alone.

"Ah, excuse me, are you ready to order?" the waitress asked.

Matt kept hold of her, holding her hand still. "Ah, two of the filet mignon with grilled prawns," Matt ordered, "and I think . . ."—he glanced at Lisa—"we'll start with the fried calamari. It sounds good."

"Great choice," Lisa said. "My favorite."

"Damn right," he replied. "May as well start here and try it at every restaurant we head to, for old times' sake. What do you say?"

"Sounds like a plan."

Lisa held up her glass and he held up his beer bottle, clinking his to hers.

"To us and the road trip of a lifetime," he declared.

"To us and our little trip," she agreed, taking a sip of wine.

He watched as she settled back in the chair, her eyes leaving his and turning toward the river. It was almost dark but still light enough to see the water, the sun slowly disappearing low in the distance. And still light enough to see the pensive look on her face, the way she disappeared into her thoughts and never seemed to be all there, not all the time anyway.

"So tell me about this market we're going to in the morning. Are you looking for fabric or just scouting for ideas?" Matt asked. "It's great you're enjoying work so much."

He'd been worried when she'd launched back into running the store, still designing everything herself without any help, but it seemed to be the only thing that made her happy and that meant he wasn't going to say anything about the long hours she was pulling. Especially not when it was usually him needing to be scolded and told to get his ass back home.

"I'm thinking super-pretty fabric, soft pinks with gold, short little skirts with stretchy waistbands to make them super-comfy and luxurious, and t-shirts. Like what I did this summer but a bit more whimsical."

Lisa had that wistful look on her face as she looked at him but through him; the look she'd always had when she'd been dreaming up a new collection or new design. It suited her. And he liked that she was passionate about her work.

"Have you ever actually used not-pretty fabric?" he asked.

Lisa loved anything that was pretty, colorful, sparkly or luxurious. He'd never seen her not looking feminine and gorgeous in her clothes, whether she was wearing low-slung pajama bottoms with cute tanks she'd designed or a dress to wear around the house.

She sighed. "I want to design the opposite of how I'm feeling. Clothes that can make women feel fabulous every day, whether they're picking kids up from school or going to work."

"Isn't that what you've always designed?" He smiled. "It's why all those women are addicted to seeing what you were wearing each day on Facebook when you posted pics."

Her smile turned to a frown, lips hovering down from the happy upturn he'd been watching. "I don't want to let them down," she said quietly. "I never explained why I disappeared for a bit, what I've been through."

"Lisa, you wouldn't have let them down," Matt said firmly. "And anyone who doesn't give you a break after what happened? Tell them to fuck off." Anger pulsed through his body. Was that what she was worried about? What people thought? He hated to think she was feeling any more guilt than she already had to shoulder.

After she'd lost the baby, been given her cancer diagnosis, she'd shut her Facebook and Instagram pages down. And then when she'd finally left the house, she'd started to post again—he knew because Kelly had told him and he'd checked it out for himself. She'd started to pull away from him at the same time she started reconnecting with everyone else.

"Those women were real; they were friends to me. They shared so much and then I just shut it down," Lisa confessed. "I didn't feel right just letting that go, and it started to make me feel better, at least while I was plugged in."

"It's good," Matt said, sitting back as the waitress approached and put the fried calamari between them. "You want to work and do everything that you used to do—why the hell not? It's you."

"Because I feel like a fraud, like I'm pretending to be someone I used to be when I post pics of me smiling and wearing a cute dress."

Matt had no idea what to say to that, how to respond. "Lisa, you're still the same person. We just have such damn big battle wounds. I don't get why you have to feel guilty about smiling or dressing up nice."

"We?" she asked, as if she hadn't heard anything else he'd said.

Matt took a big breath, looked down at his food. He didn't want to start an argument. All he'd wanted was to be helpful, to say the right thing. He didn't want to engage; he decided to change the subject.

"So tell me what you've been posting lately," he said.

The waitress returned and he nodded when she offered them fresh cracked pepper, only taking his eyes off Lisa for a moment.

"Everything. Nothing," Lisa said absently holding her fork as she glanced between him and the food on the table. "I want to share our road trip, make it look fun."

He heard what she wasn't saying. "Let's hope we can make it fun. Then you won't have to pretend."

"Me too," she whispered, a light in her eyes, a shimmer there that used to be there every time he looked at her but came and went these days. But it gave him hope at least, even if he felt like he was messing things up between them more times than he was getting it right.

"They'll love it. They always do," Matt said, pleased they'd managed to avoid anything too heavy. "Don't you have something like one hundred thousand followers now?"

Matt picked up his fork again, stabbing a piece of calamari and dipping it into a bit of the miso-ginger aioli. Lisa leaned in closer and did the same.

"This is really good," she said.

Matt took another piece. "When I was growing up, I'd have shuddered at the thought of trying sauce like this. But it is good, surprisingly damn good."

"So you're saying I've made you more cultured?"

They both laughed away quietly, and it felt good. Matt had missed their easy feeling, the way they'd always been so chilled out with each other, not taking anything too seriously except their work. They'd always been like that, just comfortable in each other's company, until recently.

He sipped his beer and ate a few more pieces of calamari, watching Lisa as she did the same. When they'd finished, he pushed the plate away. "Come around here."

Lisa hesitated, but he waited, kept his arm up, kept his smile fixed in place. Eventually she scooted around to his side and tucked up against him on the chair he'd pulled closer. It was a table for four, and he had no idea why they were sitting across from each other anyway.

"I didn't mean what I said. This is going to be a great trip. It's just hard to let go," Lisa said.

"I know," he said.

"We're going to be okay, aren't we?" she whispered, holding on to him tight. "Tell me it won't always be like this."

Matt nodded, even though the question scared the shit out of him because he had no idea what the answer was. "Yeah, we are. Of course we are."

∽

Lisa sat back and looked at Matt, wondering how the hell she'd managed to get a guy so gorgeous. He'd been nineteen when she'd first met him, had a reputation for hooking up with all the girls on the cheerleading team in his final year of school, getting into trouble, drinking too much. She knew that he'd changed when his mom died, had become more of a troublemaker, falling out with his dad and doing a whole lot of stupid stuff to piss him off, but she got that he'd probably wanted to blame someone. Hell, she'd love to pin all the blame on someone, *anyone*. She wondered how hard it had been, what he'd really been through back then. Because even though she knew what had happened, he'd never wanted to talk about, unless it was to tell her that she'd made everything okay for him.

When they'd met, he'd looked at her and something had happened. She'd never been that into boys, never cared about having a boyfriend even when her friends were hooking up with guys. And then along had come Matt, way too old for her and just finished senior year, and the girl who'd never been self-conscious or been gaga for any boy had suddenly cared about how she looked, how she smelt, how she spoke . . . *everything*. And she had known that

Matt felt the same, had been crazy embarrassed when her sister had stared at her long and hard and demanded to know if she had a crush on him. Or if he'd tried to make a move. The only other time she'd felt that kind of pull toward a guy had been watching football and admiring the sexy quarterback—and she'd soon realized after meeting Matt that he *was* that guy.

"What are you thinking about?" he asked, voice husky as he took a pull of his third beer. They usually didn't drink a whole lot, but tonight was different. It was grittier and more real, and she actually felt like she was being herself instead of pretending, even if it was a new version of herself.

"Us, how we met."

"What about it?"

"I was so happy being the good girl, doing well at school, hanging with my friends."

"And then I corrupted you." Matt's chuckle made her smile. "Right from that first day when I stubbed out my last cigarette and saw you at your parents' pool."

"You made me see things differently. And I was pretty okay about the corrupting part, if I remember correctly."

"Hey, I can't take the full blame," Matt said. "You were pretty happy to skip school and meet me behind the bleachers. I used to blush just thinking about what you wanted to do to me!"

She cracked up big time, laughed so hard tears trickled down her cheeks, and through her blurry eyes she could see Matt almost doubled over. And it felt damn good. He was repeating her words, had always teased her about what she'd said to him the day he'd pushed his luck and tried to unzip her jeans with one hand, the other already slipped beneath her t-shirt. Matt was experienced and confident, and she'd been shy with no other experiences to compare it to—she'd been all talk, and he'd been all action. It had been forbidden and exhilarating for her; and from what he'd told her, it had been just as exciting for him. She'd been young and just as forbidden in different ways.

"You're mean, taunting me with that."

He winked, beer bottle paused against his lips. "But it was just so cute."

"You loved that I was all doe-eyed and inexperienced." She sipped her wine, feeling a familiar flush rise through her body that was only a little to do with the wine and a lot to do with the man seated next to her. Even after all these years he still managed to make her pulse race with one long look, one wink. They hadn't been intimate in so long, but now she wanted him, wanted to rip his clothes off and forget everything else. She wanted hot and sweaty sex—now, not later.

"Damn right I did! But it was more than that. There was an innocence about you I didn't want to change. Maybe I still don't. Maybe that's why this has been so hard."

She liked that about him, how primal he was about her. Right from the start he'd wanted to protect her, look after her, and she'd never seen the asshole Matt who'd given his dad a black eye one night and never come home on countless occasions, the guy who'd missed football training because he was too stoned when previously he'd been the school's star quarterback. He'd gone from star athlete and scholar to heading off the rails fast, and she knew his dad was eternally grateful that he'd met her and gone back to the nice, easygoing guy he'd been before his mom died.

"I love how you go all 'caveman protecting his woman' when it comes to me."

"And I love how you bring out that man in me."

She gazed at him, fingers playing up the stem of her glass. Their food arrived then, but she thanked the waitress without looking at her. It was unlike Matt to be so . . . she didn't know what it was. He didn't usually talk like that, never told her how he felt very often.

"Eat your dinner," he ordered, obviously buzzing from the beer. "This caveman is ready to drag his woman back to his man-cave."

She laughed, knowing she was blushing, which was so stupid when it was her husband talking to her. It was insane that he could still have that effect on her. Matt was still staring, still intense, his blue eyes twinkling as he watched her. Maybe she was just embarrassed because it was *she* who wanted him so bad right now, and because it had been a while.

Lisa looked away, down at her food as she picked up her fork, appetite almost gone. When she glanced back, he opened his mouth to say something but obviously changed his mind.

"What?" she whispered.

"I was just thinking how nice this is, being here just the two of us, in a bittersweet kind of way."

And there it was. No matter how happy they were or what they were doing, it always circled back to her cancer, to what had happened. Happy now felt like a different kind of happy to the happy they'd once enjoyed.

She pushed the evil thoughts away, had to so she didn't ruin the moment.

"Yeah, me too."

Lisa held her fork tighter and took the knife into her other hand, making herself smile at the beautiful food on the plate in front of her. She was sitting in a gorgeous restaurant with a gorgeous man, about to eat what looked like amazing food. She needed to push it down, lock her thoughts and memories away before she ruined what was good in her life.

She took her first mouthful of prawn and savored the flavor. It was divine.

"Good choice," she said, smiling up at Matt.

He'd already eaten a few mouthfuls to her one. "It's seriously good."

Lisa ate a mouthful of steak and shut her eyes for a second. It was heavenly. She sipped her wine once she'd finished chewing, sat back and took in her surroundings, the buzz of people as the outdoor area of the restaurant started to fill up. She was so lucky to be here right now, and nothing could take that away from her. She just needed to keep reminding herself that she could have been dying or even dead right now, and instead she was alive, still breathing, still walking. She had a lot to be thankful for. She just needed to start acknowledging it.

14.

"Stop!" Lisa laughed as Matt tried to grope her from behind, pushing up her top, wishing she hadn't had so much to drink. He had his hands on her butt and he wasn't giving up. "Matt!" she hissed, fumbling with the keys as she tried to get them into the lock. "Someone will see us."

"So? You're my wife."

"It doesn't mean other people need to see us naked!" she laughed.

Lisa shoved him with one hand and eventually managed to get the key into the lock. She ran through the door, half-heartedly tried to close it on Matt and failed. His big frame filled the door, eyes never leaving hers. She walked backward, the piercing blue irises following her every move, his wide shoulders pushing into the door as he nudged it shut, biceps flexing as he yanked his t-shirt over his head and faced her bare-chested. This was what she wanted. Something to take her mind off *everything*.

She ran her tongue over dry lips, feeling trapped, exhilarated, *alive*. Matt was stalking her, his intention clear, the way they'd been looking at each other over dinner still sending licks of anticipation through her. But the way he was staring at her now was so primal, and as much as she wanted to play the game, to tease him, she wanted him, too.

"You remember the night in the cabin?" Matt asked, one eyebrow arched as he waited for her response.

"Always." She slipped the strap of her dress down, stared back at him. "Only that girl was blushing every time you looked at her naked, and this woman knows exactly what she wants. Right here, right now."

Matt chuckled. "You're saying that you don't think I could make you blush anymore?"

Lisa stopped walking backward and decided to stalk straight back toward him. She slipped off the other strap, paused so her dress could fall off her body into a puddle on the floor, leaving her in just her bra and panties. She grinned when he let out a low wolf-whistle.

"Oh, I know you can." She stopped in front of him and ran her fingernails down his bare chest, took a deep breath as she thought about what they were about to do. After so long . . . it was a relief to finally *want* this again. "In fact, I'm counting on it." She needed him to make her forget, to pleasure her and make everything else go away.

Matt stayed still, took a big breath that she felt against her hands when she laid them flat to his body. Her own breath was short and sharp, her eyes trained on his, lips parted, waiting, knowing what was coming.

"You asked for it," he muttered, scooping his hands beneath her butt and walking her backward, throwing her down onto the bed. She watched as he undid his belt and ripped his jeans off in record time, body slamming into hers.

The weight of him, the feel of him, everything felt so right. Lisa raised her chin, didn't resist when he roughly claimed her mouth, all of the softness of earlier long gone. But it was just what she wanted, *needed*, and she hungrily matched his movements, rocked her pelvis up into his, legs wrapped tight around him to lock him in place.

"Don't stop," she demanded when he pushed hard against her.

"Wasn't going to," he muttered straight back.

Lisa sighed into his mouth when he kissed her again, hungry for him, wanting him closer. She arched her back as he reached for a bra strap, moaning as his mouth closed over her breast, using her heels to try to get his boxers off when she couldn't reach low enough.

"Slow down, tiger," he said with a chuckle, smiling down at her as he half-rose to oblige her.

Lisa took her chance, stripped her panties off and parted her thighs to let him fall back into place above her.

"Damn," Matt muttered, his voice husky as hell and making her laugh.

"Screw '*slow*.' I want you now," she demanded.

"What my wife wants, she gets."

Lisa fell back and held her arms above her head, arching her back when Matt settled his weight over her and took hold of her wrists to pin them in place. After months of not feeling like sex, of not wanting Matt or feeling the attraction toward him she was used to, he'd managed to make her pulse race and her body hum just like old times.

༄

"You know, this *is* kind of like the cabin," Lisa said, stretching out beside Matt and pulling the sheet with her.

Matt promptly pulled it down again, hand claiming her skin, skimming past her breast and making her smile.

"If you squint your eyes to blur out the fact that this place is actually a whole lot nicer."

"I mean just the lying in bed part. No house to worry about, no commitments, just you and me. And it feels naughty for some reason."

Lisa tickled his nipple and received a slap on the hand in response.

"It does feel kind of naughty," Matt agreed. "We need to do this more often."

Lisa stretched out again, this time not caring about the sheet slipping down. It was stupid to be modest about her body with Matt, she knew that, and the hungry look in his eyes the night before and when they'd woken up this morning told her that he liked what he saw. For some reason, though, she felt shy in the light of day; the alcohol had helped take the edge off the night before.

"You ready to go to the market soon?"

"Do I look ready?" he asked, sitting up and leaning against the headboard.

"In a woodsman kind of way, all mussed up and unshaven," Lisa said, pulling up beside him and brushing a kiss against his jaw before reluctantly getting up. "I'm jumping in the shower. We can grab breakfast at the market."

Matt lay back down, flashing her a grin just as she turned. She envied him getting some extra bed time, but then again she wanted to wash her hair. She'd spent long enough hiding in bed at home— this trip was about moving forward and changing all that.

Lisa got in the shower, running through her usual routine as fast as she could. She wrapped herself in a big towel and wiped the mirror clear when she got out, pinning her hair up and rubbing on moisturizer over her body. Then she went back out into the room to catch Matt rising, still naked as he stretched. He kissed her on his way past before disappearing into the bathroom. She dressed while he was in the shower, staring at her cases full of clothes for what seemed like forever before finally pulling out a pretty long dress that had been part of her last summer collection. It had a bright orange piece of contrasting fabric under the bust, and she dug around in her jewelry bag until she found a cute orange bracelet that she'd made by hand when the collection came out. She slipped it over her wrist, found some equally cute sandals and then joined Matt in the bathroom to put on her make-up and dry her hair. Today felt different, in a good way. She felt so much closer to him now than she had in a long while.

"You look good," Matt said, rubbing his hair with a towel.

"I hate how easy it is for *you* to look so good." She applied her foundation with a brush and watched him in the mirror. He looked so damn amazing naked. His skin was golden, arms thickly muscled from all the heavy work he did on the building sites. His shoulders were just as good, and she had to resist the urge to turn and run her fingers over them.

Lisa went back to applying her make-up and Matt walked out with his towel slung low. She quickly dried her hair, putting her head down and blasting it with heat. She was lucky it was long and easy to do—all she had to do now was run her fingers through it with a little product in and it would be done.

"Ready?" she called out as she walked back into the bedroom space.

Matt slipped on a t-shirt, taking his phone from his ear and pushing it into his pocket. "Ready."

She reached for her purse and dropped her lip gloss into it. "Who were you talking to?"

"Kelly."

Lisa glanced up. "Is Blue okay?" She missed their dog so bad, wished they'd just bundled him up and brought him along, although she wasn't so sure they'd have been able to sneak him into their accommodation that easily given the size of his body, not to mention his bark.

"Blue's fine. Still having a blast with the girls."

She blew out a breath. "Phew. Bet he's snuggling up on their beds with them and driving Kelly crazy."

"She was just checking in," Matt said with a shrug. "Maybe she doesn't trust us to behave."

Lisa rolled her eyes. "Oh yeah, us and our rock star lifestyle."

"Come on, baby, let's go get into some trouble. Give your sister something to worry about."

She swung hands with Matt as he reached for the car keys.

"How about we have brekky first, *then* go get into trouble."

They both laughed as they walked out the door.

"Want me to take a pic of you or are you doing selfies?" he asked as he locked up.

Lisa thought for a second. "You take it. But wait till we get to the market. You can snap me looking through some stalls or something."

"Sounds like a plan."

It took them just minutes by car to find the farmers' market, and Lisa forgot about everything when she stepped out and saw all the people already milling about, smelled the fresh coffee and food in the air, and felt the sunshine beating down on her bare shoulders.

Lisa waited for Matt and they walked together, side by side, until they reached the first stand.

"We need more bags," Lisa said, throwing Matt a smile and receiving a "here we go again" look in reply.

"We're not carting around a bunch of organic fruit," he said firmly. "Or anything else."

She completely ignored him and smiled at the man behind the stand as she looked at the berries on offer. What she needed was to keep busy, and if that meant buying crazy amounts of fresh fruit, then she was just going to have to go with it. "We'll take these strawberries."

Matt made a moaning noise but she flapped her hand at him without looking. "I could get more," she cautioned.

"I'm going to get us coffee," he announced.

"Matt! You're just disappearing because you don't want to be my packhorse!"

"Exactly! The more you have to carry yourself, the less you'll buy!"

Matt headed off in search of coffee, casting one last glance over his shoulder to see Lisa with her head bent low looking at something else. She was infuriating and gorgeous at the same time, but he liked that. He liked when she was sparky and made him react, because that was what she'd always done. When she wasn't keeping him on his toes, that's when he started to worry.

He found a coffee stall and stepped up to the counter past others waiting for their coffee to be made.

"Two lattes, please," he said.

"About ten minutes," the man replied.

He paid his money and gave his name, then had a look around. It took him only a few minutes to spot someone selling French pastries. Matt scanned what was on display, smiling when he saw what he wanted.

"Can I help you?"

"Pain au chocolat," he said. "I know I'm not saying it right, but it's my wife's favorite."

"What the wife likes, we buy, eh?"

Matt laughed. "Yeah, that sounds about right."

"One or two?"

"I may as well have one, too," he said, his stomach rumbling in response. It had been a long time since dinner, and after the workout they'd had this morning *and* the night before . . . A smile pushed his mouth up and he thought about exactly what they'd been doing. It had sure been a nice way to start their vacation.

"Are you sneaking pain au chocolat without me?"

A hand on his side made him turn.

"For you, baby, always for you."

"Beautiful couple! My wife and I were just like you." The old Frenchman smiled at them, nodding his head.

Matt turned and stole a quick kiss from his wife before collecting the paper bags and passing one to Lisa. He was liking the fact that she hadn't turned away from him lately after pushing him away for so long.

"You're so sweet," Lisa cooed at the man. "Any chance you could point me in the direction of anyone selling fabric or clothes?"

He pointed out the way and Matt thanked him, taking Lisa's hand to drag her away before she talked the man's ear off for the rest of the day.

"Let me collect the coffee and then we can go trawling," he said, rolling his eyes just to get a reaction out of her.

"Let's sit a bit. I'm starving."

Matt heard his name called and retrieved his coffee, then followed Lisa over to a tree that had children playing on one side while their parents picnicked.

"Here." He dropped down and held out his hands, drawing her with him and tucking her against his body as he leaned against the thick tree trunk.

He watched as she nibbled at the pastry. "Good?"

"Amazing. Can I have yours too?"

Matt grunted. "Let me take a pic of you sitting there looking all cute. Then you can steal mine."

"With pastry crumbs on my lip gloss?"

"Yeah. It's real and you look gorgeous."

Lisa shrugged. "Go for it then."

Matt brushed his jeans off when he stood, pulling out his phone and taking a few shots of her.

"Do you want a photo together?"

Matt hadn't even realized anyone was approaching. He saw straight away that it was the kids' dad, who'd nodded at him earlier when they'd sat down.

"Yeah, that'd be great." Matt passed him the phone. "Thanks." They could have just tried for a selfie, and he wasn't one to volunteer to have his photo taken usually, but he wanted some memories of this trip so Lisa could stick them on the fridge with all their other pics.

"Come here," he said, dropping down beside her again and slinging an arm around her shoulders. Lisa looked up at him and smiled, staring into his eyes before they both turned to the stranger holding Matt's phone.

"Thanks."

"You're welcome." The guy laughed. "And I was kinda hoping you might be able to do the same for us if we can wrangle our kids."

Matt slipped his phone into his pocket and held out his hand. "They say never to work with children or animals, but I'll give it a go. Lisa, come help."

Lisa gave him a puzzled look. "What are we doing?"

"Reciprocating. You can get the kids looking at us, I'll take the photos. These guys want a family shot."

"Oh, hey!" Lisa said when a little boy and girl came whizzing toward them, only just stopping before they crashed straight into their legs.

"Sorry! Just a sec."

Their dad was trying to catch them and their mom looked embarrassed. Matt knew it was crazy, especially when the kids were clearly acting out, but it only reminded him of what he'd wanted with Lisa. What they'd lost. Anger swelled inside him, made his skin hot, but he forced it down just like he always did. Him losing the plot wasn't going to help anyone, least of all himself. He thought of what she'd been through and what made her so damn angry and sad all the time.

"Quick kids, come on!" the mom called out, sitting down by the tree and beckoning them over.

Matt glanced at Lisa, saw she was watching the children as they raced into their mom's arms and almost knocked her back against the tree. The dad sat down, they all looked up, and Matt quickly took a few shots before they were off again. He knew it was hard for Lisa, hated that seeing a happy family might knock her back when they'd been having fun together all morning.

"You've sure got your hands full there," he said.

"Tell me about it," the dad moaned. "Thanks," he said when Matt passed him his phone back.

The woman was pretty, her hair tied back in a ponytail. She smiled broadly and held out her hand to Lisa.

"I'm Kate," she said. "It means a lot to us to actually have a family shot. It's usually only one of us with the kids."

Lisa introduced herself and then gestured to her husband. "And this is Matt."

"Pete," the man said.

They all shook hands.

"So do you two have any kids?" Kate asked. "Or is that a stupid question given that you're here at lunchtime, just the two of you?"

Matt hesitated, wasn't sure what to say. He knew Lisa hated people looking at her and thinking she didn't want a family, that she had no interest in being a mom. He doubted anyone actually thought that, but it was one of the few things she'd been sensitive about since they'd gone through all the IVF treatments. And now she was being questioned after losing her baby. He was ready to jump in but she answered.

"We would love a family one day," Lisa said in a deeper voice than usual that told him how hard it was for her saying the words. "We've tried so hard, but it just hasn't happened for us."

The other woman reached for Lisa, placed her hand over hers. "We tried for years before these two came along, had a miscarriage in between, too. It's so painful at the time, but it's worth the heartache when it finally happens."

"We lost a little one too, at around four months."

Matt saw tears in Lisa's eyes as she spoke and wished he could take her pain, but the truth was he felt it, too. It wasn't like he'd ever talked about it with the guys, got it off his chest, but there wasn't a day that went by when he didn't look at their little black and white ultrasound photo. Not a day when he didn't think about the boy they'd lost, what he would have looked like, talked like, cried like, smelt like. Hell, it woke him in the night thinking of the decision they'd made, the fact that he'd told his wife to do it, chosen her so easily over their unborn child. Matt swallowed, hard. He'd never said the words to her, never been able to get it out. Instead, he'd buried it, drinking when his thoughts became too dark, drowning his sorrows instead of showing the hurt.

"Your little one's with God, that's what we believe," Kate said, still holding Lisa's hand.

Matt suddenly didn't want to be having this conversation with strangers, and he could see that Lisa was treading water. Or maybe she was about to drown. "It was great meeting you guys," he said, "but my wife stole my breakfast so I need to go grab something else before all the good stuff sells out."

"Thanks," Lisa mumbled as he dragged her away.

"No problem."

"I just . . . I don't know," she said, when they were out of earshot. "I guess I thought I was okay talking about it to a stranger, that I was ready to admit it. Guess not."

"Want more to eat?" Matt asked, happy to move on and not discuss their lack of children with anyone else ever again.

"I thought you'd never ask."

Tomorrow they were heading for Napa, and he hoped that the surprise he'd planned took them back to a happy place, before cancer and terminations and IVF. And then maybe he could bring up the whole adoption thing again. If he could just make her see how many babies there were out there that she could love, give her what she wanted, he was convinced it would make everything okay.

15.

att wound the window down and pushed his elbow out to rest it on the door frame. He drummed his fingers across the car to the beat of the music.

"How much longer do we have to go?" Lisa asked.

He smiled over at her. "Sick of being stuck in a small place with me already?"

She smiled back over at him and he hoped it meant no. She was clearly trying to be upbeat, but it was obvious the encounter in the market had knocked her.

"Maybe another twenty minutes. It's not far," he told her. He couldn't wait to get to Napa Valley; she might not like surprises but he was sure she was going to love this.

The rest of the drive passed quickly and soon they were there, rows of grapes growing in picturesque vines welcoming them to the valley. Matt rolled his shoulders back, pleased the drive hadn't taken long. They'd talked about coming back for some time, and it felt good seeing the place again. It brought back memories of good times, and he was hoping like hell it would help Lisa, especially since she'd been so quiet since the market. She hadn't even wanted to go to the drive-in after being so excited about it the day before.

Matt pulled off the road, taking the turn that he knew Lisa would recognize.

"Matt, this is where we got married," she blurted loudly.

"Oh, yeah. So it is." He knew his mock innocence wasn't fooling her when she spun in her seat to stare at him, grabbing his arm.

"Are we staying there?" she asked, her tone uncertain.

"Yeah, actually, we are," he said, taking a hand off the wheel to reach for her. "Happy?"

"But, isn't it too expensive or, I mean . . ." her voice trailed off and he saw she was staring out the window now.

"It's not too expensive and we are staying," he told her, finishing her sentence for her. "I booked it as soon as you said yes to the road trip."

"Matt, we can't."

He wasn't sure why she was so hesitant, whether it was actually just the money or something else. "Don't go shooting down the one seriously romantic thing I've done for you in a decade."

He listened to her sigh. "I'm sorry—it's just I wasn't expecting it. It's brought back a lot of memories."

"And that's a bad thing?" he asked. He wasn't sure what she wanted these days, what she meant half the time. He'd expected her to be over the moon that they were staying in the same place.

Lisa finally took his hand and squeezed it. "I just wasn't expecting it, that's all."

"When I told you Napa was going to be amazing, I meant it. We can pretend we're honeymooners again."

Lisa nodded but he was left with an uneasy feeling. If he hadn't done the right thing now, he doubted he'd ever be able to.

"Thanks, Matt. I'm sorry I wasn't more excited."

"You're worth it," he said. "Every damn thing I do for you is worth it." The huskiness of his tone, the gruffness of his words, surprised him. But he was speaking the truth. He might not know how to show it sometimes, but he loved Lisa, and all he wanted was to make her happy.

Lisa's phone rang and he sped up a little when she pulled away to answer it, keen to get to their accommodation.

"Hey, Kelly," he listened to her say. He was pleased Kelly had just phoned Lisa this time—he didn't like being the middle man between them.

Lisa and Kelly had always been so close, but Lisa had been closed off from everyone lately, her sister included.

"We're in Napa Valley. Matt's booked us into the same place we got married."

Matt smiled as he listened, enjoying the upbeat tone of her voice.

"How's Blue? Everything okay? I wish he was with us."

There was a long silence and Matt glanced over at Lisa. He hoped everything *was* okay.

"Well, tell the girls that they can share him with us. Maybe he could do weekends."

Matt relaxed. He'd thought something might have happened or that the dog was being too much of a handful for Lisa's sister. He tuned her out while she spoke to Kelly, focusing on the scenery and loving how green everything was. He'd often imagined them having some land, being away from everything when they raised a family of their own, and driving through the countryside reminded him of those dreams. Then again, he loved their house, and given the hours he'd put into remodeling it, the last thing he really wanted to do was move. Plus, he didn't think he could convince Lisa to trade pretty clothes for mud and animals.

"You're going to laugh at this," Lisa said, interrupting his thoughts as he turned into the entrance.

Her easygoing voice made him smile. "The girls won't give Blue back?" he asked with a chuckle.

"Even funnier. They've worked out a shared custody arrangement!" She burst out laughing as she told him. "Apparently one of Eve's friends has parents going through a divorce, and her friend was telling her what custody means and what nights she'll be spending with her dad. So Eve and Zoe decided to draw up a plan on paper to show us what days they want Blue and what days we're allowed him back."

"So in other words, if we want our dog back, we have to buy them a puppy of their own?" he suggested.

"I don't think we'd need a dog if we both did that because we'd be dead. My sister would kill us."

Matt slowed down and smiled over at Lisa. "We're here," Matt said, stopping the car.

Lisa went silent again and he suddenly wished he'd driven even slower so he could enjoy her being happy for a bit longer. He opened his door and got out to stretch his legs before moving around to open Lisa's door, holding out his hand.

"I can't believe we've come back," she whispered to him, and he folded an arm around her when she stood, dropping a kiss to the top of her head.

"Believe it," he said.

"We had some of our photographs taken over there. I remember how big Kelly's stomach was because it was so soon to her due date, and she was trying to disguise it by turning into that row of grapes."

Matt smiled at the memory. "It was a great day."

Lisa turned into his arms, eyes searching out his. "I don't know if I can do this." Tears filled her eyes and he had no idea why.

"I wish I could help you, but I don't even know what's wrong."

She shook her head and looked away, and in that moment he felt like he'd lost her again. Like a wall had gone up between them that no amount of chipping away could break.

"Me too," she murmured. "I wish I knew how to fix me, too."

"Lis, I know you keep getting angry every time I bring this up, but if you really want a baby, if you want to be a mom—"

"Don't," she whispered. "Why can't you get that I want *our* baby? A baby of our own?"

He steeled his jaw. He got it, because he wanted it too. But that wasn't going to happen, so why the hell couldn't she consider another path?

∽

Lisa sat and looked up at the bright blue sky, thinking how blissfully perfect it seemed. Everything about where they were right now was perfect; there was just no other way to describe it. The sun was shining, birds were singing, there was a faraway hum of a harvester or something working nearby, and the breeze was gentle. So why couldn't she just focus on all those beautiful things? Why did she have to keep thinking about what they didn't have? What was wrong with her?

Matt was off running, and it was nice to have some time without him. They'd had some lovely moments together, but the thoughts inside her head drove her half crazy sometimes, and those moments made it hard to be upbeat all the time. She just wanted to sit, and she sure as hell didn't want to take a walk down memory lane like he wanted to. Because being here reminded her of the dreams they'd had, the things they'd planned for the future. Things she was never going to have, no matter how badly she wanted them.

But the problem was that she didn't want to be alone; she just didn't want to be with Matt right now. They'd always been so easy with one another, but now he was suffocating her again.

Lisa reached for her phone, needing to talk to someone. Her sisters were always good at talking her down from any ledge she needed rescuing from, and that was exactly how she felt. Instead of calling Kelly, she decided to phone Penny. Her big sister already had Lisa's dog to contend with twenty-four-seven; she didn't need Lisa to deal with too.

It rang for what seemed like forever, and just when Lisa was expecting the voicemail to kick in, her sister answered.

"Hey!" Penny panted, sounding breathless. "I'm so sorry I haven't called!"

Lisa smiled. Her sister always talked a million miles an hour and hearing her voice was exactly what she'd needed.

"It's fine. We've been having fun driving so it's no big deal."

"Hey, as much as I want to talk, can I call you later? I'm just running in to see a customer, and I have my arms full of crap and . . ."

Lisa tried not to be disappointed. Her sister was busy and she got it. "Of course! No hurry."

"You're okay, though, right? I mean, as okay as you can be considering everything."

Lisa clutched the phone tighter. "Yeah, I'm okay. It's weird, though. I feel like I'm looking down on my body, kinda numb all the time."

"You could always try getting stoned."

Lisa laughed. "Only you could make me laugh when I'm feeling like shit."

"Hey, I haven't done it since high school, but if it took your mind off things, I'd happily take a walk down memory lane with you."

"You don't have to break the law to make me happy. I'll be fine, honestly." She knew her sister was only kidding. They hadn't exactly been pot-heads when they were in school.

Lisa said goodbye to her, still smiling at her younger sister's words. She was too cute.

She dialed Kelly after all, wanting to keep the happy vibe going, to stop herself sinking back into her own thoughts.

"Hey!"

Both her sisters were bright and easy to talk to, but the fact that Kelly picked up so fast told her that Penny had probably already texted her and told her she needed cheering up. She'd probably have her mom calling soon to talk to her, and for some reason Lisa found it a whole lot harder to hold it together when it came to her mom. Maybe because she knew her mom could see through any cracks, no matter how well she thought she'd patched them up.

"How are the girls? And Blue?" Lisa asked.

"Great and great," Kelly said. "I'm just getting the kids an after-school snack ready, so I'll put you on speaker."

Lisa could imagine the scene, could see Blue sitting at Kelly's feet, tail thumping as he drooled over whatever food she was fixing. His tongue would be lolled out to the side, blue eyes bright, ready to catch any morsel that dropped before it even touched the ground. Her sister would be putting home baking or sandwiches or something else yummy in little containers, ready for the girls to eat in the back of the car after she collected them from school so they had something to fill them up before swimming or dancing or whatever activity they had to get to.

"So, anything to report?" Lisa asked, sitting back with her phone to her ear, eyes shut as the sun beat down on her. "Any gossip?"

"No. We're just doing the same old here. You? Is Napa beautiful as ever?"

"Did you know that he was bringing me here? To the same place we got married?" Lisa sighed. "I can't believe you didn't tell me."

"Matt was so excited about taking you back, and I thought he was right, that it would do you good to remember those times."

Lisa listened to Kelly's sigh and tears filled her eyes. She hated how emotional she'd become. "I don't know if I want to remember anymore."

"I can still see you two, holding hands and staring into each other's eyes. I was always so worried that he'd break your heart, but Matt changed when he met you. It's been tough on him too, but he loves you. You just need to let him in."

"I know," Lisa murmured, not wanting Kelly to hear her tears even though she knew her sister would have guessed already by her voice. "It used to be so easy, but now it's just . . ." She didn't know what to say. "I'm not that same woman anymore, and I don't know if I'll ever get back to being her. And he is trying so hard, but I wish we didn't have to try, you know? Because we've never had to before."

They were the words Lisa had been holding close, not wanting to admit. But it was true. Would she ever be the same again? Would she ever be able to get past what she'd done? What she'd lost?

The phone muffled for a second and then Kelly's voice was clearer. She must have taken her off speaker.

"I know this is hard, but you're so lucky to have Matt. Some people spend their lives searching for what you two have, and they never find it. You just need to open up to him and get past this. And where better than Napa?"

"I don't want Matt," Lisa whispered. "I just want my baby." The words cut her in half, made it almost impossible to breathe. She'd said it; she'd finally admitted it. That's what the dark cloud had been; those were the thoughts she'd been hiding behind. "I blame him."

"Lisa, they're dangerous words. I know you want your baby back, but not without Matt. He lost just as much as you did that day, but men deal with these things differently."

Kelly was silent and Lisa felt sick, wished she'd hadn't unloaded on her sister after promising herself that she wouldn't burden Kelly any more than she already had.

"I don't want to think like that—I don't want to think at all, but my brain's just mush. I can't get past it, any of it."

"Life's a bitch and you've had a serious serving of bitch lately," Kelly said. "But you can get through this. You *will* get through this. Just don't make Matt out to be the bad guy. Once you paint him as the villain, you'll never get past it, and it's not his fault, so you can't let that happen, okay?"

Lisa took a deep breath, sat up straighter and glanced over her shoulder to make sure Matt wasn't approaching. It was easy to put blame on to her husband, but Kelly was right: it wasn't his fault.

"Matt deserves to have someone to have a family with," Lisa said quietly. "It breaks my heart to think of him never being a dad because of me."

"Look, it probably breaks his heart that you can't be a mom, but he'll get past that and so will you."

"I don't know if it does break his heart," Lisa replied flatly. "I don't know how he feels."

"You need to talk to Matt about this," Kelly said. "These are dangerous thoughts to have circling in your head. Do you hear me? And you need to get it all out. Talk it through with your husband, and if not him, then someone else."

Lisa knew her sister was right, but it didn't make it any easier. "I don't even know where to start."

"You know why?" Kelly said.

Lisa waited, shutting her eyes as clouds parted and made the sun shine even more brightly.

"You guys were childhood sweethearts," Kelly said. "You've never had to deal with anything like this, none of the hardships that other couples have faced who've met later in life. You've hit little road bumps, but your relationship has been easy up until now. Neither of you have had your hearts broken or been through those awful breakups that the rest of us have."

Lisa heard what she was saying, knew it made sense. "I hear you."

"Go find your husband, and don't go saying anything you'll regret. And then just try to enjoy yourself. Take a walk, sleep, eat, have great sex. Make the most of it."

"You're right," she admitted. "It's just been rough coming back to the place we were married. It's bringing back old feelings, reminding me of the promises we made, of all the things we'd talked about and planned."

"You're going to be fine."

Lisa thanked her sister and said goodbye before ending the call. She was still holding tight to her phone as she shut her eyes and basked in the sun. She pushed her sunglasses back up her nose as they slid down, tried to breathe deep and fill her belly before exhaling.

"Hey, baby."

It felt like she'd only had her eyes shut a few seconds when Matt's hands landed on her shoulders, his wet face brushing hers as he leant in for a kiss.

"Eww," she muttered, wrinkling her nose and pushing him away. "You're sweaty and gross."

"Sorry."

He flopped down on the seat beside her, hair as wet as his running t-shirt, which he'd just pulled off. He had his earbuds slung around his neck, iPod tucked into the waistband of his shorts. His legs were long and tanned, shoulders muscular and even more golden. He'd always had a good body, and even though he'd put on a little weight over the years, he still looked fantastic. His face had filled out, body not quite as lean but sexy as hell in a more mature way than the lanky guy he'd once been, still filling out his frame when she'd first met him. She still loved him so much, which was why she knew her sister was right. She could only push so hard before he started to pull back.

"Good run?" she asked.

"Yeah, great," Matt said, sinking back further into his chair with his feet stretched way out in front of him. "I ran way out around the property, then did some sprints down the rows of grapes. Doesn't get much better."

They sat in silence for a bit, before Matt pushed up to his feet beside her. "I'm going to have a shower. Meet at the restaurant for lunch? We can take a walk down memory lane, see if we can eat outside like we did on our wedding day."

Lisa nodded and let him go, watching until he disappeared. Then she sat back in the sun again, shutting her eyes and refusing to acknowledge the sting of tears even as she braced for them. She needed to tell him how she felt, before it all became too much. Before it ruined everything.

"Matt," she called out, her voice so hoarse she wondered if he'd hear her. But he did, because when she sat up, he was already walking back.

"Yeah?"

"I don't think I can do it," she forced out.

"Do what?" he asked.

This, she wanted to say. But for some reason she couldn't push the word out. "I can't relive all this. I . . ." She took a deep breath. "I feel like I'm suffocating."

Matt frowned. "I thought you'd love coming back. I thought this would make you happy."

She didn't want to be angry with him, but she couldn't fight her feelings any longer. They wouldn't simmer down, no matter how hard she tried, and now that she'd opened up to Kelly, she couldn't stop the words.

"I don't know how to be happy anymore, not like I used to be," she told him, wishing she didn't hear so much sadness in her voice.

"Baby, we can be happy. Just try. Please."

"No!" she choked as he closed the distance between them and took her hand. She shook off his touch, didn't want to be placated. "It's not that easy."

"Lisa, come on," he said, looking confused.

"You can't just tell me to be happy, Matt. I can't change the way I feel." Did he even care? Did he even feel the way she did at all?

"Maybe if you told me how the hell you were feeling instead of leaving me guessing, then I'd get it," he growled back. "But instead, I'm playing a fucking guessing game, wondering what the hell to do to get back to what we had. Wondering what I've done to deserve you pushing me away."

Lisa felt stung, like he'd slapped her across the cheek. "We're never going to get back what we had. That's gone. How can you not get that?"

"You know what I don't get? You," he said, voice low, his smile long gone.

Tears flooded her eyes. "I don't get me either anymore, Matt. That's half the problem. Can't you see?"

His gaze softened, face falling as he looked at her. "Then let me in. Give me a chance to make things right."

"You really want to know what's wrong?" she said, needing to get it out, no longer able to keep it all locked away inside.

"Yes," he muttered.

"You chose me," she blurted out. "You chose me when all I wanted was for you to fight for our baby. I wanted you to tell me that no matter what, you'd look after him. That the life we'd created was more important than me, that it was worth the risk to wait until I'd given birth." Now she'd started, she couldn't stop, even though Matt had walked backward a few steps, even though she knew she was pushing him away, driving a wedge between them. Because the words were like venom and they'd been eating her up inside, and now she was spewing them at him. "I hate you for not telling my doctor that nothing was worth me being infertile. For not telling him that I had to have children to be a woman, that it was so important to me. I hate that we made the choice to terminate the baby growing inside of me, as if it was okay to just suck him out of me and discard him. Because I *wasn't* more important than him, Matt. I wasn't then and I'm sure as hell not now." She gasped. "I hate that I can't give you the family that I know you'll start to resent not having."

Matt stared at her, his glare like ice, his jaw steeled. "You finished?" he asked.

She wiped away the tears that were pouring down her cheeks. "Yeah," she whispered.

"I'm not going to pretend like I did the wrong thing, because I didn't. I married *you*. I love *you*. What the hell did you want me to do? Did you honestly think that I was going to choose a baby I'd never met over my wife? That I'd want to raise a baby alone without you? Haven't we already had this conversation?" He folded his arms across his chest, shook his head. "I lost something too that day, Lisa. I lost our baby, in case you've forgotten. I was his goddamn dad! But I was so damn happy that I still had you, and I wish you were more damn grateful that you're alive. Because I lived the flipside of that when I lost my mom, and I don't ever want to live through that again."

"*Fuck you*," she muttered, hating him for being so honest, for speaking the truth. "I *am* grateful that I'm alive, but you weren't the one with a child growing inside of you. I know you lost your mom— I can't imagine what that must have been like, but I can't think about anything other than what *I* lost right now. You won't ever understand. And if you'd loved him like I did . . ."

"If you hadn't shut me out since it happened, then maybe I would understand! And don't you dare try to tell me I didn't love him, because I did. That's bullshit."

"I'm grieving, Matt. How can you not see that? Just because he wasn't born doesn't mean that it hurts any less. I want a family, and I'm never going to have one. And it makes me a shitty wife because I can't ever give you a family either."

"For Christ's sake! There are plenty of babies out there in the world we could adopt, and then there's surrogacy and fostering. Why won't you even talk to me about all that?"

"Stop!" she yelled at him. "I don't want to adopt. I don't want another baby. I want *my baby*! You can't just fix this, Matt. You can't just offer me another baby and give me a pat on the head and think everything's going to be okay! Don't you dare mention adoption again!"

"You know what? I wish we had our baby, too. Every god-damn day I wonder what he would have looked like. Did you even know that I still carry our scan photo in my wallet? That I think about him?"

Lisa gulped, eyes burning, hands shaking.

"No, of course you don't," Matt yelled. "Because you've been acting like you're the only one who's lost something."

Matt turned to go, then stormed back toward her.

"You want to know the difference?" he asked in a low, gravelly voice. "I can live with what happened because I still have you. But don't you dare act like I don't care or like I didn't want our child."

Lisa sucked back air, gulped it down, felt like she was going to be sick. Her entire body was shaking, bile rising in her throat. She frantically swallowed it down.

"I thought bringing you here would help, that we could talk and move on," Matt told her, his voice quiet now. He shook his head, his gaze impossibly sad. "I've been so scared of losing you, but it's like the good parts of you left me anyway the day you were wheeled into that operating room. And I'm not talking about the parts of you that've stopped you from being a mom."

Her heart ached. Every part of her body seemed to be screaming out, telling her to throw her arms around him and say sorry, but she couldn't. She was frozen solid to the spot.

"I wanted you to fight," Lisa whispered. "I just wanted you to demand a way to save our baby."

"I was too damn busy trying to save you instead," he ground out, turning away this time and not looking back.

Lisa's hands were shaking violently now, her lips were trembling, tears were still dripping down her cheeks, and she fell, dropped to her knees. She was powerless to move, to do anything but collapse and let silent screams fight to be heard as she broke down and watched her husband walk away.

Maybe it was what she'd wanted, to blame him and push him away. To make him feel her hurt. Only now she'd done it, she didn't feel any better. She'd been so self-involved, so lost in her own thoughts and unable to see anything else but her own pain, but Matt wasn't wrong. Not about everything. Maybe not about anything.

She felt as bad as she had that day her baby had been taken from her. Because if she didn't have her baby and she didn't have Matt either, then what was she left with?

16.

Matt turned on the faucet and stripped off his clothes. He stood naked in front of the vanity, waiting for the water in the shower to go hot. He stared into the mirror, into eyes that didn't look like his anymore. What had he done? Why had he exploded like that? Why couldn't he have just kept his shit together, let her vent, then tried to pick up the pieces?

Instead, he'd said everything he'd been trying so hard to keep in.

He braced his hands on either side of the ceramic bowl, wondering if he should shave, wondering . . . He stopped thinking and turned to step into the shower, letting the hot water blast over his body. The run had done him good, cleared his head and made him just focus on the pounding of his shoes with every step he made. And then he'd seen Lisa and everything had crashed around him. He'd known it was coming, that one day she was going to get it all out, all the things that were trapped inside of her, but he hadn't expected that. It was like she hated him and it scared the hell out of him.

He ran his fingers through his hair, soaked it through and reached for the shampoo bottle. He washed it, rinsed it out, tried to stop thinking . . . A sob escaped from his mouth, an animal-like, guttural sound that he couldn't stop. His entire body shuddered, the air choking in his lungs, the pain so real it was like a knife to his stomach, twisting and turning. Stabbing deep.

He'd kept it in for so long, been so determined that he'd be able to save her, that he wouldn't lose her just like he'd lost his mom, but he couldn't. Because he'd lost Lisa, too, just in a different way. He'd been so sure coming to Napa would change things, but the way she'd looked at him before . . . It was like they were already a lost cause.

"*Fuck!*" he cursed, trying to stop crying, trying to stop the sobs that kept shattering his body.

Matt dropped, slid against the tiled wall of the shower and slumped on the floor. Water slid around him, ran down his face and into his mouth as he sobbed. The shudders had stopped, replaced by a steady stream of tears that fell from him like they'd been waiting a lifetime to be shed.

He'd lost his mom to cancer, memories that he'd buried with everything else he'd been through all those years ago; then his wife had gotten cancer, then his baby had been killed to save her . . . The tears wouldn't stop, the burning in his throat almost impossible to bear.

"Matt?"

"*Shit*," he swore, trying to get a hold on himself, wanting to pull himself up but feeling like he didn't have any strength left.

"Matt?" Lisa's voice was louder now, echoing out.

He sniffed, wiped at his face, tried to get it together.

"Matt!" Lisa ran to him across the bathroom. "Matt!"

When he saw her through the foggy glass, his eyes meeting hers, he lost it again. Matt hated himself for being so weak, for crying in front of his wife, but he'd lost all ability to pull it together.

It took her only seconds to fling the glass shower door open and drop in front of him, arms tight around him as she cradled his head to her chest. She was still wearing her dress, the one she'd been sunbathing in, but she didn't seem to give a damn and neither did he.

"I'm sorry," he heard her whisper as she held him. "I'm so sorry."

Matt moved, put his legs out straight so Lisa could straddle him. She never let go of him, held him and rocked his head like he was a baby she was trying to comfort.

"I'm sorry too," he managed to say once he'd started to get a hold on his emotions.

"Shhh, it's fine," she said, her wet hair stuck to his face.

"I shouldn't have said those things . . ." he started.

"No," she muttered. "We both needed to get it all out."

Matt knew he shouldn't feel guilty, but he did. He wanted to be there for her, didn't want her to see his pain, but there was only so long he could hold it all in. He cleared his throat and sat up a bit, arms around her so he could move her with him.

"I'm sorry," he said again, wiping at his face now that he'd managed to pull himself together.

"It's about time you had a damn good cry," she said in a low voice. "All this time I just thought you didn't care like I did."

Matt listened to her words, hated that he'd done the same thing that he'd despised so much about his dad all those years ago. Seeing his father stand stoically, like everything was okay, had hurt him as much as seeing his mom suffer and then die. But he got it now: everyone coped differently. But knowing that wasn't about to save his marriage.

"I don't know if I can be here," Lisa confessed, pulling back and leaning against the glass.

"I know," he replied, watching her, thinking how damn beautiful she was sitting there all wet.

Lisa gave him a small smile, but it was enough to make a difference to him. They were both miserable, both suffering, but sitting here with her in the shower, he could almost pretend like they were going to be okay.

"You're wet," he said, stating the obvious.

Lisa gave a small laugh and held up her arms, attempting to pull her dress over her head. Only it was completely plastered to her body, and she didn't have any luck.

"Here," he said, helping and managing to peel the fabric off her skin. He tugged until it finally came off, and then she was sitting in her underwear, legs still connected with his.

They stared at one another. Matt wanted her. The only thing he was sure of right now was that he wanted his wife, wanted to be distracted by her body so he could forget about all the shit they'd said, all the crap they'd been through.

"You look good wet," he said, hesitating before leaning forward and cupping the back of her head, softly kissing her.

Lisa moaned and he kissed her again, the water falling between them and around them from the faucet above.

"So do you," she whispered back, reaching for him, pulling him close, mouth covering his.

Lisa wrapped her arms tight around him and he kissed her some more, ran his hands through her tangled wet hair. He skimmed his hands down her body, undid her bra, cupped her breasts and groaned as she brushed her wet lips back and forth over his. She reached for him, pulled herself up and onto his lap again, hair catching on his damp skin, her hands on his face as she rose above him, lips still locked.

"Lisa . . ." he started.

"Make me forget, Matty. Just make me forget," she begged, voice whisper-quiet.

He could do that. He hadn't been able to do much for her, but this he could do.

❦

Lisa kept her fingers interlinked with Matt's as they walked barefoot across the grass. There had been a wedding that day, and the fairy lights that had been strung up through the vines closest to the restaurant were glowing and casting a twinkling web around them. It only made her nostalgia worse, the feeling of intense suffocation that kept coming over her in waves, but she was trying so hard to forget their fight, the hurtful things they'd said to each that were so painful but so truthful at the same time.

"It feels like only yesterday," she said.

"I know." Matt pulled her closer and she let him. "It was a great day."

The sky was inky dark now and Lisa tipped her head back to look up at it. "I love it here," she confessed. "I always thought that if we could move anywhere in the world, I'd choose right here. A house overlooking a vineyard, so I could open the windows each morning and watch our kids run across the grass, filthy dirty and having the time of their lives."

"We still can," he said firmly. "We can still do all those things; you know we can."

"What I wanted hasn't changed—that's the problem," she told him. "And no amount of pretending that you have a solution is going to change that."

"So you do want to move or you don't?" he asked, sounding genuinely confused. "Because I'm perfectly happy where we live. It's just the whole lifestyle thing here that I love the idea of."

"I want what I can't have," she said bitterly. "I wish I could get past it, but I can't. And it wouldn't matter where the hell we were living; that wouldn't change."

"It will," Matt said, stopping and staring down at her. "I know it will."

"Don't tell me to give it time," she muttered. "Because I seriously doubt time alone is going to heal me."

"Never," he said, a harshness to his tone that surprised her. "Because I heard that a million times after my mom died and it's bullshit. You learn to live with it, but it never gets easier."

Lisa watched him, looked into his eyes and saw a pain there she hadn't recognized before, or maybe she just hadn't known what she was looking for.

"You've never really talked about your mom, not properly," Lisa said.

"Because it's something I'd rather not talk about," he said gruffly, starting to walk again.

She stayed still, waited for him to stop when he realized she wasn't following.

"Why don't we ever talk about it? Why have we just cruised through the past ten years like everything was perfectly fine?"

"Maybe because it has been fine." Matt had turned, was looking back at her now. He slowly started to walk toward her. "We've been happy. What was there to dwell on?"

"Talk to me about her, about what you went through," Lisa said, needing to know. "Maybe I was too immature in the beginning to understand, but I need to know. I need to know what happened and how you felt. What it did to you. Why everyone acts like I saved you."

"Lisa, don't push me on this. I buried it all a hell of a long time ago."

"Like you're trying to make me bury this? Acting like adopting a new baby will make me forget? Like that will make me feel less guilty for robbing you of being a biological father?"

Matt shook his head, fists clenched at his sides. "Don't throw words around like that."

Lisa wrapped her arms around herself. Things were going from bad to worse again. But the hurtful things they'd said earlier couldn't just be erased, just like what had happened to her couldn't be forgotten. Their moment of closeness in the shower seemed like a lifetime ago.

She started to walk, stopping when she came to a table placed amongst the vines, surrounded by twinkling fairy lights that made the ones she'd been smiling over earlier look insignificant. "*Oh . . . my . . . god*," she whispered, hardly able to expel the words, each one coming out slowly.

"It's the exact same place we were married, the same place we had that bottle of champagne, too," Matt told her, following not far behind her. "I wanted to do something to surprise you."

"You organized this today?" she choked out, looking from the table back to him again.

"Before we even arrived," he told her, hands thrust into his jeans pockets now as she turned to look at him again. "My lame attempt at doing something romantic, and I can see that I've screwed up again."

Tears welled in her eyes. She wished it was enough, that there weren't so many thoughts running through her head, that they didn't have so many issues to work through. But she couldn't deal with this.

"Is it the wrong thing?" His voice was gruff and starting to choke up, but she didn't want to look at him again, her eyes stuck on the beautiful table now and the waiter making his way toward them, a smile on his face that should have been replicated on hers.

"Matt, I don't know what to say," she whispered.

He came up behind her. She heard him but still didn't turn, even as his hands closed over her shoulders.

"Tell me this is enough, that we can get past this," he said into her ear. "Tell me we can forget all those things we said."

"I'm sorry," she murmured, finally spinning so she was facing him. She fisted her palms, twisted in his arms and pressed them to his chest. "I can't do this, Matt."

"Can't do what?" he asked.

"This. *Us*," she whispered. "I hate the person I've become. I need . . ." Her voice trailed off.

"Just tell me what to do."

"*Let me go*," she said, unable to disguise the sorrow in her voice. "Please," she begged, "just let me go."

Matt stared at her and she looked back at him, blinking through her tears. "I'll tell the waiter we're not staying for dinner then."

"No, Matt, I mean I need to *go*," she said, finding a strength she didn't even know she had. Matt had been her love, *her life*, for so long. "I need to be alone for a while, away from you."

"You're breaking up with me? You're calling time out on our *marriage*?" he asked.

She nodded, biting down hard on her bottom lip. Sadness engulfed her, but she knew she'd said the right thing, that there was no way she was going to get past how she was feeling by not being honest.

"Lisa, come on. All because I keep bringing up adoption? Because I won't talk about the shit I went through after my mom died?"

"No," she said, knowing that he was angry and lashing out, that he hadn't been expecting her to say she wanted out. "It's everything that's happened; it's me needing to spend some time alone and find my way back. It's me dealing with the person I've become." *And hating her.* She couldn't say that to him out aloud, but it was true. She didn't want to be this person but she had no idea how to get the old Lisa back.

"You're sure about this?" he asked, shaking his head.

"No," she admitted. "But I think it's for the best. I'll find my own way out of here in the morning."

"Fuck that," Matt swore.

"Please Matt, just let me go."

"Fine," he ground out. "I'll leave for home now. If you change your mind, pack your stuff and meet me at the car. Otherwise, I'm getting the hell out of here."

Lisa watched him, hated how badly she'd hurt him, but taking a break from her marriage was what she needed. If Matt kept smothering her, trying to pretend like everything was okay, then she was going to explode.

She walked away, wanting to give him space to leave. And she didn't want to be tempted to go jump in the car and head home with him at the last minute. She craved her own bed, was desperate to see her dog and throw her arms around her sister and cry, to be back in the home she loved so much and had always thought would be theirs for a lifetime. But she also wanted to find herself, to not have to think about anyone else. And this was her chance. To see if she could ever find the old her and be the girl Matt knew and loved.

Tears dripped down her cheeks, but as she disappeared into the darkness amongst the vines, she didn't bother to wipe them away. It was okay to cry, especially if there was no one around to see her.

17.

att stayed statue still, waited, looked around in the dark, expecting her to come running. But she never did.

He was actually leaving his wife in Napa, the one place he'd never expected things to turn so bad, the place that he'd thought would make things right between them.

He stormed back inside to gather the last of his things. She'd told him to go, and that's exactly what he was going to do. He was getting in the car and getting the hell out of Dodge. At least at home he could work, he had Blue . . . *fuck it*. Going home without Lisa was just goddamn wrong.

When he got to the car, he slammed his hand against the roof.

"*Fuck!*" He yelled, not caring who could hear. "Fuck!"

Matt kicked his tire, needing to hurt something, anything. He swung his bag into the back and got behind the wheel, hand shaking as he put the key in the ignition. Everything had turned to shit. It had been the worst year of his damn life, and now he was about to lose his wife. Just like he'd lost his mom years before, he was going to lose his wife; it was just a matter of time. Only this time it wasn't cancer.

He'd never wanted to hurt like that again, never wanted to experience the raw pain of loss and grief like when his mom had died. But the roller coaster was starting; he could feel it building deep within him. Lisa had kept him on the straight and narrow, but without her, he had nothing. For ten years she'd been his rock; for ten years he'd loved her. And now he didn't know what to do to make things right. Everything he said was wrong; everything he did just seemed to push her further away.

So he was going home. He could spend the night in Sacramento, which would mean he'd be home by morning. So much for a damn road trip. They'd only made two stops in what was supposed to be the trip of a lifetime.

Matt pulled his shit together and opened the trunk, reached for the plastic bag he'd hidden away. He'd been saving it to give her, and he couldn't see the point in taking it back home with him. He went back in, bent over one of her bags and stuffed it into the bottom. She might not want him anymore, but he'd put money on it that she'd still want to draw.

18.

Lisa dipped her toe in the water, testing the temperature. Her body felt numb. She looked back over at her white towel, thrown over the sun lounger, and thought about just wrapping herself back up in it and going back to the room. But then all she'd do was sit, and she didn't want to think. Not yet.

She stared into the liquid blue, imagined the warmth of the water, sucked in a big breath and then pushed off, propelling herself in. The first splash made her feel good, the second her body was submerged, and then she pushed her body to keep going, surfaced just long enough to take a breath. It took only five long strokes to reach the end, and then she tumbled under the water and came back up, doing laps, not ready to stop. On and on she went, forcing herself forward, legs kicking just enough without breaking the water, arms rhythmic. Until, after six lengths, she forced herself to halt, held on tight to the edge of the pool, knuckles white.

What had she done?

Lisa gasped, caught her breath, sank down one last time, body falling as she pushed her arms up to help propel her down, to force her body to the bottom of the pool. She came up slowly, thought about staying down, thought about what it would be like to end things now instead of waiting for the slow onset of what she had coming. Her lungs screamed, wanting air, and she opened her eyes and slowly resurfaced.

She didn't want to end her marriage. She didn't want to be without Matt. But she couldn't be with him right now either.

Lisa pulled herself out, heaved her body up and crossed to the lounger to retrieve her towel. She rubbed her body dry, patted down her legs, focused on breathing. Then she wrapped herself up tight and started to walk. How could it be less than one day since she'd last seen him, barely twelve hours, and yet she missed him so much already?

What had she done?

She went back to the room that she'd been sharing with her husband only a day ago, opened the door, dropped the towel and stood still. Tears started to run down her cheeks, silently escaping from the corners of her eyes. Maybe she should have left, shouldn't have decided to stay and try to confront all her issues head first in the one place that hurt the most.

This was supposed to be better; it was supposed to be easier being alone. But it wasn't.

What had she done?

Her body was numb. Her teeth started to chatter.

She had the best husband in the world, so why was it so hard to make things right? Why was it so hard to get past what had happened? Why couldn't she accept what had happened?

Lisa dropped to the soft carpet, her sob silent, the scream lodged in her chest a noiseless choke. She reached for the towel she'd just dropped, clutched it, stuffed it into her mouth and bit down on the cotton. The hurt was even worse now, the pain greater than when Matt had still been there. But she didn't want him to see her like this, had needed the time to suffer alone, to work out what had happened. To stop blaming the one person in the world who'd fought so hard for her.

What had she done?

19.
FIVE YEARS EARLIER

M att!" Lisa hissed, giggling as she grabbed his hand and pulled him into her room. "What are you doing?"

His grin was infectious, the devilish look in his eye telling her that he wouldn't leave even if she told him to.

"I wanted to see you," he said, scooping his arm around her and pulling her close, blue eyes bright, sandy blonde hair messy.

"What happened to not seeing each other the night before the wedding?" she asked. "We're supposed to be apart until the ceremony." The last few words were mumbled because he kissed her, mouth so soft over hers, and it felt so damn nice that she decided not to bother protesting and melted into him instead. When it came to Matt, there wasn't a lot he could do to annoy her, and there weren't many times that he couldn't distract her with his kisses.

"You do realize that Kelly will kill you when she finds you here," Lisa muttered against his mouth.

"Your sister won't find us. Come on."

Lisa looked down at her little boxer shorts and tee, not convinced that she wanted anyone to see her in her sleepwear. "Um . . ."

"You look gorgeous," Matt said, slapping her bottom and making her laugh as she swatted him away. "Now come on."

"Where are we going?" she asked, scanning the gorgeous honeymoon suite until she saw her flip-flops and quickly slipped her feet in, wondering what she was going to tell her sister. Her mom and sisters were going to come back to her room to check on her, and Kelly had said she'd stay with her until late to chat.

Lisa threw her hands up in the air and grabbed a sweater, not about to freeze her butt off wherever he was taking her. She followed behind Matt, taking his hand. He peeked out her door and made her laugh, like he was kidnapping her and didn't want to get caught. Only she guessed he kind of was, given that her family was super-traditional—her mom had given her *the look* when she'd suggested that they weren't following tradition too much, which was why she'd agreed to separate sleeping quarters from Matt's in the first place for the night before. A shiver ran down her spine, a delicious feeling that pooled in her belly and made her feel naughty, like the first time Matt had kissed her.

"Lisa! Get back here!" Kelly yelled out.

She burst out laughing, clutching Matt's hand tight. "Run!" she whispered.

Lisa glanced over her shoulder, saw her younger sister, Penny, doubling over in laughter, her mother standing behind her and looking less than impressed. Maybe it was because Lisa had always been the good one, never done anything to make her parents angry, but now she was with Matt, it felt kind of good to rebel a little. He had always told her that she'd pulled him back into line, made him feel again and want to be a better kind of man, but he'd done the opposite to her, in a good way. With Matt she felt alive, felt like she was living life and not missing out on anything. And it was the kind of feeling she loved: it exhilarated her and made her love life. He believed in her, and if it hadn't been for him, she would never have believed that someone her age could have been capable of opening a clothing store, let alone stocking it with all her own creations. She had the drive, but he believed in her, and the confidence he'd given her was impossible to describe.

"Matthew Williams, you bring my daughter back here this minute!" her mother called out.

Lisa blew her mother and oldest sister a kiss, catching a glimpse of Penny and giving her a thumbs-up. They all adored Matt, but they also knew that there was nothing they could do when it came to him. They hadn't had any control over that since the day he and Lisa had started dating in secret.

"They're going to kill us," she said as they escaped outside into the darkness. Lisa was breathing hard, not used to running.

"No," Matt said, spinning her around so she landed with a thump against his chest, dipping his mouth to hers. "They're going to kill *me*. I'm the bad guy here, not their perfect girl."

She was wondering exactly how he could be the bad guy when he ran his hands down her back, fingertips trailing across the thin fabric of her tee.

"Come with me," he said in a husky voice.

Lisa obliged, palm against his again as they walked. The moon was bright, almost full above them as Matt led her across the large area of grass and toward the rows of vines. They stepped between them, heading down through the grapes, farther and farther away from where they were staying. But it was close to where they were getting married the next day; the wedding was scheduled to happen outside as long as the weather was Napa Valley perfect.

"Where are you taking me?" she asked.

"Somewhere to be alone, where nobody will find us."

She was pretty sure no one was going to find them outside anyway, or bother looking in the first place, but she was happy to oblige.

They walked in silence, slowly, across the grass, the air still warm from the balmy day. They'd had their rehearsal dinner the night before, but today she'd been busy with the girls, doing spa treatments, sunbathing and chatting. After a girly day she was definitely ready for some alone time with Matt.

She stopped. There was a champagne bottle sitting in a bucket and two glasses, smack-bang on the ground in the middle of nowhere. Her jaw dropped.

"You planned this to be just like our engagement?" she asked.

He shrugged. "All I had to do was find a spot."

Matt made out like it wasn't a big deal, but she disagreed. "I don't know what to say."

He sat and dragged her down with him, pushing her gently right back until she was lying on the ground. Matt stared down at her, stroked her cheek as he pushed some stray locks from her face.

"Tomorrow is going to be crazy and it'll probably pass by in a blur. I wanted this to be just for us," he told her, lying down beside her. "Look up and see the stars. It's kind of perfect out here."

She dragged her eyes from her man and did what he asked. "It is beautiful," she agreed.

"This is what I want to remember about our wedding," Matt said gruffly.

"Stars?" she asked.

He pushed up on one elbow beside her. "No, us. Just me and you. Not all the bullshit fuss."

She smiled as his palm touched her cheek, lips covering hers for a delicious second before he pulled away and reached for the champagne as she watched him. She jumped when he popped the top, taking a glass and holding it up so he could pour hers. Once they were both full, she held her glass up and tapped it to his.

"To us," she murmured.

"To us," Matt repeated. "Matt and Lisa forever."

"You don't even like champagne," she giggled when he bent to kiss her.

"I know."

⌒⌒

Matt sat up in bed, sheets covering his lower half and strewn across Lisa's naked body as she looked up at him. He thumbed absently across her skin and she smiled at his touch.

"Why did we stay up so late?" she whispered when he bent down to kiss her.

"We had a lot to talk about," Matt replied, stroking her hair and running his fingers down her back when she turned into him. "And then we had a lot of other things to do."

Her laugh was muffled against his chest as she tucked in tight. "We were so bad last night. It was only *one night* we were supposed to be apart."

Matt kissed the top of her head and she sighed.

"I think it's time for me to sneak out," he said.

"Do you have to? Can't we just snuggle a bit longer?" Lisa begged, holding him tight. "I don't want to get up."

Matt pulled Lisa closer and she obliged.

"Maybe we should just cancel everything we have planned and stay here all day," he muttered.

"Uh-huh," Lisa said with a giggle, arms around him. "We can get the celebrant to pronounce us man and wife in bed right here, tell all our guests to travel back to wherever they've come from because the ceremony is off."

Matt groaned when she ran her fingernails down his back. "I was thinking they could still all go through with it, enjoy the food we've already paid an arm and a leg for."

They both laughed, then froze when they heard muffled voices. They got louder. Fast.

"Shhh," he whispered, finger to his lips, as he pulled away from Lisa and sat upright.

"What? Who is it?"

The muffled voices became louder again, followed by knocking on the door.

"Lisa? Lisa are you up yet?" Kelly called out through the door.

"Shit," Lisa swore, looking back at him wide-eyed.

Matt jumped up and grabbed his boxers, quickly pulling them on and then fumbling for his jeans. He tugged them on as she watched, leaving the scuffed boots he'd been wearing the night before and grabbing his t-shirt as he ran for the door.

"See ya, beautiful," he muttered, running back and kissing the top of her head. "I'll be the guy up front waiting for the bride."

Lisa laughed and got up, pulling the sheet with her and wrapping it around her body.

"Lisa, open up!"

When he swung open the door, the chatter stopped abruptly and Lisa cringed.

"Matt?" Penny burst out laughing.

"Matt!" Kelly growled, hitting him with a bag she'd been holding, eyes wild as she swatted at him. "Matthew Williams, you couldn't keep your hands off my damn sister for *one* night?"

"I'm sorry, I'm sorry!" he howled as Kelly whacked him again.

Lisa's hand flew to her mouth and she tried not to laugh.

"And you!" Kelly turned her attention to Lisa. "You shouldn't have let him in!"

"Go, Matty!" Penny called as he ran.

Matt turned and ran backward, and Lisa stood in the doorway watching him, still wrapped in the white bedsheet as the others moved past her. He blew her a kiss and she blew him one straight back, until Kelly grabbed hold of her arm.

"I don't want to see you until the ceremony!" Kelly yelled down the hall after Matt.

Lisa laughed at her sister and pulled her in for a hug.

"Seriously?"

"Hey, if I didn't want to sneak him into my room in the night, then I'd be marrying the wrong guy."

20.
PRESENT DAY

Matt sat alone, his elbows pressed hard into the wooden counter at the dive bar. He was drunk. His lids were heavy, his movements were slow, and he was finding it hard to stay sitting on the barstool.

"Another," he slurred.

The bartender leaned closer, smiling as he poured him a water. "No more for a bit. I think you've had enough."

Matt opened his mouth to argue, then shut it. "Fuck, sorry." He lowered his head, pressed his cheek to the cool wood.

"You don't seem like my kind of regular," the bartender said, nudging the water closer to him. "But I don't care if I know you or not, I think you should sober up a little."

"My wife's left me," Matt said, raising his head just enough to sip some water, his head starting to thump. "She hates me and there's not a goddamn thing I can do about it."

"*Damn,*" the bartender muttered.

Matt watched as the bartender poured a shot of whiskey into two glasses, sliding one his way.

"I'll let you have one more." The bartender raised his glass. "To your marriage."

Matt held up his own glass, staring at the golden liquid before downing it in one gulp. He'd drunk enough that it wasn't even burning anymore, just giving him a nice warm feeling that he'd like to hold on to for a bit longer.

"This is her," he said, pulling his wallet from his back pocket and opening it, showing a photo of Lisa on the day he'd proposed to her. She was grinning, her hair all windswept, eyes big and blue.

"You must be the last guy around carrying an actual picture of his girl in his wallet."

Matt shrugged. He didn't give a damn.

"She's beautiful. Why'd she leave you?"

"I know," Matt said, staring at her, wishing he was with her right now. "She had cancer. And we lost our baby. And now everything's turned to shit." Going back to Napa was supposed to make things better, was supposed to take them back in time. He'd wanted to remember the night before their wedding, in bed together instead of apart, not wanting to be separated for an hour, let alone an evening.

"It sounds rough," the bartender said, wiping down the counter, putting away glasses.

Matt looked around. He was the last man standing. The bar was deserted.

"Rough doesn't even start to cover it."

"Look, I'm gonna be here awhile. Why don't you drink some more water? I'll make you a coffee, and you can crash over there,"—the bartender pointed to a corner that had a big old sofa in it—"while I mop the floors."

Matt stood up, about to say no, that he had somewhere to be. But his legs almost buckled, the room spinning.

"Yeah, okay."

He stood, holding the counter, and knocked back the water. The bartender refilled his glass and he downed that too.

And just like that, he was back to being the Matt before he'd met Lisa, drinking away his sorrows, doing anything to try to put a hold on the pain. And just like old times, it never worked.

"You all right?"

He took the black coffee that the bartender passed to him, shaking his head. "Yeah."

Matt waited for the coffee to cool, thought about what an idiot he'd been. Lisa was the love of his life, but no matter what he did, what he said, what he thought, he'd still managed to lose her.

Why the hell didn't he know what to do to make things better? Why did the pain of his mom dying still haunt him? Why did he still shoulder so much guilt for the way he'd treated his dad?

Why didn't he know how to help his wife?

"I'm just going out back for a bit. Don't spew on the sofa," the bartender called out.

Matt drank the coffee and stumbled toward the sofa, needing to lie down. If he didn't, he probably would be sick. Once he was alone, he pulled out his wallet again, took out the black and white photo that he hadn't looked at for a week now. *His son.*

He hit the sofa hard when he stumbled forward, his movements clumsy. What he needed was some sleep. With numb fingers, he pushed the picture back into his wallet. Once his head stopped thumping and the room stopped spinning, maybe then he'd know what to do.

21.

Lisa woke slowly, stretching, smiling as sun streamed in through the window. She'd forgotten to pull the drapes, and she loved the feel of being bathed in warmth before she even opened her eyes.

She reached out, stretched out her fingertips across the sheets searching for Matt. Only she didn't connect with anything other than a pillow and more empty sheet. Lisa sat up, rubbed at her eyes and looked around.

She'd forgotten Matt wasn't there, just like she'd forgotten the morning before, and the morning before that. She blinked a few times as her eyes adjusted and forced herself up and back into the bathroom. She stepped into the shower, turning the water on and waiting until it ran warm enough for her to step under it, letting it soak every inch of her. The water cascaded down her face, over her shoulders, her hair instantly plastered to her head. And she let the tears fall. Disguised, mixed with the water so she couldn't even feel them on her skin, but she could feel the burn as they left her eyes.

She'd pushed Matt away because she'd found it impossible to be around him, but being without him was feeling just as impossible.

She slumped down. Slithered to the floor and sat there, the water falling over her. Part of her wanted to give up, if it meant continuing on without Matt, but another part of her wanted to do anything to pull herself up and out of the grief she'd fallen into. Facing a future without Matt was scarier than she'd realized it could be, but then so was facing a relationship that was so much more grown up. They'd laughed their way through life, had so much fun and made so many plans, but the only big hurdles they'd faced were work related. She'd never seen Matt grieve, never seen him cut up about something to the point that it put them in crisis. Just like he'd never seen her hit rock bottom before.

Lisa cried some more, got it all out, and then finally hauled herself up and washed her hair, went through the motions of rinsing it and soaping her body. Then she got out of the shower, dried herself and pinned her hair up to keep it off her back. She slathered her body in her favorite coconut moisturizer, put on her face cream and some make-up, then went to find her hair dryer. She blew it out, left it loose and falling over her shoulders, and decided to put on one of her favorite dresses. The room was so quiet, the silence almost deafening, and she quickly turned on the television to drown out the nothingness.

Then she grabbed her phone, scrolled to her favorites and selected Kelly's number. She'd been wrong: she couldn't do this alone. She needed someone to talk to; it was just that that person wasn't Matt right now. And unless she found a professional, her big sister was her best option. She dug her nails into the duvet as she waited, staring at the door, hoping by some miracle that her husband would walk through it in his sports gear, all sweaty from a run, that it had all just been a nightmare, a bad dream that she could laugh about later. *All of it just a bad, bad dream.*

"Morning," Kelly answered.

"Hey, how are you?"

"Kids driving me crazy, but they're at school now so I can breathe. How are you?"

Kelly had always been worried that Matt would break Lisa's heart. From the moment they met, when Matt had made her fall head over heels in love with him, her sister had bitten her nails down worrying that Matt wouldn't be able to stay on the straight and narrow. But he always had, and Kelly had eventually realized she had nothing to stress about. So Lisa needed to tell her the truth in such a way that she didn't flip out and think that Matt had walked out on her when the going had gotten tough.

"Matt isn't with me. We're, um, we're taking a break."

"*What?*" Kelly asked.

"It was my choice. I made him go," she confessed.

There was silence down the line. Lisa gulped and then folded one arm around herself.

"I need you, Kel," she said in a low voice. "I need someone with me. I don't know how to get past this, how to live with the pain I'm feeling. I need you."

Kelly was silent for a beat and Lisa waited. Hopeful.

"Tell me where and when and I'll be there," Kelly said firmly.

"You will?" Hope filled her body, calmed her. "I know I shouldn't be asking you but I don't know what else to do," Lisa told her honestly. "I need someone to talk to, to help me." She'd finally admitted that she was struggling, that she needed her sister, and the relief hit hard.

"Penny's flying in next week anyway, and she can help out with the kids. And I'll get Mom to come and stay too; then you can see her when you get home. Richard will be fine looking after the kids. It'll do him good to have to cope without me for a little bit." She could almost feel Kelly's smile down the phone line. "You're my little sister, and if you need me to help you get back on your feet, then I'm all yours. My girls are old enough to go without me for a little bit."

"I don't know how to thank you," Lisa said, wanting to collapse now she'd finally asked the question.

"You don't need to thank me. Because I know you'd do the same for me in a heartbeat."

It was true, she would, but that was different. "The difference is that I don't have to leave two little girls behind."

Kelly made a chuckling sound. "It doesn't do them any harm to see me being a good sister, and also seeing that their dad is capable of looking after them. I want to help you. If you're ready to work through this, then I'll be there."

"Thank you." Lisa didn't know what else to say.

"You're still in Napa, right? I'll be busy making lists for Richard so he knows what to put in the girls' lunches, about their afterschool activities and everything else I do that he has no real idea about, but I'll be in the car by mid-afternoon."

"Thanks Kel. I'll call Mom, tell her we could really do with her help back at your place. I need to tell her what's going on so she doesn't worry about Matt going home without me."

"Okay. But she's going to worry anyway. You know that, right? We're all worried about you."

"I know, Kel, I know," she said, wishing she'd called her sister sooner. "I'll see you tomorrow."

"Bye."

Lisa kept the phone pressed to her ear a bit longer, listened to the beep and then the silence once Kelly had gone. And then she sat alone, staring at her bags where she'd left them on the floor. She had pretty dresses in there that she'd been saving for Mexico, kaftans that she was going to wear as she sipped cold drinks and lay around the pool with her husband—things they'd talked about even if she'd known deep down she couldn't go through with them. There were so many things she should have been looking forward to doing with Matt on this trip, but instead she'd felt empty, although maybe not as empty as she felt right now.

❧

Lisa was starting to like running. There was something therapeutic about the steady thump-thump of her feet, listening to music and just staring ahead at the road, because it forced her to concentrate, which meant she had little time to think about anything else. She missed Matt, like a limb had been torn from her body, but the time alone was soothing her in a really weird kind of way. Reminding her of the good times they'd had without having to keep a smile plastered on her face, without having to fight tears when they suddenly came out of nowhere, time after time, like a vicious cycle. Her emotions were all over the place, but it was oddly okay.

"I can't keep going," Kelly yelled out.

Lisa was panting as hard as her sister was, but she guessed her sister wasn't running from demons, which gave her a whole lot less incentive to keep going under the burning hot sun.

"Let's crash under that tree," Lisa called back, pointing and jogging over.

They both collapsed in the shade and Lisa was pleased they'd decided to run with drink bottles. She swallowed her water down until there wasn't a drop left.

"You're going to kill me here," Kelly muttered. "Seriously."

"Can I ask you something?"

Her sister nodded but shut her eyes at the same time, lying back.

"Do you think childhood sweethearts can ride out an entire lifetime of ups and downs?" she asked. "Do you think it's possible to meet the person you're supposed to spend the rest of your life with, before you've experienced life with anyone else?"

Kelly opened her eyes and hauled herself back up, staring back at her. "Are we talking about you and Matt, or just generally?"

Lisa shrugged.

"I think any couple can stay together or split up regardless of when they met," Kelly said. "And I think some people can meet a lifetime of wrong people, and others can get it right first go. Maybe it's just luck of the draw."

"Yeah, I guess." Lisa had been thinking about it for days, letting it circle around in her mind. But then if they'd just gotten pregnant and started a family like they'd expected to, maybe she'd never be asking the question in the first place.

"But if you're asking me if you and Matt can stay together, then I'd say hell yes," Kelly continued, wiping sweat from her forehead with the back of her hand. "I think you guys need to figure out how to tell each other what you want and what's going on. Doing anything for the first time is tough."

Lisa thought about what her sister was saying. "I just can't deal with how he thinks he can fix our situation like a house that needs fixing up. Why he can't get that I'll never be the same again. Why does he have to keep offering solutions and acting like . . ." She didn't even know what she was trying to say, she was so lost.

"Lisa, I lost a baby a year before I had my first full pregnancy."

Lisa swallowed hard, couldn't believe what she was hearing. "What do you mean?" She stared at Kelly.

"We didn't tell anyone we were pregnant in case anything happened, and when I miscarried at six weeks I just kept it quiet. Then we didn't try again for a while because it just felt too raw for me."

"Kelly, I can't . . ." she stared at her sister, heart breaking. "I can't believe you went through that alone. I wish I'd known so I could have been there for you."

Kelly nodded. "I think we're just so well trained, as women, to keep these things quiet. It's stupid, and the more I see you grieving the more I realize that women should be open about their early pregnancy rather than waiting until that first scan to share it. So many women out there are grieving the babies they've lost in silence, and it's horrible, because no one around them even knew they were pregnant."

"Did you?" Lisa asked, hugging her knees to her chest. "Grieve, I mean? How bad was it?"

"I felt like I was mourning that little unknown baby until the day I conceived again. Now that I have the girls I don't think about what I lost, but it doesn't make what I went through any less real." She sighed loudly. "Maybe that's why I threw you that party before you were through your first trimester, because I didn't want you grieving alone if it happened to you, too."

"Thank you for telling me," Lisa said, still in shock that her sister had been through so much without telling her.

"You know, Matt might be annoying sometimes, but he was only trying to help you in his own way. Just like I was with the party."

"He just kept going on about adoption and fostering, like giving me a new baby would help me to miraculously get better."

"I don't mean to side with him, but in a way he's right."

Lisa stared at her sister. "How can you say that? Especially after what you just told me?"

"I'm not saying it will take away the love you had for your unborn child, but loving another *is* healing in itself. It's okay to move forward and hold on to the past inside, even if it does feel scary and make you wonder if you'll forget."

"So you're saying I was too hard on him? That I shouldn't have . . ." Lisa felt confused.

"I'm just saying that when you're ready, it's okay to move forward," Kelly said gently, only lightly panting now as they both continued to catch their breath. "I would carry a baby for you and be your surrogate, Lisa, because I know what a great mom you'd be, but that's something you can think about in the future if and when you want to. Just don't write off all the wonderful plans you had with Matt—not yet. You might still be able to have those things, and I think that's what he was trying to tell you, just a bit more bluntly!"

Lisa shuffled over and put her arms around her sister. "Thank you."

"Hey, that's what big sisters are for."

"I don't know how I'll ever get past this, though. I just don't know how to live with the decision I made."

Kelly's smile was so kind. "Think about what could have happened, Lisa. Could you honestly have imagined Matt raising your newborn on his own while you had treatment? Can you imagine him grieving for you and bringing up that little boy without you if you'd died? Telling his son that he didn't have a mom because she'd chosen her child instead of saving herself and getting treatment when she needed it? How impossible that would have been?" Kelly had tears in her eyes as she spoke. "Matt needs you, Lis, and your baby would have needed you. The fact that he agreed with the doctor and wanted to save you doesn't make him a bad person. It makes him a person who loves you."

"I know," Lisa acknowledged. "And the truth was that I made that decision too: I was the one who signed the papers, I was the one who could have said no at the last minute." She wiped away a few stray tears that she hadn't been able to hold back. "I guess I thought that it would be okay, that if the surgery went well then I'd just bide my time until I could get pregnant again. And then I would be able to forget," she sobbed.

Kelly held her in her arms. "You need to talk to Matt. You need to figure all this out and be with him, because men seem like they don't care sometimes just because they process things like grief differently."

Lisa wiped at her eyes again with her knuckles. "You were friends with him then, when his mom died. I wish I'd seen what he went through. It feels like we've been together so long but it's a part of him he's kind of kept at arm's length."

Kelly smiled but shook her head. "I was more friends with him after, and it wasn't something he ever wanted to talk about."

"I was selfish not making him tell me more, not asking more questions about what he'd been through and how hard that must have been on him when I got my diagnosis," Lisa said. "Hindsight's a bitch, that's for sure."

"Sweetheart, you weren't selfish. You were grieving and in pain and going through cancer treatment. And maybe he likes that you didn't know him then, didn't see him in that raw state."

"I love him," she admitted. "But seeing him just reminds me of what we've lost. Reminds me that he'll never be a dad, that if he stays with me, he'll never have what he wants. That he's having to settle for a sad, unfertile woman."

"He loves you," Kelly said. "For god's sake, that man *adores* you."

Lisa shrugged, not sure whether she believed her sister anymore.

"Take as much time as you need, but don't take so long that you lose him."

Lisa stood, not wanting to talk anymore, desperate to run again and burn away the thoughts.

"Ready?" she asked.

Kelly laughed. "I'm walking. I'll meet you back there."

Lisa broke into a jog straight away, heading back through the vines and across the grass. Being here with Matt had been tough, but being here without him was starting to help in a weird kind of way, even if it was seriously depleting her bank balance. But what Lisa had said before kept playing through her mind.

What would it have done to her son if he'd lived, growing up knowing that his mother had sacrificed herself for him? What if he'd known her just long enough to remember her? Or not long enough at all? What if Matt had become so lost in his own grief that he hadn't been able to care for him?

She'd been so angry at Matt for unwaveringly telling her that she mattered more, that her life was more important. But she was starting to realize how unfair she'd been, that she'd blamed him because blaming him had been easy.

Lisa ran faster, not wanting to think, just wanting to be free. She knew her sister wasn't going to be able to stay hidden away with her forever, but it was nice to have her while she could. And then it was back to the real world, trying to figure out how the hell to deal with the hot mess that was her life.

The only good thing that had come out of being alone was her designs. They were fun and bright and vibrant; the complete antithesis of how she felt. When she woke in the morning or couldn't sleep at night, she sketched. Designing what was in her heart. It wasn't Matt, but it was a part of her life that had always calmed her and fulfilled her, a part of her soul, and it was starting to feel like therapy, showing her that there was something in her life that made her whole, that gave her purpose. And for that, at least, she was grateful.

22.

FIVE YEARS EARLIER

Lisa ran her hands down the fabric of her dress, trying to stop her breath coming in uneven short pants.

"Sweetie, calm down. You're going to be fine."

She shook her head, grabbing hold of her sister's hand. It was just she and Kelly standing in front of the vanity, staring into the mirror, side by side. Her big sister might be bossy, but she was one hell of a support crew when Lisa needed her, and Kelly was the only one who loved Matt as much as she did.

"It's just Matt. It's just the two of you."

Lisa blew out a long, shaky breath, squaring her shoulders and staring back at her reflection. Her hair was out, full and slightly wavy after an hour sitting with rollers in, tiny crystals like a crown on her head as they sat loosely where she'd placed them.

"It's just all those people watching, and what if he doesn't show? What if he changes his mind or something?" Her fears were stupid—logically she knew that—but it wasn't the rational part of her brain screaming at her right now.

"Lisa," Kelly said, her arm draped around her now. "First of all, there are only a handful of people here, and we all love you and want to be here to support you. And second, we are both talking about the same groom, right? Because the Matt I know couldn't keep his hands off of you for one night! He adores you!"

Lisa nodded, knew her sister was right, but for some reason her hands wouldn't stop shaking and she was starting to feel woozy. "I just . . ." her breathing became short and sharp again.

"Come on, let's go," Kelly ordered. "You need to get out there and see your man."

"But aren't we supposed to wait a bit? It's not even time yet, and . . ."

Kelly took both of her hands, forced her to turn as she stared into her eyes. "Matt will be there already, so let's just go. So what if not everyone is seated and ready?"

Lisa looked down at her dress, gulped at the thought of what she was about to do. She'd spent hours, weeks, *months* working on her dress, sewing all the intricate beads and crystals. It was everything she'd ever dreamed of in a perfect dress, something she'd starting sketching the day after Matt had asked her, on his knee under the scorching sun, laughing as he asked her so that she thought he was kidding at first, heady from the bottle of champagne they'd shared lying on the grass between the vines. It fitted her like a glove, the zip at the back hidden to make the fabric look seamless, a pretty puddle of a train showing off the exquisite lace. She twirled slowly in front of the mirror, deciding to focus on her design rather than herself.

"You're Matt and Lisa," Kelly said with a laugh. "Everyone is rooting for you because you guys are the couple everyone else wants to be. There is absolutely no reason for you to be worrying right now!"

"Let's go." She managed to force out the words, held her chin high as Kelly smiled at her.

"You'll have to give me one minute to get into my dress first," her sister said dryly.

Lisa burst out laughing when she took a step back, only just realizing that her sister was still in the cute pink pajamas they'd all been wearing while their hair and make-up was done. It was also why they'd come into the bathroom in the first place—so they could both get dressed.

"I'll help you," Lisa said, in designer mode now and feeling a lot more settled. She'd made the dresses for both her sisters, although it was her younger sister who was going to be standing by her side. Matt had Kelly beside him. They'd decided from the start that they wanted their day to be about family and their closest friends, so it had seemed pointless to have bridesmaids and groomsmen for such an intimate ceremony. But Matt had always been so close to Kelly that they'd decided to have both her sisters supporting them, and Matt's dad was going to walk up the aisle on the other side of her, too. Both their dads were so important to them, and Lisa had liked the idea of both being involved.

Kelly stripped down and Lisa took the dress off the hanger, pulling it down from the door where it had been waiting. The fabric was the softest shade of lilac, a silky satin that complemented her sister's blonde hair and golden skin. Kelly stepped into it and Lisa carefully zipped her in.

"You look gorgeous," she told her.

"Lucky I was able to zip my baby bump in!" Kelly said with a laugh. "Now come on, let's go find your man."

Lisa opened the bathroom door, feeling less panicky than she had been but with a ball of nerves still battering her stomach and making her feel sick.

"Oh, sweetheart, look at you!" Her mother stopped what she was doing and came rushing over. Which only made Lisa start to panic all over again.

"Mom, I need to . . ." She had no idea what was wrong with her, why she was struggling so much when she was usually so chilled out. Or maybe she just wasn't used to being the center of attention.

"We're going. Now," Kelly told everyone.

Kelly didn't use her bossy voice all that often, but when she did everyone tended to listen. Lisa kept hold of her big sister's hand, feeling bad about running out on her the night before when she needed her so badly now.

She gathered up her single white, long-stemmed rose from where it was resting on the bed and kept walking, pleased she already had her shoes on so all she had to do was focus on putting one foot in front of the other. They walked out into the passageway, then into the bright Napa Valley sunshine. She'd almost forgotten about the photographer who'd been taking snaps while they got ready, and he was now running in front of them to take pictures of them walking to where the ceremony was taking place.

"Lisa?"

She stopped dead the moment she heard Matt's voice. All her fears, all the worries that were pooling in her stomach, everything just faded away the second he spoke. She turned and saw him standing there, tie hanging around his neck not yet knotted, but with a grin on his face that melted her heart.

"Matt!" Kelly gasped. "I thought you'd be down there already. We . . . I'm sorry Lisa, I shouldn't have hurried you."

"It's fine," she said, not sure whether she'd just thought the words or actually said them.

Matt came closer and stopped in front of her. Her breathing became more even, a smile curving her lips before she even realized what she was doing. Her fingers found their way to his tie, worked the fabric until it was tied perfectly and resting against the collar of his shirt. It wasn't until then that she looked up at him and realized he was silent, that he was staring at her like he was seeing her for the first time. Lisa didn't know if the others had stopped talking or if she just couldn't hear them, but when Matt slipped his hand into hers, it felt so right.

"You look . . ." he started, whispering in her ear as his lips brushed her cheek, "*so beautiful.*"

Lisa felt weightless, everything washing away except her man standing in front of her.

"Shall we go and get married?" she whispered back.

Matt grinned and pulled her close, in her favorite spot, tucked under his arm, his body tight to hers as they walked. Even Kelly didn't bother telling them off, just let them do their own thing. Maybe it had been real nerves that had been stressing her out, or worry that Matt didn't feel the same, or maybe that she was going to do something stupid as she walked past everyone, but Matt had her now, and that was all she needed.

Time passed so fast . . . The people sitting alongside the vines on their beautiful white covered chairs tied with big white satin bows were just a blur as she let go of Matt's hand and let him walk to the front. She took her dad's arm on one side, his dad's on the other as the soft music started, and made her way toward Matt again.

And then she was there, Matt pulling her close, holding her before placing a soft, gentle kiss on her lips.

"We're supposed to wait," she murmured, loving that he didn't give a damn what anybody else thought.

"I know," he said back.

When they parted, the celebrant started, but Lisa hardly heard the words, was too busy staring into Matt's eyes, staying calm because of the open, easy way he watched her. Then it was her turn to say something, and she repeated the words, her vows, which they'd rehearsed only days earlier. The vows were traditional, simple; she wasn't the kind to bare her soul to the world, and neither was Matt.

Or at least she'd thought he wasn't.

"Lisa, from the day I met you, I knew I had to do everything in my power never to lose you. So," he cleared his throat, his back turned slightly to the small crowd gathered as he stared into her eyes.

Lisa felt the tears prickling, pooling, and the moment he paused, one slipped. Then another. Tear after tear started to slide down her cheek as her hands trembled against Matt's.

"So yeah, I want to be your husband," he continued. "I will care for you and love you and hold you, in sickness and in health, as long as I have you by my side. I promise I will love you, a hundred times over, if you'll have me."

"Yes," she whispered, as he stepped in, his big body blocking everyone and everything from her as he gently wiped her cheeks, his thumb gliding so carefully across her skin, head dipped to look into her eyes.

"Well, ah, there was a little bit missing from those vows, but I'll take that as both of you consenting to be man and wife," the celebrant said with a chuckle.

A murmur of laughter echoed out, but Lisa ignored it. Just stared up at Matt.

"So we're husband and wife?" he asked.

"Yes. You may kiss the bride."

Lisa gasped a little breath, paused, waited as Matt's mouth slowly moved toward hers. His kiss was as gentle as his caress had been, lips so soft as they moved back and forth across hers. And then he scooped her up, her rose long forgotten on the ground as he twirled her around and around, lips still pressed to hers.

The crowd clapped and cheered as Lisa hung on tight to Matt, arms clasped around his neck. She was dizzy, drunk on love, happier than she'd ever felt as the sun beat down on them and she kissed her husband, the man she'd just pledged to spend the rest of her life with. When he finally stopped, she held him tight, didn't let go, kept him tight against her.

"I love you," she whispered.

"I love you too, baby," he murmured straight back.

Everything she'd worried about was long gone, and when she finally pulled away, her sisters were surrounding them, her mom and their dads. The only thing that was wrong with their picture was the fact that Matt's mom wasn't there to celebrate with them.

As arms reached for her, hugs that she was happy to return, she tipped her head back and looked up at the blemish-free sky, hoping that the woman who'd raised such a beautiful son was looking down on them. Because if there was one thing she would wish for if she had the chance, it would be to hold that woman tight and tell her how much she loved the man she'd just married and that nothing in this world could make her stop loving him. Never. Not a thing.

23.
PRESENT DAY

Matt gulped away a shudder that was making its way up his throat, blinked back tears. He never broke down around Lisa, and he'd sure as hell never cried to his dad, but it was getting damn hard to hold it all back these days. But his father had been there, experienced the same kind of darkness, only he'd had a son full of even more darkness to deal with at the same time, had had so much more to hold together. And his dad hadn't had a choice, had lost his wife, whereas Matt's had been saved.

He sat outside his house, one hand on Blue's head as he clutched the phone. He dialed his dad, hanging his head for a bit as it started to ring, clearing his throat when his father's husky voice came on the line.

"Matt?"

"Hey, Dad," Matt said, coughing to try to pull himself together, not wanting his father to hear the crack in his voice, not again.

"Son, it's after midnight. What's going on? Is Lisa okay?"

Matt could imagine his dad sitting up in bed, bleary-eyed, with the bedside lamp on, phone pressed to his ear. He shouldn't have woken him, but he had no one else to talk to. There was no way he was going to call one of his guy friends and break down, talk to them about something they couldn't understand, and he'd already leaned on Kelly so much. Besides, the last thing she needed to worry about on top of her kids and their dog was that her sister's husband couldn't hold it together.

"Hey, son. Where are you?"

Matt waited a beat, swallowed as he stared out through the outdoor lights at the pretty yard that had taken him and Lisa so long to landscape on their own.

"I'm home. Alone."

His dad didn't say anything.

"Lisa and I are taking some time out."

"I see. You okay about that?"

Matt nodded even though his dad couldn't see him, got a handle on his emotions. He wasn't okay, but that wasn't why he was calling. He was calling to tell his dad what he'd wanted to say for so long but had just never found the words for. Just like he'd waited so long to tell his dad that he loved him, words that should be so simple but just weren't.

"Every day, every single day, Dad, I think about you, about what I put you through. You never even got the chance to just grieve for Mom because I was such a shit, and I want to say that I'm sorry. I should have said it a long time ago, but this is me saying it now. I'm sorry, so goddamn sorry."

Matt hated thinking back to the day his mom had died, seeing her body, chest no longer rising and falling, making him want to be sick. His beautiful mom who'd have done anything for him, who was always waiting for him after school, who was at every football game cheering him on, who never once complained and always smiled. The day she'd gone, a light had gone out in him, too. A switch had been flicked and he'd turned into the asshole kind of teenager who'd have horrified his mom, the kind of son he'd never have been if she'd been there to see it. He'd given his dad hell, and it wasn't until he'd fallen for Lisa that all of that had changed, because he'd known she wouldn't look twice at the kind of kid he was then. He'd pulled his shit together for her, and even though the guys had all made fun of him for how he'd changed for a girl, he'd known it was his chance. That if he blew it with Lisa he might never find anything worth changing for again, worth stepping up for. But he'd never opened up to her about it, never admitted his pain, deciding to bury it instead. Along with all the apologies he owed his dad.

"The past is the past. You don't need to say sorry for anything," his dad said. "You're a good son—is that what you need me to say? Because you are, and you've more than made up for it over the years."

"I just need you to listen to me, to hear me say how sorry I am. It's the only thing that'll stop me feeling like the worst son in the world." Matt felt like he'd aged twenty years, like what had happened between him and Lisa had made him grow the hell up real fast.

"Tell me about Lisa. What happened?"

"I don't know if I can keep going," Matt confessed, swallowing hard over and over, trying to get rid of the lump of emotion stuck there wanting to choke him. "I don't know if *she* wants us to keep going."

"You can and you will," his dad said firmly. "Now you tell me what's happened, get it off your chest, then pull it together and go back to your wife."

"She wanted time out, on her own," Matt told him, finding it hard to believe that he was telling his dad this. "I'm not going back to her because she doesn't want me to."

"Okay. Well, that could be a good thing, couldn't it?"

His dad had always been patient, but they'd never exactly had heart-to-hearts. They'd played ball, watched games on TV, chatted over beers as he'd gotten older, worked in the garden and on the house. But he'd never had to open up to him before, and it wasn't easy. The only person who had ever truly seen the raw him was Lisa, and before that his mom when he was a teenager.

"It's just . . ." He laughed, despite the pain he was feeling inside. "Shit's getting real, Dad. There's no other way to put it. I just can't believe that Lisa doesn't want to be with me anymore."

"You'll get through this."

"I thought I was going to lose her to cancer. We got through that, but . . ." Matt coughed, pushing the emotion down. "I think I've lost her anyway."

"Matt, when I lost your mom, I was all cried out. I was terrified of losing her, but when she finally passed, it was a relief to not see her suffering anymore."

"I never saw you cry," Matt admitted. "It was what made me so angry, thinking you didn't care like I did."

He listened to his dad breathe deep. "I should have let you see me break down, but I was trying so hard to be strong."

Matt wished that his teenage self had had this conversation with his dad.

"The difference is that you and Lisa have a fighting chance. You can make this work if you both want it to; you just need to find a way to move past what happened."

"Easier said than done," Matt replied.

Matt didn't want to bring up the past, didn't want to dredge up memories that they'd long put behind them, but talking was helping. He'd pushed it all down for way too long, and he'd also never imagined he'd be going through the same thing as his dad, thirteen years later. Only he wasn't, because his dad had had a child to deal with, and Matt only had himself. And a dog who'd probably mope at the door for the rest of his life if Lisa never came home.

"So what do I do now?" Matt asked, voice hoarse, every word like silk dragged over jagged rocks.

"You do what you need to do: yell at me if you want, curse the bloody world for the hand it's dealt you, then you pick yourself up off the ground and figure out how the hell to make things right with your wife." His dad paused. Matt could hear his breathing and it soothed him for some strange reason. "And when she lets you close again, you hold her and tell her how much you love her, tell her that you'll be strong for her. You don't blame her or pull away because you know how bad it's going to hurt; you just listen and love her. She's been to hell and back, and you have too, but right now I'm guessing she just needs you to step up and look after her like she's looked after you all these years. Don't go thinking you've got to keep it all in to be a man, because you don't."

"Okay," Matt said. "Thanks, Dad. I needed to hear that, to have you just tell me what to do." He didn't think he'd ever heard his dad talk so much in his life before, let alone open up like that.

"It might not get any easier, son, not for a while. The only thing you think about is to keep on going, one foot in front of the other. But you're lucky, because she made it. The tough part is finding a new way to move forward. That's what she's struggling with."

His dad was right. They needed a new path, instead of trying to tread the old one. But every time he'd tried to bring that up, she'd clammed up and gotten angry.

"Sorry I woke you up," Matt said. But it had helped. It had given him something, the strength to keep going, to just do what he was already doing.

"I love you, Matt," his dad said. "I should have told you more often when you were growing up, but words didn't always come so easy."

Matt's laugh was rough. "Yeah, and I wasn't always that easy to love."

They were both silent for a beat.

"Water under the bridge. You just keep your chin up and be ready to look after that beautiful wife of yours. And don't give up," his father told him. "There's always hope, right until the end. Marriages aren't supposed to be easy all the time."

"Thanks, Dad." Matt smiled. "I love you, too."

After they said goodbye, Matt sat alone in the dark, head in his hands as he rocked forward, heels of his palms nudged tight into his eyes. His dad was right, but he still didn't know how to reconnect with her to give himself a second chance.

In his heart, he knew the truth; he just wasn't used to having to open up, to let his feelings be so raw when he usually managed to cruise through life. He didn't just want Lisa to be his beginning: he wanted her until the end, and he wanted every damn bit in the middle, too. And he needed to tell her that.

Emotion wracked his body, threatened to suffocate him as it clawed at his throat, strangled every breath from him. Silently he suffered, gulping for air, fighting the pain. *Why?* Why did this have to happen to them? Why did his beautiful wife have to have so much taken from her? Why did they have to lose their little baby boy? *Why?*

Matt wanted to yell, to scream a bloodcurdling cry that could be heard back in Napa. But he didn't. Instead, he dropped to his knees and quietly sobbed until there was nothing left inside.

And then he slowly pulled his body up, squared his shoulders and wiped at his face. Matt walked back inside, blocked out every thought and walked down the hall.

He stopped outside the nursery door, held up his hand, thought about pushing it open but couldn't. Not without Lisa. So he continued silently into the bathroom and splashed cold water on his face in the near-dark, then finally turned, stopping in the doorway to stare at the bed where Lisa should have been asleep waiting for him. Only the bed was empty. For the first time in what felt like forever, there was no beautiful, warm body lying there in wait.

Matt stripped off and moved around to the other side of the bed, lifting the covers and sliding silently in. He missed her body, the warmth of her smile, the way she looked at him. He craved the scent of her shampoo, the softness of her skin.

He missed her. He missed his wife.

Lisa had meant everything to him, and he had no idea in hell how he was going to survive without her if she wouldn't give him a second chance.

24.

It's driving me crazy," Matt confessed, twirling his beer bottle between his fingers. "I just . . . I can't explain it. What's it like not being with her after all this time."

"I get it. You guys haven't spent a night apart in forever," Penny said.

"It's not just that. It's the fact I haven't spoken to her; I don't know what's going on with her, what I can do." Matt sat back, shook his head as he leaned into the seat on the porch of Kelly's house. "I've been fighting in her corner for so long, and now I don't even know where that corner is. What I can do to get her back."

The girls came running past, dressed in princess costumes and giggling. He grinned and pulled a face, which sent them into even more giggles as they ran out into the yard toward their tree hut. He adored the girls, wished he could tell Lisa right now how much they missed her. *How much* he *missed her*. He was ready to step up and be the man she needed, if only she'd give him a chance.

"Look, just give her the space she needs," Penny said, sitting down beside him. "She's fine. I promise."

"What if she doesn't want me after being apart?" Matt said bluntly, finally getting it off his chest. "I will do anything for her. I just need to talk to her and show her that I'm ready to change."

"She . . ." Lisa's younger sister frowned at him and started over. "I'll speak to her for you."

"You will?"

"Yeah. This has gone on long enough."

Matt nodded. "It's all kinds of screwed up, us being apart when she's hurting so bad. But maybe she was right that we needed time apart. It's sure as hell showed me how miserable life is without her." He took another pull of beer. "And what I need to do."

"The three of us are stubborn," Penny told him, patting his hand. "Add to that what she's been through and how rough it's been. She just needs some time. She's holed up somewhere, and she's fine, and Kelly's doing a good job of keeping her busy, getting her talking. It'll be killing her being apart from you, too."

"But she won't even take my calls. She's completely blocked me." Matt blew out a breath. "I'm not so sure she's going to come back. It feels kind of final, like I'm not going to get that chance to convince her that we can make it."

Penny stood and looked down at him. "Then fight dirty. Show her what she means to you; make her see without having to talk to you."

"I'd be on her doorstep before morning if I thought she'd want to see me," Matt muttered.

"Tell her how you feel—make her listen," Penny said. "If you were ever going to be Mr. Romantic, now's the time."

"I've been leaving voicemail messages," Matt admitted. "But I doubt she's even listened to them. But I've been thinking about emailing, writing it down so that one day she'll read them."

"Then I'll make sure she does," she said confidently. "I'll go call Kelly now."

"Thanks," Matt said. "I just don't know what else to do."

"Matty, you know she loves you, don't you? Because she does," Penny said softly. "We all love you, but you guys were made for each other, and if anyone can make it, you can. You just need to find a way past all the shit that's been thrown your way."

He nodded, took a deep breath. "That's why I need her to hear me out before it's too late, before she gives up on us."

"You get us another beer, and I'll call Kelly," Penny said. "And you figure out what you're going to say to make my sister fall head over heels back in love with you."

Matt laughed. When he'd married Lisa, he'd gained two sisters. And while they loved ganging up on him sometimes, he wouldn't give them up for anything, because they were as much his family as his dad was. And for a kid who'd grown up without siblings, it was good for him.

He pulled out his phone to email Lisa, trying to figure out what the hell to say. There was so much in his head, so many feelings he wished he had the words to express. Trouble was he'd never had to talk like that, never had to find the words to tell his wife because he'd always kind of taken for granted that she knew how he felt. He'd also never had to worry that they could break up before; until now. Now reality was fast setting in, and while she was in flight mode, he was fully engaged in fight mode.

She could avoid him all she wanted, but he wasn't just giving up on what they had. Not when it came to Lisa. And as easy as it would have been to snarl and limp off to lick his wounds, this was his marriage. It was the one thing in life he couldn't afford to be an asshole about, because he would only be hurting himself. He needed to open up to her, be honest, and make sure she knew how he really felt. No more burying everything; it was time to be real. He *needed* to step it up.

"Hey, Blue," he said, reaching a hand down to his dog as he came bounding up the porch. "Those girls too much for you, huh?"

He rubbed his dog's head as he used his other hand to scroll to his emails. This was it. He'd been closed off about his past, not open enough about his feelings, but now was the time to start. Before it was too late.

25.

L isa watched as her sister packed. Being with Kelly had meant so much to her, but she knew her sister couldn't stay any longer. She had a family of her own to go home to, a husband who was holding down the fort without her and pretending like everything was fine so Kelly could be with her. Lisa already felt guilty about the length of time— just over two weeks—she'd had her by her side, and even though she knew her mom and little sister were helping out back home, and that Kelly had more than deserved some time away, they couldn't hide forever.

"You need to call him."

Lisa stared out the window, pretending she hadn't heard her. She was talked out, and she didn't want to go over old ground again.

"Lisa?" Kelly was her big sister and Lisa knew when she was about to throw her weight around.

"I heard you," Lisa replied. "I just . . ." She didn't know what to say. Being without Matt was beyond tough, but she was also scared of talking to him again, of seeing him and trying to get everything that was in her head out in the open with him.

"You just what? What are you scared of? What really happened between you guys?" Kelly stared at her. "Penny told me that Matt doesn't know if you'll ever want to work it out, that things could be over for good, but I don't believe it for a second. Am I right?"

Lisa swallowed, ran a hand through her hair, absently playing with a tiny fairy knot at the end. "I miss him so bad, but I'm scared. Everything's changed and I don't want to be that person I was around him for the last few months. I don't know how to get past what I said to him the day before he left."

Kelly was sitting beside her now, her weight putting an indent in the bed that made Lisa slide closer to her. She leaned into her sister when Kelly held her arms out, let herself be held. There were only a few years between them in age, but Kelly sometimes cared for her like she was the mom, not the sister, and Lisa would never take her big sister for granted.

"Look, just turn your phone on and check your voicemail. I'll bet it's full—he's tried to call you so many times. I know how hard it's been for him being cut off from you, and it's not fair to just tell him to leave and then never give him the chance to talk it through with you."

"You've spoken to him?" Lisa asked, staring at her sister's face.

Kelly looked away before standing up and going back to packing her bag. "Matt loves you. Whatever happened between you hasn't changed the way he feels, and I know you feel the same. You guys can make this work. Because the issues you have? They're not going to change; they're going to be there for the rest of your life. But with Matt you can find a way through it."

"It's not that easy. We can't just go back to what we used to have. We can't just pretend like nothing happened."

"Lisa, you can move past it. We've gone through this. You'll never forget, but neither of you did anything wrong here. It's not like moving past an infidelity." Kelly held her hand, looked into her eyes and smiled. "Matt hasn't had to be sensitive or careful with you before because you've always been able to stand on your own two feet and look after yourself. Think about how hard it must have been for him to suddenly have to care for you like you were breakable, when you've probably always seemed indestructible to him!"

Lisa nodded, biting down on her bottom lip. She missed Matt, craved him like a drug, wished she could do something to turn back time and go back to the easy way things had always been between them. "I need to tell him that I understand," she managed to whisper. "Just because I'm not speaking to him right now doesn't mean I don't love him, and I want him to know that I should have acknowledged what he was going through, too."

She watched as Kelly zipped up her bag, then stood, hands on her hips. "When I go, can you at least promise me that you'll check your voicemail and your email? I know for a fact that he's been writing to you, that he wants to tell you something, or maybe even a whole lot of somethings."

Lisa's heart started to beat just a bit too fast, her palms instantly clammy. "He told you that? So you *have* spoken to him?" She'd thought so much about what she wanted to say to him, how to bring up the things that she wanted to be more open about. She'd craved time alone, away from him, but now everything was starting to remind her of him.

"All I'm saying is that I've stuck to my end of the bargain. I haven't told him what's going on or what we've talked about, or that we've stayed in Napa, although Penny might have been easier for him to crack, but now you need to do this for me, okay? Because he's going to make my life hell if I turn up without you and he still hasn't heard a word back from the woman he loves. It's been as rough on him as it has you, maybe even harder because you were the one who wanted the space in the first place."

Lisa nodded. "Okay." She would agree to that; it was only fair. Besides, she had to talk to him sooner or later. It wasn't like she could just hide away forever.

"That man would give his life for you, Lis. You owe it to him to at least give him a chance."

She knew her sister was right, but it didn't make what she had to do any easier. Matt had been her world for a decade, even longer if she was completely honest with herself because she'd fallen for him well before they officially got together. And after a couple of weeks of trying to go it alone, with only her sister by her side, she was realizing just how impossible it would be to live without him. And he hadn't even done anything wrong, but her head had been so messed up and she was struggling to process everything, and coming to terms with what they'd done . . . She took a deep breath. Life felt empty right now, and it would be even emptier if she didn't at least try to work it out with Matt.

"Do you think he'd still . . ." Lisa shook her head, didn't know what she was even trying to say, or maybe she just couldn't say the words. "Nothing."

"What?" Kelly asked softly, dropping to sit beside her again, shoulder to shoulder. "You think he's forgotten about you after a few weeks? Give the poor guy some credit. He might not be the most sensitive soul sometimes, but he's a damn good man."

Kelly was right. He was a good man, and if he was prepared to open up to her, then to understand what she was feeling, then surely they could move forward.

"You're right. I know you're right."

"Good," Kelly said, reaching for her hand and squeezing it tight even though she was speaking so firmly. "Because he's still your husband, you're still married, and that means something."

Lisa dropped her head to Kelly's shoulder, kept hold of her hand.

"Read his emails and don't be scared of telling him whatever you need to get out. And don't be afraid to push him to open up about his mom. It must have been a really dark time for him, and maybe he's kept it locked away for too long."

Kelly eventually stood, but not before dropping a kiss into Lisa's hair.

"I love you," Lisa said, looking up at her. "Thank you for everything, for putting your life on hold and just being here for me. I don't think I could have done this without you."

"Hey, we're sisters. We're supposed to have each other's backs."

Kelly waved and hauled her bag up, wheeling it behind her, and Lisa leaned back into the pillows and watched her go. She was exhausted from doing nothing; from thinking all day, from being alone all night, from running and swimming and keeping active with Kelly. From talking with her sister.

From everything reminding her of Matt.

She'd craved calamari every time they'd eaten out, but hadn't been able to order it without Matt. They'd always shared it; for ten years, seeing calamari on the menu anywhere had made them laugh because they always shared it as a starter. Everything about Napa had reminded her of him, and as much as it hurt, it had given her the time alone to remember why she loved him.

Matt was her rock. He was goofy and childish and always running late, but he'd also protect her against anything, give his own life for her. *And he'd made the hardest decision he'd probably ever had to make in choosing her over their baby.* But that was her husband, ready to protect her whatever the cost. And she wished she'd been able to see how tough that must have been for him instead of pushing him away.

Lisa wanted to swim, to indulge in a few laps in the water before deciding what to do. She glanced into the bathroom and saw her wet bikini hanging, and decided to find another. She was sure she'd packed two, but then she hadn't seen her pink one at all.

She unzipped one of her bags, the one full of brightly colored things she'd originally packed for Mexico, rummaging around through the clothes. She saw a flash of pink, went to pull it out, but her hand connected with something hard.

What the hell? She pulled more clothes out and saw a book, one she didn't recognize. Lisa took it out, surprised that a large book had been hidden in her bag and she hadn't even realized. She ran her hand over the gold cover, the softest shade, which was interwoven with elegant swirls. It was beautiful. Then she opened it, hand flying to her mouth as she recognized a collection of her favorite fabrics from the last few summer seasons making a collage over the first few pages.

She looked at each piece, still in love with all the beautiful colors and textures she'd used.

And then she turned to the next page and saw writing she'd recognize anywhere—strong capital letters written in bold black pen.

A beautiful girl deserves a beautiful book for her designs. Love, Matt.

Lisa read the words over and over, stared at his name, felt a pang for him in her heart that almost stole her breath away. Matt had done this for her. Sometime before they'd left, he'd had this made for her and packed it without her knowing.

Lisa held the book to her chest, clutched it tight and took a big, deep breath. She needed Matt, wanted him with her. And that meant she needed to take a huge leap forward and tell him that. *That she was sorry. That she'd needed the time without him to under-stand how much she missed him. That she forgave him for making a choice he should never have had to make and that she should never have blamed him for it in the first place.*

She shut her eyes for a few minutes, focused on breathing deep and filling her belly with each breath like she'd read she was supposed to do, but the only thing she could think about was her phone. She got up, rummaged around in her handbag until she found it, and turned it on. It was usually never off, but since she'd said goodbye to Matt, she'd had it permanently switched off. Eventually it came to life and she tapped on her mail icon, quickly scrolling through her emails, deleting all the junk, all the things she didn't have the time or interest to read. And then she was left with five emails from her husband, his name alone enough to make her stomach twist in pain; pain from being parted for the first time in ten years from the man she loved so bad. The man she'd never, ever stop loving no matter what.

Maybe she just needed to be honest with Matt and make him be honest with her, get it all out before starting over, make sure they were past all this before they tried to patch their marriage back together. *If he'd still have her that was.*

26.

Lisa,

I don't even know where to start. I don't think I've ever written you a letter or even an email, because you were always there with me and if you weren't, I just called you. Baby, I miss you so bad. Ten years and we hardly spent a full night apart, and now you've been gone two weeks and I'm going crazy. I want you home. Blue misses you; he's whining every night, waiting for you to walk through the door.

You're my wife, Lisa, and I know things have always been easy for us, but I don't care if it's not easy, if we have to fight for it to work. I love you, and I wish I knew what to say to make you believe that I would do anything for you. Anything.

Matt

27.

Lisa,

I don't know if you're even checking your emails, but you won't answer your phone and I'm going crazy here. I wish I'd told you so many things. I wish I'd been honest with you about . . . I don't know how to say it. I'm even worse at writing emails than I am at talking about how I feel.

Tell me where the hell you are so I can come and get you. Blue says he'll never eat another pair of your shoes ever again if you come back to us. And I'll promise anything if you just come home.
Matt

28.

Lisa,

So I'm guessing you're either not checking these or you've decided to punish me and not reply. It's been over two weeks, Lis, and it's killing me. I'm about to go crazy. If you won't come home for me, do it for Blue. Do you know that poor dog is standing by the damn door every night waiting to hear the jangle of your keys? He's miserable, and so am I. Where are you?

I'm so damn angry but I don't want to say that because I want to tell you myself. Right after I kiss the hell out of you and tell you never to leave me again. We can get through this, can't we?

Matt

29.

Lisa,

There's something I should have told you a long time ago. I've been sitting here, wishing you were here, then I figured it out. You don't want to come home to what we had these last few months, and I get that. I don't want that marriage either. I want us to be happy and not feel like we're walking on goddamn eggshells all the time. I don't want to see you crying and not know what to do, or see you happier at work than with me. So I get it.

I just want you to know that losing my mom broke something inside of me. Then you came along and I buried all that shit in my past because it was easier than dealing with it. Until you got sick and cancer took over everything again.

I saw my mom die, Lisa. I touched her body when it was cold instead of warm. I promised on the day of her funeral that I was never going to hurt like that again and that I'd damn well never let that happen to someone I loved. I blamed my dad for so much, for so many things, just because it was easy to make it his fault. And then you got sick and we lost our baby and I realized there was not a damn thing I could do to help you.

I don't want an adopted baby either. I don't want anything other than you and our baby we lost. I cry, just not when you can see. When you're around I turn into a meathead, coming up with

a whole lot of ways to fix the problem. But we can't fix it. We can fix us, but that part of us that lost a baby? It's okay if that's always a shitty part of our past that hurts. You're the love of my life, Lisa, and I wish I'd told you all that before now. I love you and I just want a chance to prove it.
Matt

30.

Tears started to drip slowly, silently down Lisa's cheeks. She chewed on her lower lip, biting so hard that she tasted blood. Her eyes scanned fast through Matt's words, then more slowly the second time she read them through. *Why hadn't he told her more about his mom and what that had been like? Why hadn't she asked? Why had she thought she needed to be apart from him instead of being brave enough to let him close, instead of pushing him away?*

She wiped her cheeks with her fingers, her eyes with the back of her knuckles, before pushing her phone into her pocket and standing, needing to escape from the airless room, suddenly desperate for fresh air, desperate to get outside. She knew why; deep down she knew why. Because she blamed herself. She blamed herself for getting cancer, for ruining their dreams of having a family, for pushing Matt away when he'd tried so hard in his own way. And she'd blamed him for the decision her surgeons had made when she was under the knife, just like she'd blamed him for choosing her over their baby. Only Matt didn't deserve to shoulder any of the blame.

The guilt that she'd broken their marriage into shards when it had been so strong hit her hard. She'd been trying so hard to put distance between them when what she should have done was hold her Matt close, cherish what they still had, the bits they hadn't lost.

And now her marriage was in tatters.

She wanted Matt. Needed her husband. He'd started to tell her all this days and days ago, opening up to her like he never had before, and instead of responding and being a decent wife, she'd shut herself off from the world, pretended like she was okay alone. Pretended like she knew what she wanted and needed, when she hadn't at all. The guilt she felt was hers alone, and instead of just punishing herself, she'd punished Matt, too.

You're not an island, sweetheart. It's not like you to be shut off like this, and it's not good for anyone.

Her sister's words echoed through her head, words she'd said before leaving to go back to Redding, back to her family, and before telling her that she needed to talk to Matt. Or if she wasn't up to talking to him, an email, a text . . . *anything*. She might have been through hell lately, but it was no excuse to push Matt away.

Lisa kept walking until she was outside, surrounded by green fields, vines and a bright blue sky above. She sucked in air like she'd been deprived for hours, months. Then she slumped down, stared at the blank screen of her phone in her hand. Slowly, hand shaking, she swiped across and forced herself to touch on Matt's last email. She stared at his name, wondered how the hell she'd managed to go weeks without him when before she'd never left him even for two days.

They were Matt and Lisa. They were a team. They were the couple everyone had wanted to be. And she'd lost sight of how lucky she was to be alive, to be in remission from cancer, which meant she needed to fight. Fight for her marriage. Fight for Matt. Fight for her future.

She'd never been a quitter, and she wasn't about to be one now.

Matt & Lisa forever. That's what they'd carved into the big oak tree at her parents' house when they were first together, and it's what she'd whispered to him the night after they were married. She'd kicked cancer's butt, she'd survived, and now she needed to kick butt with her marriage. Just because she'd lost one thing that was so important to her didn't mean she deserved to lose another.

31.

Lisa,
I won't give up on us, not now and not ever. You know what I want? To start over on another road trip in our bright red Cadillac. That and kiss my wife and tell her how damn much I love her.
   Baby, come home.
Matt

32.

att?" Lisa's voice, so strong in her head, so steady when she'd been imagining this call, was so shaky, so weak, that it was barely audible.

"Lisa?"

She burst into tears the moment she heard him, the second he said her name. Relief engulfed her, the grief she'd felt at being parted from him washing over her in waves.

"Lisa? Lisa!"

She sucked back her sobs, tried to force away the choke in her throat. "This is me telling my husband I love him," she whispered. "And thanking him for the beautiful new book."

"Damn, Lis, do you have any idea how much I've missed you? How worried I've been?" he muttered.

Lisa clutched the phone tighter, fought a fresh surge of tears as she imagined Matt standing on a building site somewhere, tool belt slung around his waist. Being without him had been a pain so raw, so real, but she'd been so sure she was doing the right thing, that she'd needed to give them both space. And maybe she had been right. Maybe if they hadn't been apart they never would have found their way back.

"Can you meet me in Mexico?" she asked him.

"Mexico?" Mat practically yelled down the phone. "Just come home."

She shook her head even though she knew he couldn't see her. "I want some time together, just the two of us. Just tell me you'll meet me there."

"I'm there," he said, yelling at someone to be quiet in the background. "Sorry. Where exactly do you want me?"

"I need you to get on the next flight out to Cancun," Lisa said, the longing she felt just thinking about seeing him again making her squeeze her hand into a tight fist, nails biting into her palm. "I'll be waiting at the Live Aqua resort. I've made the booking." She sobbed again, furious with herself that she just couldn't keep her crap together. "Just be there."

"Lisa?"

"I love you, Matty. I miss you so bad."

"I miss you too, baby. I miss you so . . ." Matt choked. A big sob echoed down the line, then a noise that sounded like him clearing his throat. Matt never broke down like that, had always been so frustratingly strong sometimes, and she sure as heck couldn't imagine him crying on a building site. "I'll see you tomorrow."

Lisa held the phone so tight to her ear that it hurt, waited until he clicked off and the dial tone was the only noise she could hear.

She'd done it. She'd told him she loved him, and he was coming to meet her.

In less than twenty-four hours they'd be together. Now all she had to hope for was that they'd be able to find their way past everything and start over, for good this time.

33.

"M att?" Lisa had been sitting in the lobby of the resort for at least an hour. She'd checked in, paced around the pool for a while, then decided to sit with a glass of cold water and face the entrance, wanting to see Matt the moment he walked in.

"Lisa," he called back.

"Matt!" *Ohmygod, it was him.* She jumped up and ran, not sure whether to wait for him to react first or whether to just throw her arms around him.

"Hey, baby," he said when his eyes met hers.

Lisa couldn't contain herself. She opened her arms and crashed into him, desperate to feel his body against hers, to inhale the smell of him, feel him, just be with him. They'd never been truly apart, and after weeks without him, she was ready to grab him and never let go. Maybe they should have spent more time apart instead of being joined at the hip. Maybe then she'd have known what she stood to lose.

"Hey." He smiled, looking down at her. "You're the best thing I've seen in weeks."

Lisa suddenly felt shy, more self-conscious that she'd ever been with Matt. And then Matt grinned and she melted. He was gorgeous. Just the most incredible man, and she didn't even know where to start on her long list of apologies. His smiles and easygoing way had been so frustrating when she'd been in so much pain, but it was just his way of coping, of getting on with life. She could see that now.

"Matt, I'm so sorry. There are so many things I need to tell you, too . . ." She didn't even know where to start. "I'm sorry I pushed you away."

"You don't have to explain."

She shook her head, leaning back to look up at him. "But I do."

"I know why you did it, Lisa. You lost a baby, you had cancer, you went through so much and you just needed to check out and be alone for a bit, without me making things worse when you needed to figure it all out on your own." His eyes were shining, tears visible even though none had fallen from his lashes yet. "I should have given you more space."

"But I am sorry. I'm sorry for not being me all that time, for pushing you away."

"I think the time apart was good. Made us realize what we could come back from," Matt said softly, rubbing his thumb across her jawline. "It sure as hell made me realize I can't live without my girl."

She still loved when he called her his girl. She'd loved it when she was eighteen and she loved it now.

"I keep thinking back to when we first met," she said in a low voice, still with her arms around him but leaning back now so she could look at him. "You made me so aware, so in love. I felt so different around you, and being without you showed me why I can't live without you."

"Baby, it was you who made me aware. I could have ended up dead with my car wrapped around a lamp post," he said, shaking his head. "Drunk, stoned, dead . . . It wasn't looking good for me."

She disagreed. "You were friends with Kelly. She was sensible enough; she wouldn't have let that happen. You weren't *that* close to going off the rails." There were so many things she wanted to ask him, wanted to say, but this was what she needed him to know now.

"Still, she wasn't exactly going to tell me to stop drinking or smoking weed. Although she did kick my butt when I drove drunk one night, told me she'd phone the cops next time I even thought about doing it."

"We changed each other," she said wistfully, thinking back to happier times, before being a mom had even crossed her mind, before cancer was even on her radar. "And I don't want that to stop."

She had a lot to explain and a lot more to tell him, but he was here. And right now that was all that mattered. That and the fact that she finally had the time to make things right, to be with her husband and enjoy every day she had with him. She might feel like she wasn't the whole woman she'd been before, but she was here and alive and in the end she'd fought damn hard to get to where she was. She deserved to be alive, to be having a second chance with her husband.

"Lisa?" Matt said.

"I'm here," she replied, grabbing his hand as he held it out, knowing that he'd thought she was slipping back into sad memories.

"I love you," he mumbled.

"I love you, too," she said as she walked alongside Matt. It had been too long since she'd held his hand and told him those three little words, but damn, everything about it felt right now.

"Come on, let's get rid of my bag and then you can take me down to the beach or to the restaurant so we can talk properly."

Lisa grinned up at him.

"What?" he asked.

"Fancy fried calamari?" she asked with a laugh. "I've been wanting to order it for over two weeks now but just thinking about eating it made me feel like I was being unfaithful to you."

Matt wrapped an arm around her and she tucked tight into him. Back in her happy place. "I say that sounds like the best damn idea I've heard in a long time."

"Would you have forgiven me?" she asked with a laugh.

"Sweetheart, I'd forgive you a lot of things, but eating calamari without me? Not a chance. Definite grounds for divorce."

Lisa laughed. "I guess you'll have to take my word for it that I kept my mouth shut, then."

∞

They sat in the poolside restaurant, the air warm and balmy as the waiter brought them both beers.

"I don't want to ruin the moment, but there's just so much I want to say," Lisa told him. "Is that okay?"

"Yeah, it's definitely okay."

She was craving a fresh start, wanted to get everything out in the open.

"Can I start though?" he asked.

"Yeah, sure," she murmured, wrapping her arms around herself as she sat back in the chair, eyes never leaving his.

"I've kept so much inside, locked away from you," Matt told her. "When my mom died, I went running into the hospital, and it wasn't until I saw her body and touched her that it hit me. I'd thought that she was going to be okay, even when her hair fell out and she started to get so small because she'd lost so much weight. I just wouldn't, or maybe couldn't, accept it."

"I wish I'd asked you about this. I wish you'd confided in me," Lisa said.

"But I didn't want to talk to you about it. I wanted us to be happy, and when I was with you I could forget about all that and it made me feel good. I felt better that way. It was like you were this beautiful, passionate, fun girl, and everything about you made me want more out of life, because I wanted to be with you. You were the best thing that happened to me and I didn't want to burst that bubble by thinking about what I'd lost."

"I wish I'd known more, though," she said, blinking away tears. "I can't believe I never asked you more, that after all this time we never talked about how you felt when you lost her or what you went through."

"You were so young when we met, Lis. And we had so much fun. We always have," Matt said. "I've been carrying around so much guilt for the way I treated my dad, but I just never got the words out to tell him I was sorry. I tried to make up for it, but I never said it. And then you got cancer and everything I felt with Mom came back, only a hundred times worse."

Lisa thought about the way he'd held her hand in the hospital, kissed her and smiled and tried so hard to act like everything was okay. The way he'd refused to accept that she might not make it, that there was any other option other than to save her life.

"You must have been so scared when I went into surgery," she said.

"Yeah, I was." Matt said, voice husky. "I'd seen someone I love get taken by a cancer so similar to yours, and it was killing me to see you like that. That very first day we were told the news, I was terrified of losing you, because I knew what that kind of loss felt like and I didn't think I could survive it again."

Lisa filled her lungs, breathed deep over and over, the pain hitting her in waves. "That's why you said from the very beginning that you'd do anything to save me, that it was no choice to you."

243

Matt nodded, pain etched in his face. "I couldn't lose you, Lisa. I couldn't go through that again. I couldn't lose the person that had made me happy again. Not for a second time."

"I'm sorry," she sobbed, throwing herself against him, holding him tight, her arms wrapped around him. "All I could think about was the baby and all you could think about was losing me. And the more I think about what our child could have gone through, knowing he'd effectively been my death sentence? It's horrid."

"I wanted him, Lis, you need to believe that. I wanted to be a dad so damn bad, but not if the price was you." He was stroking her head now, his fingers running through her hair. "Never if the price was you."

"How do we move forward? How do we deal with never being parents?"

Matt's breath was deep; she felt the rise of his chest against her face. "We just take it one day at a time."

"Really?" she asked, pushing up so she could look at him.

"Really."

"I don't want you to blame me—I don't ever want you to wish that you'd left me for someone you could have a family with."

Matt laughed, a quiet, warm laugh that sent goose pimples across her skin. "Baby, I don't want to leave you now and I doubt I ever will. The time apart was good for us because we both lost a lot this year, but one thing I don't want to lose is you."

Lisa tucked into him again, cocooned against his body. "I'm sorry I shot you down so fast about adoption. I just . . ."

"It was way too soon. I don't care about all that—I was just trying to make you happy, to make you see that we still had options. To try to help you see that you could still be a mom if you wanted it."

"Is it okay if we don't?" she asked quietly. "I just want to be the two of us for a while, maybe forever, to just be us and start afresh. I don't want to talk about what else we could do."

"Yeah, that's fine by me," Matt said, dropping a kiss into her hair that felt so warm and comforting. She'd missed his touch. He might not have opened up about his feelings a lot before, but he'd always touched her, always made her feel loved. "All the more of you for me to enjoy without sharing, right?"

She smiled. "I just want to be me for a bit. To remind myself how lucky I am to be alive, to enjoy hanging out with you. I need to make peace with what happened before thinking about anything else. Or any*one* else."

"I do have one confession to make," Matt said. "And I can't go back on my word, so you have to say yes."

Lisa groaned. "What? Please don't tell me you've gone crazy buying anything for the house or . . ."

He held up his hand, interrupting her. "While you were gone, I promised Blue a sibling. A four-legged one."

Lisa burst out laughing and Matt joined in. She loved that they could be so serious one minute and he could make her laugh the next—it might have annoyed her when she was wallowing in her grief, but she wouldn't trade it for anything right now. But a sibling for Blue? "I guess as long as it's a rescue pup. And you've already told me that I don't have a choice in the matter, right?"

Matt tipped her face up, his fingers nestled beneath her chin. "I love you, Lisa. I love you so damn much. And not just because you're letting me get a puppy."

"I love you, too," she whispered back. "Although you'll have to love me from the floor when we're back home, 'cause there'll be no room for you in the bed between Blue, me and the new pup."

Matt groaned. "I knew there was a catch. No puppy then!"

Lisa knew it wasn't going to be easy, but she felt more at peace with her life and within herself than she had in longer than she could remember.

"Tell me we're going to be okay?" she murmured, gazing up at him.

Matt held her close, one hand stroking up and down her back. "I promise you, we're going to be okay."

She had a feeling this time that it was a promise he could keep.

34.

att looked out at the blue water, sparkling and looking more movie scene than reality. The sand beneath his toes was almost white, and when he turned back to the resort, everything else was white, too. The seemingly hundreds of sun loungers and umbrellas were placed in rows to face the pool, which he knew from his early morning walk was the perfect place to look out at the ocean.

"Wait up!"

A flash of bright pink caught his eye and Lisa came rushing toward him, past the pool and out onto the sand. Her eyes were bright, smile wide as she landed at his side, breathless but grinning.

"What did I miss?" she asked.

"Blue sky, blue water, white sand, no noise . . ." He laughed. "Same as yesterday, only better."

"Sounds like bliss."

Matt felt like a weight had lifted from him, one he hadn't even realized he'd been carrying around for so long, and looking at Lisa only reminded him of how good things were starting to feel.

"I love it here," Lisa said as she slid her arm around him. "This place has been good for me, for us. A new special place, maybe?"

Matt kissed her cheek. It had been rough acknowledging that they weren't unbreakable after so many years of all their friends and family teasing them about how loved up they were, how they were the couple everyone wanted to be, but it had been worth it. It was like a more grown-up version of what they'd had instead of the easy-going childhood romance they'd begun with.

"I know this sounds way too 'romance novel' to come from me, but I heard a song awhile back that reminded me of you," Matt said, clearing his throat, knowing it was stupid to be embarrassed about saying something romantic to his wife. "I want you as my beginning, middle and end, Lisa. I honestly mean that."

She hugged him tight, her face turned up to him, smile wide. "I want that too, Matty. I know it's going to be a different middle and end than we'd imagined, but I'm starting to be okay with that."

"Good," he said, pulling her in for a kiss, arm looped around her as he held her near. "Because I want that, too."

"Hey, did you talk to your dad when you were home? Talk about how you felt, open up about what you told me the other day?"

"Yup," Matt said. "I have you to thank for that, because when you pushed me away, I turned to him, and I couldn't keep it all in any longer."

She hugged him again. "Good. We need to move forward with everything out in the open. No regrets, no secrets."

They strolled a bit longer, toes digging into the soft white sand.

"Would you mind if we kept the nursery for a bit longer? I know we're not going to be using it, but I think I need to spend some time in there. Think about our baby and make peace with that at home, make sure I've dealt with it." Lisa pushed out a loud sigh. "I can still imagine myself sitting there on the armchair, holding a baby wrapped in a blue blanket. I need to deal with that rather than bottle it up."

"Want to do it together?" Matt asked, knowing that he needed to let a lot of his thoughts and regrets go, too. "I think I could do with spending some time in there, too. We closed the door that day but I think I need to open it again and go in. With you."

"Yeah, I'd like that."

They walked a bit longer, in silence, the only sounds the ocean beside them and the birds circling above.

"Come with me," Matt said, hearing the gruffness of his voice.

"Why?" she asked as she followed him.

"Because I want to stop talking and start dreaming about our future," he replied. "I fully intend on taking you on a real road trip in the very near future in that shiny red Cadillac of ours."

Lisa was laughing as he dragged her along by the hand. "Where are you taking me? You know I hate surprises."

"What are you talking about? You *love* my surprises!" He listened to her groan and ignored her.

The beach was pristine so Matt couldn't find a stick to etch the words in the sand that he'd wanted to. Instead, he bent down in the damp sand and put three fingers together to trace the letters, starting with his name. Then he spelled out Lisa's name directly beneath it, before encircling them both in a big heart.

"That's so beautiful," she said, tears twinkling in her eyes.

"I hardly ever saw you cry, in all our years together, until that first cancer diagnosis," Matt said, rubbing his thumb gently across her skin to wipe the tears away. "That's why I always thought you were unbreakable, so damn strong that you would always be okay. It's why I struggled so hard with everything that was happening to you, because the only other person I'd ever seen with such strength was my mom."

"And now I'm a big crybaby all the time," she said, shaking her head.

"No, you're not," Matt told her. "I just hope that from now on you don't have so much to cry about, that's all."

He pulled her close, dropping his mouth over hers. Their lips moved in perfect harmony, the ocean lapping behind them, threatening to wipe out their names in the sand as they embraced. Matt's hands ran down her body, skimming her hips, landed on her butt and stayed there.

"I'd like to scoop you up and carry you back to our room," he muttered.

Lisa giggled and slapped her hands on *his* butt. "That sounds good."

"Race you," Matt whispered, slapping her butt.

Lisa jogged ahead, looking over her shoulder, smiling as she stayed just far enough in front of him, teasing him. It was the woman he'd always known; the smiling, carefree, constantly happy beach-blonde who'd stolen his heart when he hadn't even known he had a heart. He'd always loved Lisa, but seeing her suffer from the moment of that diagnosis through to the termination and everything else that came after it had been rough. Trying to be the guy who could hold it together, who was strong enough for both of them—that had been harder than rough: it had almost broken him.

But he had his Lisa back now. His girl. And he was going to make the most of every damn day they had.

"Wait up, beautiful," he called.

Lisa turned again and stopped, walking backward, laughing at him. Just as he was reaching for her, wanting her, she moved out of his grasp again and he wasn't about to chase and tackle her when someone would probably see and not realize they were joking around. But Mexico was the perfect place in the world to be, and Lisa was the perfect person to be sharing it with.

"We could always go have some lunch," she suggested, raising an eyebrow. "I know how you like to fill up before using all your energy."

She squealed as he made a grab for her, laughing so hard that he couldn't help but join in.

❦

"Stop," Lisa said, laughing, trying to push him away. But Matt was relentless. "Matt!" Her feet were bare against the cool porcelain tiles, the backs of her knees suddenly pressed against the soft white sheets of the bed.

He pushed her back instead, standing over her as she fell back onto the bed. She was only wearing a little summer dress, so it didn't take much for him to shove it up and have half of her bare straight away.

"This is what I've been dreaming about," he said. "My naked wife in Mexico."

"Oh really?" Lisa said with a laugh.

"Yes, really," he muttered, leaning over her, then falling forward, just missing crashing into her. "Shit!"

Lisa happily took charge, taking over.

"We need to go easy," she said, softly kissing Matt's lips as she bent forward. Lisa sat up slowly and grabbed the hem of his t-shirt, pulling it up. He obliged. "Take this slow."

"A little over two weeks apart and I'm not interested in slow," Matt grumbled.

Lisa didn't let him keep speaking. She traced kisses across his abdomen, sucked and licked so slowly that it made him moan. And then she undid his shorts and pulled them down.

Then she raised her arms as he nudged at her top, slipped out of her dress and pulled it over her head before throwing it away.

"Damn, you're gorgeous," he growled.

"I've missed you," she suddenly said, falling down on top of him, arms wrapped around him, skin to skin.

Lisa kissed him as tears fell from her lashes and merged with their lips, salty and full of love. The weeks without him had been so tough, almost impossible, but it was worth it for what they had now.

"I love you, Matty."

"Good," he said, hands tracing up and down her spine before slipping beneath the lace of her g-string. "Because we're Matt and Lisa, and we've got to keep on making all the other couples jealous, right?"

She laughed against his mouth, tears long gone.

They were Matt and Lisa. And they were going to make it.

ᕦᕤ

"So tell me," Matt said, tracing invisible circles across her skin as they lay naked on the bed. It was so warm that they hadn't bothered pulling the sheet up, their bodies no longer slick with sweat, slowly cooling beneath the overhead fan. "What are we going to do in Mexico? Because I've told my guys and your crew at work that we're not coming home for at least two weeks."

She moaned when he stopped stroking her skin, curled tighter into him like a cat wanting to be petted. "I'm not even going to argue with you. I want to stay here forever. How about you teach me how to surf?" she asked.

"Finally!" he said. "I'll go rent the damn boards now!"

Lisa laughed. "And I want to write our names in the sand every day for the next two weeks and drink margaritas every night."

"I'm loving you even more right now. You're the perfect woman."

"You better believe it." Lisa stretched out, brushing a kiss along his jaw as she changed position. "Because I want us to both learn paddle-boarding, too."

"You do all that, I'm gonna promise to tell you I love you every day for the rest of our lives."

"You know, I could get used to this new romantic version of my husband," she murmured, running her fingers through his hair and stretching her naked body forward so she was brushing against him.

"Dangerous move, baby, very dangerous move," Matt growled.

She laughed. "Maybe I like dangerous."

Matt kissed her, softly at first. She pushed into him, kissing him back, as hungry as he was.

"We're gonna do all those things," he muttered, mouth pulled away from hers just enough to talk. "Every goddamn thing."

Lisa didn't answer, her mouth hungrily searching out his again. What they'd had might not have been perfect, but if this was flawed, then he didn't give a damn.

EPILOGUE

"Are you sure?" Matt asked, holding Lisa's hand and studying her face.

She nodded. "Uh-huh. I'll be fine."

He doubted it, but he pushed open the door anyway and entered. The noise hit straight away, the barking and whimpering, and the sight of the dogs behind wire broke his heart.

"*Ohmygod*," Lisa whispered, letting go of him and walking forward, hands to her face. "There's so many."

"I know," Matt said with a grimace. "I know."

He'd wanted to tell the helpful woman out front of the Haven Humane Society what they were looking for. She could have picked out a dog and brought it through to them, and they wouldn't have had to see just how many animals were waiting to find a forever home. But Lisa had insisted.

"And we're only getting one?" Lisa asked, glancing back at him, her eyes full of pleading.

"Baby, you know we can only get one," Matt said, shoving a hand through his hair. "We find the best dog for us, and then we go."

"I can't," she said, shaking her head.

"Yes, you can," Matt said firmly, imagining their entire car full of new four-legged friends. Knowing his wife, he wouldn't put it past her. "This is why I wouldn't let you come alone."

"No, I mean I can't just turn my back on these other dogs. I can't just pick one dog and go."

He wasn't following her, but he didn't interrupt, just slowly scanned all the sad faces waiting for someone to pick them.

"I'm going to take pics of them all, each dog, and every day I'm going to post one on my Facebook and Instagram and try to find homes for them."

Matt blew out a sigh of relief. "That sounds sweet." She had a determined look on her face that made it clear she'd made her mind up. And he didn't doubt for a second that she'd be able to talk people into wearing her clothes *and* copying her by adopting a rescue dog.

"So, do we even know what we're looking for? I mean, there's a nice Labrador down here, and we already know we love that breed."

"No," Lisa said, walking ahead, bending to talk to a tiny little fluff-ball that he was seriously praying she hadn't fallen in love with. "I bet all the purebreds like that find a home, and all the cute little tiny ones, too."

"So you want . . ." He wasn't even sure what she was trying to say. "The ugliest one? The biggest one without a pedigree?"

"This one," Lisa said, dropping to her knees, hands on the wire of the divider.

Matt caught up with her and glanced in, saw exactly why she'd fallen in love. He was scruffy, with big expressive eyebrows and even bigger brown eyes that were focused lovingly on his wife.

"He looks like he needs a bath," Matt said, bending beside her and looking him over. "And a haircut."

"He looks like he wants to be loved," Lisa said quietly. "Along with every other damn dog here. But he's the one."

"Okay, he's the one, then," Matt agreed, not about to argue now that she'd chosen. The dog might not be beautiful like Blue, but he was big and friendly looking, and he sure beat a poodle.

"You go tell the lady. I'm going to sit here with him, so he doesn't think we're not taking him," Lisa said.

Matt walked back past the other kennels and out through to the front of the adoption center.

"How are you getting on?" the lady asked.

"My wife has fallen in love with the scruffiest dog. He is in kennel thirty-two."

"That's Benji. He's been here for months. Literally walked in off the street himself one day, like he knew where to look for help." The woman walked over to get a leash, pausing to smile over at Matt. "You know, everyone else keeps walking past him, so he's gonna be real happy to go home with you."

"Do you mind if we bring our other dog in?" Matt asked. "Make sure they get along okay?"

"Sure thing. We'll go into one of the dog visiting rooms."

Matt pushed the door open and went to his Chevy, letting Blue out and clipping on his leash. Trust Lisa to find the one dog straight away that deserved a home more than the others, the one that had been overlooked by everyone else.

"Come meet your new friend," Matt told Blue. He laughed. "And you'd better like him because your mom's already in love."

❧

"He's seriously gorgeous," Lisa mused, sitting back with a glass of water in one hand as she watched the dogs play around the yard. They were sitting outside, the doors to the house all flung open, white drapes billowing out toward them in the soft breeze.

She met Matt's gaze and he burst out laughing. "He's not gorgeous, but he's a cool dog."

She knew that he wasn't the most handsome or perfect-looking dog, but his face was so expressive, and there was a sadness in his eyes that told her he'd been through a lot. Just like her. She was scarred and flawed, too. She'd been through hell and survived, just like their new pooch. She'd managed to move on and be happy, which was exactly the life she wanted for this perfectly flawed dog.

"A few months ago, I thought I'd never smile again," Lisa said. "I couldn't imagine being happy like this."

"Me neither," Matt admitted. "We're so lucky to still be together, to have been given this chance."

She smiled. They'd had a shit run of luck, but she knew what he was saying. "Lucky, given the crap hand we'd been dealt," she said, seeing the look pass over his face, the look that said he'd just figured how bad that sounded.

"Yeah, exactly."

Lisa pulled Matt down on top of her, lying back on their outdoor sofa and drawing him close, eyes closed as she parted her lips, sighing as he kissed her. Matt traced his fingers up her body, tickled her stomach.

"Woof!"

"Aw hell!" Matt cursed, pushing up from her.

"What?" Lisa mumbled.

Benji had his hackles up, back all prickly as he stared at Matt. Blue was sitting to attention, big tail thumping as he watched what was going on.

"He thinks you were hurting me. How sweet," Lisa said, standing up and calling out to the dog. "Benji! Come here, buddy."

He obediently crossed over to her, sitting on her feet and glaring back over at Matt.

"He's protecting you. Great," Matt said. "Back to the shelter!"

Lisa bent and put her arms gently around the dog, cradling him. He needed love, and she had a whole lot to give. "It's okay. You go back and play. I got this," she told him, pointing over to Blue.

Matt threw a ball and Blue ran to chase it straight away. She pointed for Benji to follow and he did.

"I can't believe we have two fur babies," Lisa said, going back over to Matt and slinging an arm around his waist.

"Do you still think about our baby every day?" he asked, kissing the top of her head as she snuggled closer.

"Every day," she admitted. "But that's okay."

"Me too," Matt said. "I'd love to think we'll have kids one day, that they'll be rough and tumbling on the lawn with the dogs and running barefoot through the house, that everything we went through was some kind of bad dream. That I can build the tree house with my own hands and know that little people will be playing pirates in it. But only if you want that to happen."

"We just have to change our dream," Lisa said, her heart still close to breaking just thinking about what they'd lost. "We talked about that future for so long. That's why it hurts so bad, but it was never real. It was just a picture we had of what our family was going to look like, of our biological children. Or what we thought we were supposed to have."

"So what does our new future look like?" Matt asked, turning his body into hers. "Have you thought about that lately?"

She put both arms around him, looped her fingers into his jeans and leaned back. She was okay with him asking now, had pushed through and come out so much stronger.

"It's still just you and me for now," she said, staring up into the brightest blue eyes she'd ever seen, the dark ring around the ocean-blue making them even more mesmerizing. "Spending our days together, happy that we have each other. And one day if we decide we're ready to adopt, or take up Kelly's offer of surrogacy, then that'll be okay too. I just want to see what happens, how we feel."

"That sounds like a pretty damn good plan," Matt said, voice gruff.

"Yeah, I reckon," she said with a smile, standing on tiptoes to kiss his cheek. He turned his face fast and she ended up in a lip-lock with him instead.

"And you're okay with that?" he asked, tone more serious this time. "Are you sure you're okay?"

"I'm okay," she reassured him. "I promise."

A loud woof echoed out again and Lisa burst out laughing, cheeks hurting as she stared at Benji. He was glaring at Matt like he was about to attack.

"We have to do something about this damn dog!" Matt cursed, obviously deadly serious but managing to make her laugh. "Seriously!"

"He just needs a little time to adjust, that's all. He's been through a lot," she said, straight-faced.

Just like her. Which was why she was prepared to give the poor canine all the time in the world.

"Fine," he grumbled. "But he's not sleeping on the bed."

"Aw, sweetheart, don't get your hopes up there. Of course he's sleeping on the bed!"

Matt glowered and she laughed so hard tears welled in her eyes. Happy tears that felt so damn good.

∾

"Lisa Williams," Matt said, turning and holding out his hands for both of hers. Lisa was about to say something, then clamped her mouth shut and placed her hands in his.

"Six years ago I married the love of my life," Matt said, his smile sweet as he stared into her eyes, his blue irises so bright, so piercing and intense, just like they'd always been. He was a man's man, the kind of big, burly, sexy-as-hell guy that loved downing beers and watching ball, wielding a hammer during the day and fixing anything that needed tending to. But he also had a softer side to him, a side that not many other people in their life ever got to see, a side that she'd seen a whole lot of lately. To everyone else he was an ex-football player who fixed up houses and had a cute wife on his arm.

"Me too," she murmured, refusing to blink, not wanting to miss a moment of Matt looking at her like she was the most beautiful girl in the world.

"What's next?" he asked, eyebrows shooting up.

Lisa gulped, swallowed the emotion and fear that threatened to engulf her. "I don't even remember our vows!" she hissed.

"Baby, you'll remember the important ones," Matt said, the gruff edge to his voice telling her that this wasn't easy for him either. "Come on, let's do it together."

Lisa cleared her throat, held on tighter to Matt. "I promise to love you, Matt. Always and forever."

"To have and to hold from this day forward," he said.

"For better or worse, richer or poorer," she remembered.

"In sickness and in health." His smile was sweet; his head dipped as he continued to meet her gaze. "Until death do us part."

The sun made her squint as clouds parted above them. "Is this the bit where you kiss the bride?" she asked.

"Hell yes," Matt whispered, hand leaving hers to press to the back of her head instead, pulling her forward, possessive and strong as his lips crushed hers. Just like their wedding day, when Matt had kissed the hell out of her in front of everyone gathered when she'd been expecting just a polite, chaste peck on the lips.

❧

Lisa looked around the table at all the people who meant so much to her. As the sun started to set, making the sky a fury of dark pinks and soft reds, she cleared her throat and stood, holding her champagne glass tight. She took a sip for an extra burst of courage.

Everyone was silent as they turned to watch her, and she looked at every face, every single person who'd traveled to gather with them. Her sisters, Kelly and Penny, her gorgeous nieces, who were such strong-willed, beautiful girls; her parents and Matt's dad.

"Ten years ago, Matt and I stood amongst the vines with you all and pledged to spend the rest of our lives together," Lisa said, smiling down at her husband and taking his hand, her heart skipping a beat when he stood, still holding her hand, beside her. Close enough that their hips were touching. "We took vows that for better or worse, we'd stay together." She took a shaky breath, nodding her head. "I'm proud to say that through thick and thin, this beautiful man has stood by me. One year ago Matt and I came back here, and I didn't think I could get through what was a very dark time, but we did. And I'm so grateful that we're standing here, together, today."

Matt tucked his arm around her and placed a gentle kiss on her cheek. "I love you," he whispered in her ear, just for her.

"I couldn't have made it without every single person here, and it means so much to us that you came to celebrate not only our sixth wedding anniversary, but also my first year of being in remission. I'm blessed to be so loved. Thank you."

Matt held up his glass and she did the same, smiling at him through tears. Happy tears that she was okay about shedding.

"You okay?" he murmured.

"I'm good," she whispered, just for him, before clearing her throat. "To us, to all of us. I'm so proud to call you all family, and I'm so proud to have this man as my husband," Lisa said, in a louder voice this time.

Everyone clinked glasses. The table was covered in food, the air warm, peaceful in a way that only Napa Valley could be, as they sat together amongst the vines, surrounded by twinkling fairy lights in the near-dark.

"I'd like to say a few words."

Lisa looked up, sat down as Matt's father rose to his feet. She glanced at Matt but it was obvious he didn't know what his dad was up to either.

"None of you knew Matt when his mother passed away, but I will be forever grateful to Lisa. The day he met you, Lisa, something changed inside of him, and I used to wonder if his mom had sent you to save him. You gave me my boy back, and when I saw him struggling with your cancer, when I saw the pain he was going through and knew what that felt like, my heart broke."

Lisa held on tight to Matt's hand, leaned closer into him. The tears in her eyes now weren't happy tears—they were full of heartbreak. Because she knew now that Matt still suffered, that his heart had a crack through it that would never mend, one his mom had left when she'd passed. And she hated that she'd brought him back to his knees again when she'd been so close to leaving him, too.

"So to you, Lisa. For loving my boy, for being there for him and making him the man he is today. And to both of you for coming through this stronger than before."

Matt cleared his throat and stood again. "To Lisa," he said, giving her a tear-filled wink. "And to kicking cancer's butt so you could be here with me today. We lost a lot, but we still have each other. And I say cheers to that."

They all held up their glasses and Lisa watched as Matt sipped from his before putting it down and walking around the table to his dad. They embraced, Matt holding on to his dad tight, hugging him like they had a lifetime of them to catch up on.

She was happy. So happy. And no one and nothing could take that away from her.

The End.